THE STARS IN HIS EYES

BY

JOSEPH & JILL TANTILLO

ISBN: 1544995687
ISBN 13: 978-1544995687

This is a work of fiction. Names, characters, businesses, places, events, and incidents are either the products of the author's imagination or used in a fictitious manner.

DEDICATION

To my best buddy and favorite boy in the world. You truly are a legend. Always stay awesomellent.

"God may have made it more difficult for you to learn, but he also made it easier for you to love, and that is a more important task. Your purpose is to love people, and you are the best person I know for the job."

- Author Unknown

FOREWORD

The idea for this story came about because I have a special needs son. I freaking love this kid—he is funny and quirky and awesomellent (a word he made up). In my dream he was cured of his genetic disorder (Williams Syndrome). It was an awesome dream as it was happening, seeing my son's face and body evolve into that of a normal 13-year-old boy. In real life he looks about six years old and has many facial characteristics and issues that make him look special as well. He has the mental capacity of a much younger child, and loves Barney, Chuck E. Cheese, etc.

So when I awoke from this dream, I was faced with the question: what would I do if given the chance to change him? That led to the writing of this book—so here we go...

- Joseph Tantillo

PROLOGUE

"Billy's reading comprehension is still improving consistently every month," the petite woman said while carefully adjusting her bifocals and retrieving her pen from her white lab coat pocket. She looked back down at her chart to review the full list of results while trying to anticipate the doctor's next question.

"And how were his speech pattern tests this past week?" the doctor asked as he wrote something down in his journal.

"He's performing better than normal. The results of his expressive and pragmatic language tests are pretty amazing actually. And there are little to no delays in his responses," she said.

"What about his height?"

"He's grown about two inches over the past six months. I'd say he's going through a bit of a spurt," she answered with a smile, hoping to finally get a positive reaction from her boss. But his expression remained stoic.

"He's also gained about seven pounds and still has a good BMI for his size," she continued.

"And what about his vitals? Blood pressure readings?"

"Normal today. All good. And they've been very consistent for the past month."

"This is all encouraging news, Tamara. Proceed with the next dosage," the doctor said nonchalantly, never looking up from his work.

The doctor had always been good at guarding his true emotions. On the inside, he was ecstatic, lit up, over the moon about how their secret trial was proceeding. He would finally have something to prove that he was a worthy physician and researcher to all of his colleagues who doubted him. He was so involved with thoughts of redemption that he didn't realize his assistant was still lingering behind him.

"Is there something else you need?" the doctor asked her, now sounding impatient.

"Um Dr. Meron, there's something else we should discuss that may or may not be important at this stage of the—"

"What is it?" the doctor interrupted, finally turning and looking up at his assistant. Tamara looked away, feeling the perspiration beginning to develop on her brow. Whenever the doctor was forced to look up from his work, his demeanor changed and he could be very intimidating.

Tamara hesitated for a moment, and then finally said what had been on her mind for the past month.

"There's something happening to Billy's eyes that I can't explain. They're...different."

CHAPTER 1
The Tale of Two Photos

They are sitting together on their favorite beach. It's the same beach where little Joey T made his first sand castle at seven years old. The same beach where Joey's parents took their wedding pictures. At that beach, both of Joey's younger sisters took their first steps and both fell face down in the sand. Joey's big sister was stung by a jellyfish and developed a slight phobia of ocean water.

He reaches over and embraces his son with a reassuring shoulder hug. They look at each other for a long moment and smile. He loves his son unconditionally. He admires his son's big smile and of course his sparkling, starry eyes.

Suddenly, Joey is compelled to jump up and make a beeline for the shore. His father instinctually looks around for his son's mother, who would be having a fit by that time, but she was nowhere to be found.

By the time he is finally running toward the shore after his son, Joey is already deep in the water. In the next moment, Joey is completely submerged in the waves and doesn't come up immediately.

He's in a panic and screaming his son's name at the top of his lungs as he rushes into the waves, which seem to be pushing him back with every step. Finally, he arrives at the place where his son has just disappeared and Joey rises out of the water with his signature smile spread across his face. But that's the only thing that his father recognizes about him.

Joey's features have changed, as well as his stature. He looks like a carbon copy of his father at 13 years old. He is in shock as he gazes at the new version of his son. Finally, he reaches out to touch his face and Joey suddenly disappears into thin air…

"Joey!"

Joseph Sr., called out his son's name and sat up in bed. This was a recurring dream, which seemed to visit him right before the William's Syndrome counseling group sessions that he and his wife, Jill, attended every third Thursday of the month.

"He's in his room honey," Jill said as if this was a common routine. It was 3 a.m. and she had again been awakened by her husband calling out Joey's name.

Joseph was still in a daze as he pulled the covers back and headed toward his son's bedroom next door. He needed to see his son immediately.

When he arrived by Joey's bedside, he knelt down and gazed again at his son's face, which was perfectly lit up by his favorite Barney night-light. Joseph could clearly see the distinctive outline of his small cherub-like face; the tiny chin, the pronounced cheeks, and the button nose. It was only after he touched his son's hand that Joseph realized he wasn't dreaming anymore.

The next day at breakfast, Joseph Sr. was the last to make it to the table even though he was the first person who had to make it out of the house. Joey was already bouncing around the table from his older sister to his mom to his two younger sisters and back to his big sister. Mornings were never boring because of the energy young Joey brought to the room. He was always up at 5:30 a.m. like clockwork, even on weekends, eager and ready to start his day.

"Mom, he keeps pulling my ponytail!" Joey's 11-year-old sister Sophia complained. His 5-year old sister Mia just laughed and wriggled around in her seat anxiously.

"Stop pulling your sister's hair Joey," his mom said casually as she read a recent report from her son's English teacher. It said that he was having problems paying attention in class, distracting the other children and having challenges developing his vocabulary.

"Hey, Joey T!" his dad said immediately when he entered the room and Joey ran over to give him a high five. Joseph then leaned over to kiss each of his girls on the forehead before stealing bacon from his older daughter Grace's plate.

"Come on Dad, there's plenty of bacon left on the counter," Grace said with a grin as she scrolled through her cellphone.

"But the bacon from your plate tastes better," he replied with a wink.

"Tell me you're not going to skip breakfast again," his wife, Jill, asked him as she saw him packing up his briefcase.

"Gonna be late, they need me there to meet with a manufacturer.

Seven o'clock tonight right? I promise I'll be on time," he answered.

"Righttt. You said that last time," his wife said as she started putting some bacon and an English muffin on a paper plate for him. "Take this with you."

"Thank you. I love you," he said and gave her a lingering kiss. Every day his wife managed to remind him of why he married her. She was industrious, smart, funny and always thinking of others—sometimes to a fault.

"Ew!!! Why don't you guys get a room!" Joey screamed at his parents.

"Hey, this *is* our room buddy! Now get upstairs and brush your hair for school," Jill said as she held onto her husband. She turned back to him with a reassuring smile. "You have a great day at the office and don't let anyone stress you out."

"I'll try. The same to you," Joseph said before heading out of the house to his car. Coincidentally, his talkative neighbor Paul was coming out at the same time. This happened so often that Joseph was starting to have suspicions that Paul was waiting for him to leave the house in the morning.

"Hey Joseph!" he yelled and waved as he invited himself over.

"Hey Paul, really don't have much time to talk today," Joseph said as he held his car door open, trying not to be too rude. Paul was one of those guys who didn't really catch the hint too quickly.

"Sure. Just wanted to ask, how's little Joey doing?" Paul inquired. He made it a point to gather as much information he could about everyone he knew so that he could show a genuine interest in their lives. It was both admirable and irritating at times.

"He's awesome, doing great. Thanks for asking. How's the family?" Joseph asked. He could kick himself because that simple question would inevitably lead to at least a five-minute-long conversation. But he wanted to deflect attention from his son. He rested his arm on the top of his sedan and settled in to listen to Paul talk about what he did with his family that past weekend, who went to the doctor and how long he would be away to visit his in-laws.

Finally, at the five-minute mark of "yeas" and "ah huhs," Joseph glanced at his watch and decided to wrap things up.

"I'm sorry to interrupt you, Paul, but I really gotta get on the road. Meeting," Joseph said as he extended his hand for a shake.

"Oh, no problem, Joseph. Why didn't you tell me you had a meeting?" Paul said with a polite smile. "I've got a conference call in a while myself. Wanna come over for a beer after work?"

"Can't. We've got a group meeting tonight. Maybe another time," Joseph said as he slid into his car, still clutching his breakfast plate.

"No problem." Paul stood and waved as Joseph backed out of his driveway and took off down the street.

Everyone on their block knew about Joey's Williams Syndrome diagnosis, but Joseph wasn't sure how he felt about that. He didn't want anyone feeling sorry for his only son or treating him differently. The neighborhood kids had started teasing him when he first began to display clear symptoms of the syndrome, but soon enough he turned them into friends and acquaintances. Joey had a quality that made people naturally gravitate toward him. Though the neighborhood kids invited him to play with them from time to time, Joey preferred to hang out with his father and sisters whenever possible. He had just one close friend his age named Tommy who he felt a strong connection with because they had the same condition. Unfortunately, Tommy went to a school over an hour and a half away and they only occasionally met up on Saturdays. Only 30,000 people in the entire country had Williams Syndrome and only a portion of them were children. Finding friends nearby for Joey that he could relate to was a challenge.

As he pulled onto the freeway, Joseph thought about the time when he slept under Joey's crib the night before they had to take him to the hospital for open heart surgery. The doctors informed the family that there was a 15 percent risk of death when performing this procedure on a 10-month old baby. Joseph was so terrified that night that he made a quiet deal with God to help his son through the ordeal.

Please let him live and I'll be cool with whatever.

The first signs that Joey had a genetic condition came very soon after he was born. He would cry all night long and no one in the house would get any sleep. Joey's first surgery was at three months old to remove a hernia. Then he had to get ear tubes. Months later he was diagnosed with a heart murmur and soon after that was scheduled for heart surgery. To everyone's relief, baby Joey came out of it okay, but his heart would always have to be closely monitored. A week after doing a FISH test to detect genetic issues, the doctors finally told Joseph and his wife what they already suspected by that time—that Joey had Williams Syndrome. A small number of genes were missing on one of his chromosomes.

They were distressed when they learned that their first and only born son would forever have to struggle with health issues and developmental delays throughout his life. That he would always be different from other kids. It took him longer than usual to say his first words and take his first steps. He had to attend special classes. Every day was a struggle and yet a blessing at the same time.

Joseph loved his son with every bit of his being. At the same time, he couldn't help but wonder what Joey would have been like if he had been born without gene complications. His son was slight in stature for a 13-year-old and had behaviors that were comparable to a six-year-old boy. While normal 13-year-old boys at his school were talking to girls, beginning to rebel against their parents and playing video games, Joey was still begging his parents to go to Chuck E. Cheese, asking for his Barney night light to be turned on, and clinging to his mom tightly whenever he saw a spider.

Joseph couldn't help but wonder if there would ever be a cure for Williams Syndrome so that one day he could watch his son do what other boys eventually do: compete in sports, go off to college, get married to a great girl and eventually have children of his own. It was a thought that nagged at him more and more—ever since Joey officially became a teenager.

❧

"Any new developments or questions that anyone would like to discuss before we close the meeting for the night?" the head counselor, Marilyn, asked as she glanced around the room with a gentle smile. She was an older lady who had a daughter with Williams Syndrome who was now 32 years old. She had been counseling families for over 15 years and now had a solid group with seven sets of parents from all over the state.

The room was quiet for a while, and then Jill spoke up.

"I received a report from Joey's school yesterday. His teacher says…"

Jill stopped talking as she glanced over and saw her husband, Joseph, trying to tip toe into the room. It was close to 8 o'clock and the meeting would be over soon. He slid into the seat next to her and mouthed the word "sorry." She nodded.

"…uh, so his teacher says that he's having major problems with his vocabulary," Jill finished her thought.

"I know a tutor who can help," Marsha Rogers immediately volunteered. She was the mother of Joey's friend Tommy. "He specializes in working with children with Williams Syndrome who have learning challenges. It's a bit of a drive for him to go to your house, but I'm sure you could work something out once or twice a month? Maybe you can bring Joey to see Tommy this weekend and meet with him?"

"Thank you Marsha, that sounds like a plan," Jill agreed with a smile. She admired how proactive Marsha was at finding the help that her son needed to be well-adjusted. Jill wished she could do the same, but with her demanding work schedule and keeping up with Joey every day, it was difficult to stay on top of every new study, specialist, or development.

"That's great, thanks guys. We're stronger together," Marilyn said as she usually did at the end of every meeting. "If that's all, I was hoping I could introduce you all to someone before it gets too late?"

Most of the group reluctantly nodded their heads in agreement. They were eager to get home to relieve their sitters of their duties.

"Okay then, it won't take long. He's a doctor and scientist who has a medical facility in St. Louis. He wants to talk to you all about something that could help your sons and daughters." Marilyn stood up and walked out of the door to her office. When she returned, she had a tall man with her who was trailed by a petite young woman. She was holding a clipboard and a large portfolio. Both of them had on bright white lab coats.

"Hello everyone, my name is Dr. Howard Meron, and this is my assistant Dr. Tamara Goodwin," the man began. He looked very serious and confident as he glanced around the room locking eyes with everyone in the group.

"I'm here because I specialize in helping young children between the ages of seven and 15 who have been diagnosed with Williams Syndrome. I would like to talk to you about an experimental treatment that could—"

"Nope, no," John, one of the parents immediately waved the doctor off. "Our child isn't going to be anyone's 'experiment.' Come on Deb, let's go. We've got a drive."

"At least allow Dr. Meron to finish his presentation," Marilyn pleaded as John and his wife Debra started to gather their things.

"No thanks. See you in a few weeks guys," John said abruptly as he grabbed his wife's hand and led her out of the room.

"It's okay," Dr. Meron reassured Marilyn as he turned back to the group, hoping he hadn't lost them also. "Maybe I'm taking the wrong approach here. Let me just get right to the point."

Dr. Meron gestured to his assistant and she pulled two large poster boards from her bag. He took off his lab coat, realizing at that moment that a more informal presentation would have been better for this group of families. He grabbed the first poster board, which was a photo of a child with Williams Syndrome. He had all of the distinctive features, including small stature, wide mouth, puffy eyelids and an upturned nose.

"This was 11-year-old Billy one year ago. He was diagnosed with Williams Syndrome at eight months old," he said as he took his time displaying the photo to each individual member of the group. They nodded and smiled. Some of the mothers commented on how beautiful he was. When he was finished, he grabbed the second poster board photo and placed it next to the first one.

"This is 12-year-old Billy as of yesterday afternoon."

The entire room gasped, and Joseph sat completely still, trying to process what he was seeing. The latest photo of Billy showed a pre-teen boy with normal features. He had a contoured chin, proportional nose and face. He was casually smirking in the photo, as is usual for a boy his age who was taking a school picture whereas in the first photo he was smiling from ear-to-ear.

"Is this some kind of joke?" one of the fathers finally spoke up.

"I assure you that this is no joke, Mr…?" Dr. Meron said and then paused to wait for his name.

"It's Ray Smith," the father responded. He and his family lived over an hour away. He had a son with Williams Syndrome who was about to turn 15 soon and they had been thinking about withdrawing from the monthly group counseling sessions.

"Thank you, Mr. Smith," Dr. Meron continued. "This is not a joke of any sort. I am proud to announce that I've developed a treatment that promises to cure many of the symptoms of Williams Syndrome..."

His assistant, Tamara, bristled when she heard the doctor tell the group that he alone had developed the treatment. She had spent sleepless nights over the past five years researching Williams Syndrome, studying the genetic abnormalities associated with the condition and helping to develop the serum that had now been successfully tested on Billy.

"…It is a series of injections that are administered each week to the patient. We began to see improvements as early as two months with Billy. Not only has his appearance changed, he's also made significant advances in his ability to learn, read, and process information. We've been monitoring his cardiovascular health, and things are looking very, very good."

Everyone in the room looked at each other incredulously. Their expressions were a strange combination of disbelief, relief and a growing excitement at the news, but many of the faces were also full of great concern. Jill's face was unreadable.

"I'm happy to report that a year after starting the treatment, Billy is now functioning as a normal, healthy 12-year-old boy in every way," Dr. Meron said with a smile. "As a disclaimer, the results may vary depending on the child's specific case, the number of deleted genes, age, and maybe even gender, but I am confident that my team can help you see some degree of improvement in your child's condition. We've set the cut off age at 15 because of certain changes that may occur in the child's body around that age. Also, at this moment the formula has only been tested on young adolescents, but there may be a new formulation in the future for older teens."

The looks turned into murmurs and gradually grew to louder conversations and rapid-fire questions being posed to Dr. Meron.

"What are the side effects?"

"How can an injection affect missing genetic material?"

"Is this considered a medication?"

"Is this treatment FDA-approved?"

"Would they have to take these injections forever?"

Dr. Meron held up his hand to quiet the room, which was now full of parents who were sitting at attention. His chest swelled with confidence, knowing that he had won them over. He could tell that their minds were swimming with ideas, visualizations, and possibilities. It was an indescribable feeling that he hadn't experienced in many years. He couldn't wait until his colleagues saw the progress on his trials.

"I have a folder of information for each of you to look over, including my office phone number so that we can schedule individual appointments with each family. Take a good look at the information provided before you make your decision. Rest assured, every question that you have will be answered at your one-on-one appointment."

When Tamara walked around the room extending folders to the parents, Joseph eagerly reached out to grab one. Jill just looked at him with her arms folded. He recognized that look very well—she was not happy about what she had heard. Not one bit.

"I can't believe that you're actually considering this!" Jill exclaimed, finally letting her feelings out to Joseph when they were alone. She stood in the doorway of the bathroom in their bedroom with a look of amazement spread across her face. Her eyes were wide like saucers.

Joseph sat on the edge of the bed. He had been gingerly flipping through the paperwork provided by Dr. Meron. It included an initial consent form that said they were interested in learning more about the treatment and agreed to keep the information confidential.

Jill hadn't said a word about the proposed treatment since leaving the group session. They drove home in separate cars. She was quietly caught in a web of conflicted feelings about what she had just heard.

On the other hand, Joseph couldn't stop thinking about the two photos that Dr. Meron revealed—the degree of contrast was amazing. It was like looking at two different people. Billy would now have a chance to live the life of an everyday boy. And now, Joey could have that same chance.

As far as Joseph was concerned, he could have gone ahead and set the initial consultation that night with Dr. Meron. When they arrived home, Jill had listened to him talk for almost a half hour about the photos of Billy and what this would mean for families with Williams Syndrome. What an amazing scientific breakthrough it was. Jill washed her face, brushed her teeth, and tied up her hair as she endured his excited one-sided conversation. Finally, when he told her that he would be the one to call the doctor first thing in the morning, she could no longer remain quiet.

"What do you mean?" Joseph asked as he looked up at his wife. Her tone surprised him.

"What do I mean? You haven't even asked me what I think about all of this!" Jill said as she threw her hands up in the air. "And you're already talking about calling this *doctor* who we don't know anything about…"

"Well, why the heck not, it's just a consultation!" Joseph said, talking louder to match the level of her voice. "The purpose of a consultation is to learn more."

"I can't believe you," she retorted as she began to move around the room picking up clothes and socks.

"What can't you believe Jill?" he wanted to know. He dropped the folder on the bed so that she could have his undivided attention.

Jill was quiet for a moment as she threw his things in the hamper. Deep down, she didn't really know why she was so upset. She just was.

"Those don't need to be washed yet," Joseph protested.

"So why didn't you hang them up!" Jill told him as she went to her side of the bed and pulled back the covers.

"What is up with you? What did I do?"

Jill sat on the edge of the bed as she checked the list of things to do on her cellphone for that next day. "Listen, you're not calling that doctor tomorrow, so just forget it."

"Oh, so this us how we come to decisions about our son now?"

Within a few moments, the conversation between Joseph and Jill had turned into a full-blown argument that ended with Joseph grabbing his pillow and heading to the den. Down the hall, Grace peeked outside just in time to see her dad slam the door. She was glad that the younger kids were staying at their grandparent's house that evening. It wasn't often that her parents argued so intensely—and loudly.

Grace went back into her bedroom and closed the door gently. She flopped onto her bed and resumed the text conversation that she was having with her best friend Carlie, which was definitely winning out over her school textbook at that point. Anything could win out over that.

"Wonder what they were arguing about… " Grace texted.

"Did you hear anything?" Carlie texted back.

"Not much. Something about a doctor."

"Man, I dunno. It'll blow over. My folks argue all the time."

"Mine never do. R U ready for the quiz tomorrow, b/c I'm sure not."

"You're playing with fire Grace. Didn't you get a D on the last 1?"

"Yea, but it's whatever."

"You can't be serious. We'll be juniors soon Grace, college apps. This year's transcripts mean everything."

"Yea yea I know I know. Look gotta go. Scott's calling."

Grace abruptly ended her text conversation with Carlie as soon as she saw her boyfriend Scott calling. She hated talking about college and grades—she just wanted to enjoy her high school years for as long as possible. In the worst case scenario, she'd just go to a state or community college. Little did her parents know that she had been skipping most of her classes—but they were too busy with Joey, Mia and their careers to notice what she was doing at school. She had become adept at intercepting letters from her teachers and had managed to change the phone number they had on file to a private VOIP account she maintained.

She took her boyfriend's call and slammed her textbook shut. More and more, Scott was becoming the center of her life. They spent a lot of time together and he made her feel special. Within minutes of talking to Scott, she was grabbing her keys to head to a party with him on the other side of town. She tip-toed her way down the stairs and out of the door with the furtiveness of a ninja to avoid having to explain where she was going in person. After leaving, she texted her mom to let her know that she'd be back around midnight. As she pulled off down the street, she put her studies at the back of her mind. All she could think about was being with him again.

CHAPTER 2
Answers Needed

When Joey arrived at school every morning, he could hardly contain his excitement. As soon as he entered his classroom, the room filled with his energy.

Joey had a not-so-secret crush on the young teacher's assistant, Jemma, who monitored his class of 10 special needs students. Whenever an opportunity came for him to get help from her, he jumped on it immediately. He flirted with her, practicing smooth lines that he had heard on his favorite television shows. He made drawings depicting him with his family and Jemma holding his hand. That was his school "girlfriend."

Joey had some problems keeping up in class at times, but when it came to socializing he was definitely a professional. He had befriended everyone in his class and a lot of the other kids at school.

"Joey T. Come on buddy, let's have a seat and listen to Mrs. M., okay?" Jemma told him when she saw him beginning to get wound up with a couple of the other kids in his class. He looked like he wanted to protest, but since it was Jemma, he just sighed, went back to his desk and sat down.

"Cherubs, I have some *really* good news," his teacher, Mrs. Moldestad, announced. She was one of the kindest and most patient teachers in the school. She had a background in both child psychology and education, making her well-equipped to teach children like Joey.

All of the children in class jumped up and down in their seats in anticipation. They knew that when Mrs. Moldestad had great news, it was really great.

"The school's drama class is having a Christmas play in December and they want us all to participate!" she revealed. The entire class erupted in cheers and expressions of glee. They wanted nothing more than to feel included and accepted at their school.

"Some of you can work as theater engineers, some of you can do the art for stage scenery and some of you can audition for acting roles. *And* our very own Joey T. has been asked back to play a leading role!" she continued as she gestured in his direction. Joey had been acting in community and school plays since he was seven years old. His ability to memorize lines was uncanny. Children with Williams Syndrome were known for having a propensity for artistic talent and Joey was no exception.

"A leading role?!?" Joey said, barely containing his excitement. "Really?"

"Yes! But with one condition—you all have to finish your reading assignments by next week. Do you think you can do that?" Mrs. Moldestad asked as she crossed her arms with a feigned look of skepticism on her face.

The room erupted again with a chorus of "yeses." The rest of the day, the entire class listened with intensity to their teacher and barely interrupted. There was no way that anyone was going to be left out of participating in the school play.

Joseph sat at his desk, twirling his pen and staring at Dr. Meron's business card. He had to cancel a couple of staff meetings that morning because he just couldn't concentrate on work. He had barely gotten any sleep that night in the den, and Jill hadn't said a word to him that morning before leaving the house.

At first, he felt guilty, but those feelings of guilt were beginning to grow into resentment toward his wife. He couldn't understand how she could be so resistant to at least talking to the doctor about this new treatment. This was about little Joey after all—he deserved a chance at a normal life.

"Mr. Todaro?" Joseph's secretary Amy said timidly as she peered into his office.

"Yes Amy."

"There's a Ray Smith here to see you?"

Joseph searched his mind to figure out who Ray Smith was and why he would be showing up at his office unannounced. As he was processing his thoughts, he saw Ray appear over Amy's shoulder and immediately recognized him as one of the other parents from their Williams Syndrome group counseling sessions.

"Ray, wow, come on in," Joseph said as he quickly tucked Dr. Meron's card and folder into his drawer. He was actually relieved to see someone who was probably having the same thoughts after the previous night's news. He motioned to Amy to close his office door for privacy.

"Hi Joseph, I'm so sorry if I'm bothering you. I still have your business card in my wallet from the first time we met so I decided to drop by before I head home," Ray explained.

"No, it's no problem at all," Joseph said as he motioned for Ray to sit down. He kept two comfortable sitting chairs in his office that faced each other specifically for impromptu meetings like this.

"Thank you. We decided to book a hotel for the night and drive back today. My brain was too wired up and exhausted at the same time for that drive home," Ray admitted.

"I know what you mean," Joseph nodded as he settled back into his chair.

"So… interesting meeting last night huh? What did you think?" Ray asked.

Joseph just slowly rubbed the rough hairs on his chin and didn't answer right away. He preferred to get Ray's thoughts first.

"I'm not sure yet," he finally said.

Ray shifted in his chair and thought for a moment. "I think it's a good thing, no? Mary Ellen is hesitant, but she sees the urgency in this."

"What do you mean?" Joseph asked curiously.

"Well, Sammy's going to be turning 15 in January. The doctor said this treatment would only work on children ages seven to 15. We've got to jump on it right away."

Joseph hadn't thought of that. Joey would be turning 14 that next year, so 15 wasn't too far off from them either. They had to make a decision soon.

"But do you think it's safe?" Ray blurted. "I mean, they've got all kinds of experimental drugs out there, and the side effects…"

"I know. It's definitely not something to take lightly," Joseph said, remaining elusive. The truth was that he had a million thoughts and questions running through his mind as well. But they couldn't be answered until he set an appointment with Dr. Meron.

"I haven't called the guy yet," Ray said, seeming to have read Joseph's mind as he pulled Dr. Meron's card out of his jacket. "I guess I just wanted to talk it through with another person from the group first. My wife put the final decision in my hands."

Joseph nodded solemnly. He quietly wished that Jill would give him that freedom of choice as well.

"And I hate it when she does that!" Ray said with a nervous chuckle. Joseph could tell that he was desperate for a word from him. They weren't that close, but many of the dads in the Williams Syndrome group seemed to look to Joseph as a voice of reason.

"You know I think we're all going to have to make this choice based on our own situations. I'd say follow your intuition, Ray. That's what we're going to do," Joseph finally said.

Ray nodded, feeling relieved. "You're right. I just don't want this whole thing to blow up in my face. You know, I love my boy and we've gotten used to managing his condition. Do I really want to take a risk at this point?"

"I totally understand."

"But on the other hand, how could I rob him of this opportunity? It could be the best thing that's ever happened to him," Ray reasoned. As he said those words, Joseph's inner voice spoke up. The clarity of the message he heard jolted him a bit.

The best thing that's happened to him... or you?

"You know what. I'm just gonna call the guy, you know?" Ray said as he stood up. "While we're sitting here analyzing, there's a guy out there who might have the answers."

"Exactly right," Joseph nodded and stood up to meet Ray's handshake. He was never the type of guy to reveal his true feelings to others so readily, so he had no intentions of telling Ray what his family's plans were yet.

"Thanks 'Dr. Joseph,' it really helped talking this through. Send me your bill," Ray joked as he headed out of the door.

"No problem Ray, don't be a stranger. You've got my number," Joseph told him as he left. Joseph closed his office door again and rested his back on it for a moment. He suddenly felt emotionally exhausted.

He stood there for a while, thinking over their conversation. He finally went over to his desk and pulled out the folder of information he had received from Dr. Meron. He looked through it again, looking for some sign that he should go ahead and make that call. He thought about his wife and her shocking reaction that previous night. Could he handle that level of adversity from the woman he loved if he made this decision on his own? In nearly 20 years, he couldn't think of a time when they had had a major disagreement. He also couldn't shake the question posed to him by his inner voice.

Is this for him or for you?

"Of course it's for *him*. And she'll eventually come to see that," Joseph said as he defiantly picked up the line and dialed. "Yes…could I speak with Dr. Howard Meron please?"

Joseph decided to take the rest of the day off from work so that he could spend some time with Joey. He was too preoccupied to sit in the office after Ray Smith left. He and Joey were in the living room together watching their favorite movie starring Bruce Willis. Joey liked Bruce Willis because he reminded him of his dad.

Joey's eyes were glued to the screen, but Joseph could hardly pay attention. He was thinking about what he had done earlier and how he was going to break the news to Jill that he had gone against her wishes. He had made an appointment with Dr. Meron and planned to go alone for answers.

"Hey buddy, you know that I love you, right?" Joseph asked his son, who was sitting right by his side. That was his right-hand man.

"Yup," Joey said while nodding vigorously.

"How much?"

Joey sat up and stretched his arms as wide as he could until they were reaching behind him.

"Even more than that," Joseph said with a smile as he ruffled his son's hair. "And you know that anything I do, I do it for you and because I love you that much?"

Joey nodded again quickly, then went back to his movie. He pointed at the screen "Daddy, this is the good part!"

Just then, Jill came in through the back door carrying packages. She put them down, then went into the living room and gave Joey a tender kiss on the forehead.

"Hi buddy," she told him.

"Hi Mommy!" he said with a bright smile before returning his attention back to the screen.

"Hey," she said with a nod to Joseph before going back into the kitchen. He cringed, knowing that she was still in a mood.

"Let me know what happens next buddy," Joseph said as he pulled himself up from the couch, even though he already knew exactly what happened. He and Joey had watched this movie together at least 100 times. He tried to calm his nerves as he went to the kitchen to talk to Jill. He told 25 people what to do all day at his business and spoke with CEOs of major companies regularly, but his wife was the one person he could still get nervous around.

"Hey, how was your day?" he asked.

"Busy. Gearing up for the fall. You're home early," she said while putting Joey's favorite cereal up on a high shelf. If she didn't, he could finish off the entire box in one sitting.

"Yea, I had a lot on my mind and couldn't concentrate. Do you think we could talk?"

Jill paused and finally looked at her husband. "If what you want to talk about has anything to do with what happened last night, the answer is definitely no. I don't want to discuss it anymore."

Joseph opened his mouth to retort in anger but stopped himself when he heard Joey shriek in delight at one of his favorite action scenes. The last thing he wanted to do was spark a big argument while Joey was sitting in the next room.

"Please have him in bed tonight by 8:30 p.m.?" Jill asked before leaving the room. Joseph leaned up against the counter, folded his arms and tried to relax as a number of different thoughts ran through his head. He knew that when his wife found out that he had scheduled an appointment with Dr. Meron without her knowledge she was going to lose it.

"Daddy!" Joey shouted as he ran in to grab his father's hand. "Come on, the good part is coming on."

"Okay, okay," Joseph relented with a chuckle. His son always had the ability to make him smile.

They sat back down in front of the screen to finish watching their favorite movie.

"Here it comes!" Joey said with anticipation as he sat up in his seat.

"Yippee-ki-yay!!!" They both shouted in unison.

That night, Joseph sat up in bed thinking about the dream he had about Joey. The dream where Joey suddenly transformed into a "normal" 13-year-old boy. He thought about the many new opportunities Joey would have if he could look, think, feel, and perform optimally. Jill wouldn't have to worry so much all of the time. Grace, Sophia, and Mia wouldn't have to deal with the stresses involved with having a brother who had special needs. Finding it impossible to sleep, he decided to go downstairs and watch a late night movie in his den. He leaned over to give Jill a gentle kiss on the cheek. She stirred a bit, but didn't wake up.

Jill rarely dreamt, but when she did it was so vivid that she often recalled it as a memory or vision instead of a dream. Tonight was one of those nights when she nodded off right after her head hit the pillow and…

…she found herself lying back on a red and white checkered picnic blanket, looking up at the sunny sky. She looked to the left and saw Joey by her side, smiling at her and laughing. She smiled back.

He was just six years old—a small little boy. His face was filled with an indescribable glee and a glowing light emanated from him, like an aura. He leaned up and grabbed both of her cheeks to squeeze them…

Then she was sitting on the bleachers at a soccer game. She looked off into the distance and saw Joey standing on the field, looking much taller. She was confused.

"Joey?" she whispered to herself as she stood up to get a closer look. Then she shouted. "Joey!"

Joey turned his head and looked back at his mom. He looked different—a bit more like an adult with common features—but she could immediately tell it was him. He smiled and waved to her briefly before taking off down the field after the ball…

Then she was at Chuck E. Cheese with young Joey, tossing balls into the Skee Ball machine to get as many tickets as possible. She wanted to help him win the hockey game—the only toy he didn't have in his collection yet. She turned around and Joey was nowhere to be found. Hysterical, she began running around the room checking all of the boys with dark hair to see if it was her son. She started arguing with a man whose face she couldn't make out. He was blocking the aisle. She happened to glance over the man's shoulder and looked at the entrance. There stood a grown man with closely cropped dark hair staring back at her. He didn't look much like her Joey, but a mother knows her son. She could recognize him by his eyes, but his serious gaze frightened her. After a few moments, he just walked away, disappearing behind the building.

"Joey?!" Jill screamed as she pushed her way to the door. Outside, the parking lot was completely empty. Not a car or a person was in sight. She looked around frantically, calling out Joey's name over and over again…

"Mommy. Mommy?"

Jill jumped awake and her eyes adjusted to the darkness. She felt out of breath. Joey was sitting on the bed next to her. Joseph had left the bedroom door slightly cracked when he left the room and Jill had been yelling Joey's name in her sleep.

"Mommy, I heard you calling me," he said sleepily. "Are you okay?"

Jill sat up and grabbed his face between her hands. She ran her palms gently over his hair. Then she hugged him, finally getting confirmation that she wasn't still in a dream.

"Yes, mommy's okay. Mommy's fine, I promise," she said as a single tear streaked down her face. "I love you, baby."

CHAPTER 3
The Fast Track

Debra Jacobs was a fairly passive woman. She had been that way all of her life. She held closely to her religious beliefs and accepted the idea that the husband was the head of the household. She believed that the husband was responsible for making the final decisions for the family. In her home, her husband John made all of the calls and she rarely, if ever, questioned him.

But when she learned that Dr. Meron was offering families an effective treatment that could reduce the symptoms of Williams Syndrome, something stirred inside of her. She wanted to know more about it, and urgently. She didn't want to be left out of this opportunity.

But John didn't want to hear anything about it.

Debra stayed at home with their seven-year-old daughter Patricia. Patricia's Williams Syndrome symptoms made it difficult for her to succeed at a normal school at her age. So Debra home-schooled her with the help of a tutor and speech therapist. She loved her daughter with a passion, but being at home all day with Patricia could be more than a handful. Patricia also had two older brothers who were in high school.

John worked as a long-haul trucker, spending 12-14 hour days on the road. In some cases, he would spend long weekends away from his family for work, leaving Debra with a full load at home. He made good money and they were fully able to afford all of Patricia's expenses but more than anything Debra wanted more emotional support from her husband.

Sometimes, Debra felt guilty because she had always prayed for a girl. John was content with his two sons, but Debra was intent on having a little girl who she could dress up, buy baby dolls for and get her ready for prom one day. When she and her husband found out that their baby girl Patricia had Williams Syndrome, they were shocked and devastated by the news. John withdrew while Debra eventually developed a problem with anxiety that required her to take medication at times. Patricia was prone to temper tantrums and fits that would sometimes last for hours on end. One time, Debra had a nervous breakdown during one of her daughter's fits while running errands around town. She was nearly arrested that day for leaving her daughter in the car alone, in the parking lot of Costco for 20 minutes. Even though she knew that Williams Syndrome was caused by a spontaneous deletion of genes from Chromosome 7 and not inherited from either parent, Debra still felt somehow responsible for her daughter's condition.

Debra was dealing with a quiet struggle that she felt no one could understand—not her parents, not her neighbors and certainly not her husband John. She felt trapped in a personal prison of her own making. She couldn't pursue any real career or hobby because Patricia kept her fully occupied from six in the morning until 9 p.m. at night when she finally dozed off. Patricia looked like an angel when she was sleeping and night time was Debra's favorite time of the day.

Debra preferred to keep things close to her heart and didn't want to bother anyone else with her problems. But as noble as that may have been, every day she felt as if she was losing a small bit of herself.

So that day, Debra did something that she had never done before. She made a decision without John's say-so or approval. She called Dr. Meron to find out more about the treatment he was offering. He wasn't available, so she had a nice long conversation with his assistant Tamara. She was so reassured by Tamara's calm, comforting voice on the phone that she went ahead and scheduled a consultation appointment for that following week. She took down notes vigorously on the pad of paper she kept near the mail. Her hand shook as she put the house phone back on the charger base.

Debra felt a bit light-headed as she went to the kitchen and opened up the refrigerator. Her eyes fell on the bottle of Pinot Grigio that she had left over from the previous night and she couldn't resist pouring a little into a small thermos. She eagerly took a sip to calm her nerves.

"Mommy, look!" she heard Patricia scream from behind her and it made her jump. She turned around and saw her daughter standing there covered with a translucent white substance—her hair, her shirt, pants and the KangaROOS sneakers her father had just bought for her were a mess. On closer look and smell, Debra could tell that she had gotten into the large shampoo dispenser. She was constantly telling John to put it back up in the closet after his showers because Patricia loved the smell and consistency of the goo.

"Oh Patty!" she exclaimed with a frown as she set her thermos aside. She looked down the hall and saw that she had tracked the shampoo all the way from the bathroom.

"Mommy, I wash! Look!" Patty said enthusiastically as she rubbed the shampoo all over her face and hair. Debra knew that she would be spending the next two to three hours cleaning up Patricia and her mess.

It was Sophia's first year in junior high school and she had already made a lot of new friends. Some of her friends were from her old school, but she also had a new set of classmates who came from other elementary schools in the area. The new kids didn't know anything about Sophia's family or her brother Joey, who attended special needs classes at the school.

Sophia and her friends were sitting around the lunch table that they had designated for themselves, getting ready for the bell to ring. Sophia always tended to be the center of attention when she was around her peers. Now that she was in junior high, it was becoming more clear that she would be a member of the popular crowd at school. She had long brown hair, icy blue eyes, and evenly tanned skin. She resembled a young Liz Taylor, and though she was pretty she was also a little bit of a tomboy. She had been playing catch with her dad ever since she was old enough to walk. At 11, Sophia had become the star pitcher for her little league softball team.

"So are you pitching in this weekend's game Sophia?" Brendan asked as he hovered nearby. He was a new boy who had gone to another area elementary school before attending junior high with her. He had immediately developed a schoolboy crush on Sophia soon after laying eyes on her.

Sophia scoffed at the question, flipped her hair back, and kept writing in her little notebook.

"Does she ever *not* pitch?" Sophia's best friend Tessa responded to him sarcastically.

"Geez, just asking. I've never been to one of her games," Brendan said, sounding embarrassed in front of his friends. "Well, me and the guys will be there."

"Great," Sophia responded unenthusiastically. Though she was the girl everyone sent Valentine's Day candy grams to, the last thing on her mind was boys. She was more focused on softball and maintaining her grades so that she could be put in honors classes. She knew that would definitely make her parents happy.

"We'll save a seat for you guys," Tessa said, flirting with Brendan's friend, Rick. He smiled and shyly looked down at the remnants of his pizza lunch.

"Sophiiiieeee!!!" they all heard a strange sound coming closer and closer to their table. Brendan turned around and saw a small, black-haired boy barreling toward them. He was smiling from ear-to-ear.

"What the?" he exclaimed as he eyed the boy from head to toe. It was Sophia's brother Joey—he had broken free from the line of his classmates when he saw his sister sitting at a table nearby. It was the first time they had gone to the same school.

"Joey," Sophia said, feeling a burning flush of embarrassment.

"Guess what? I'm going to be in the school play!!!" Joey exclaimed as he slapped the table and jumped up and down. His smile could have lit up 10 rooms—he was always so excited to see his sisters outside of the house.

"Who's this kid?" Brendan said with a slight chuckle and smirk. Sophia shot him a glare, but he didn't see it because he was too busy jabbing his friend and getting ready to make fun. "Hey, what's your problem kid? Calm down, okay?"

"He doesn't have a problem!" Sophia said as she stood up from her seat, going into defensive-sister mode. She eyed Brendan down as if she were about to challenge him to a duel. "And don't you *ever* tell my brother to calm down, you jerk!"

Sophia snatched her lunch tray up from the table and walked toward her brother.

"Come on Joey T," she told him as she grabbed his hand and walked him back over to his classmates on the lunch line. It certainly wasn't the first time that she had to defend her brother in public.

"Boy, did you just make a mistake," Tessa said forebodingly to Brendan as she grabbed her tray to follow them.

Ray Smith did what his wife told him. He made the final decision to call Dr. Meron and she had agreed. When they mentioned the fact that their son would be 15 years old soon, Tamara put them on hold for a while as she checked something.

"Hi again. Dr. Meron would like to speak with you two," Tamara told them. "Please hold on a moment."

After about 30 seconds, Dr. Meron clicked onto the line. "Thank you, Tamara. Mr. and Mrs. Smith?"

"Yes, we're here," they responded eagerly over their speakerphone. Ray's wife, Mary Ellen, clutched her necklace charm in anticipation. It was a ceramic charm that her son had made for her in a crafting class.

"Thank you for calling. I'm glad that you're contacting me now rather than later because we have a very short window of opportunity for your son. You say he'll be turning 15 in the new year?"

"Yes, January 18th," Mary Ellen confirmed.

"Alright," Dr. Meron said as he jotted something down on a pad of paper. "Well to give you an idea of the urgency, our treatment requires a weekly injection. We've estimated that it takes a minimum of 14 injections to see any significant results."

"Okay, but we still have time, right?" Ray asked with a bit of desperation in his voice.

Dr. Meron spoke under his breath as he did some calculations. Ray and his wife waited with baited breath.

"Mr. and Mrs. Smith, we have to get you and your son… what is his name?"

"Sammy," they said together.

"We have to get Sammy into our office this week. I will be working closely with my assistant to fast-track your case. But I will need your full cooperation to make this work."

"Of course," Ray responded. "Well, how about Monday? I can take off of work."

"I will have Tamara call you back with an exact day and time. Does she have your information?"

"Yes," Mary Ellen responded with a sigh of relief. "Thank you so much, Dr. Meron."

Without realizing it, The Smiths had already made a firm decision about joining the experimental trial without knowing the full details about what it entailed. They were too struck by their fear of missing out.

"Tamara," Dr. Meron called for his assistant after he hung up the phone. "Let's get the Smiths fast-tracked."

"Sure thing sir…but…do you think they'll have enough time for it to be a worthwhile effort?" Tamara dared ask.

Dr. Meron paused and looked up at her with an expression that could wilt flowers. "Get them in for Monday or Tuesday please."

Tamara nodded. She went into her office and sat down at her desk to start filling out a new case file, but as she was typing, she kept making small mistakes that caused her to have to start over again. She didn't know if it was because she was tired after no sleep and 20 straight hours of work, or because she was bothered by the thought of these parents being disappointed.

It was a little after 11 p.m. and darkness enveloped the Jacobs' house. Debra had finished off the last of her bottle of Pinot Grigio in the fridge and opened a new one before passing out on the couch in front of the TV. John turned his key in the door, but it locked on him. Confused, he turned his key again and opened the door, expecting to hear the alarm beep and ask him to put in the code. Instead, the "door open" charm rang and then there was silence except for Julie Andrews singing faintly in the next room.

Debra loved watching *The Sound of Music* movie over and over again. It was an obsession from her childhood that had stuck with her. John walked into the living room where she was lounging and switched on the light. He looked at the scene before him and shook his head. There was Debra, splayed out on the couch with her head turned to the side, snoring lightly and grasping the neck of a wine bottle.

"Deb!" he called out, but she was still snoozing. "Deb!"

Debra finally woke up and adjusted her eyes to the bright light. "John, please. Quiet…you'll wake Patty."

"God forbid that happen," John said with an accusing tone as he gestured to the bottle in her hand. "How many of those have you had today?"

"Just this one. Well, a couple of glasses," Debra told a little white lie as she sat up and adjusted her clothing. She felt a headache coming on. "How was your day?"

"Not as good as yours," John said snarkily as he took off his jacket and headed to the kitchen to grab something to drink out of the fridge. "Where are the boys?"

"Both of them called to tell me they're staying over their friends' houses tonight," she answered. She looked at the bottle she had been holding in her hand and knew that she had made a mistake opening it up.

"You know, you left the house completely unlocked Deb. Door and everything," John informed her as he made his way over to the mail.

"Oh. I must have forgotten. Randy usually takes care of that when he comes in. Patty really gave me a time today. She had her therapy session this afternoon and we had to end early because she had a bad fit. Then she made me read her three *Little Blue Truck* books before she nodded off," Debra said, trying to explain her day. She watched Julie Andrews sing with her happy, perfect, soon-to-be step-children for a few moments more, then stopped the DVD she was playing.

"Have you gotten through all of those *Best Behavior* books I got her yet?"

"No, not yet."

"Well I think that's a bit more important than stories about a blue truck, right?" John asked with that same sarcastic tone as he sorted through the mail.

"Well you know, she looks up to her dad, the truck driver. She loves those books," Debra reminded him as she entered the kitchen. John grimaced at her, then glanced down and saw the pad of paper she had been writing on earlier.

"I'm heading to bed," Debra said.

"What's this?" John wanted to know. He held up the pad of paper, which contained Dr. Meron's name, phone number and an appointment time. "Dr. Meron, who's that?"

"Uh…" Debra hesitated to answer. This was yet another oversight from being so overwhelmed that day. She wanted to pick the right moment to talk to John about everything. But now was going to have to be that time.

"This is that doctor from the meeting, isn't it?" John deduced.

"I just wanted to know more about the treatment. I set up a consultation."

"Didn't we agree that we weren't going to be involving Patty in any experiments?"

"No. Actually, *you* agreed on that. I didn't have a say," Patty said. Her face flushed red—it wasn't often that she argued back with John.

"How could you even think of putting her in some type of drug trial?"

"John, we don't know what it is. How will we ever know if there's something out there that can help our child if we don't ever give anything a chance?" Debra asked.

"Patty is fine. We're fine. And we're not doing this," John answered her with finality as he tore the top sheet off of the pad and began ripping it up.

"No! We're not fine John," Debra protested. "Maybe you're fine, but *I'm* not fine! And my opinion matters too. You have no idea what I have to go through in the course of a day!"

John was surprised by Debra's tone. "And what exactly do you do while I'm driving for 14 hours straight and paying all of the bills? Oh wait, I know. Popping open all of those wine bottles must be stressful for you."

"Patty! *She's* my full-time 14-hour job, and I don't get a break like you do! I'm a wreck, constantly worried about our daughter and what she might do that I have to fix," Debra revealed. "Did you know she got out of the house last week and hid in the neighbor's yard for over an hour playing hide and go seek? I had to call the police!"

"What? And you didn't tell me this?"

"You didn't pick up your phone!"

"Why didn't you leave a message?"

"I tried to," Debra answered. "Your mailbox was full. And when your daughter's missing how do you write a text about it with shaking fingers??? I can't take this anymore John, something has to change!"

"Well, maybe you're right Deb. Something *does* need to change," John said calmly as he sat down on a stool. He put his face in his hands. "We, this, needs to change, because it's just not working anymore."

"Anymore? When has this ever worked for anyone but *you*?" Debra asked. After a few moments, she realized what John was suggesting and her demeanor changed.

"John, I know you're not trying to say what I think…"

"Yes, I am. And this is a long time coming—admit it Deb. Neither of us are happy. Let's just stop playing this game," John said as he stood up to grab his jacket and headed for the door.

"John, no! That's not what I…" Debra started to say, but John had already opened the door and slammed it behind him.

"…meant," she said out loud, finishing her sentence. But she was talking to herself. "I just need some help."

Debra slowly walked over to the door and opened it back up. She watched as John backed out of the driveway in his pickup truck. He then screeched off down the street. She stared outside for a while, trying to come to terms with what just happened. Finally, she closed the door and went back into the kitchen to sit down.

What did I just do? she asked herself.

CHAPTER 4
Keeping Up Appearances

"You'll really like this tutor, he's amazing. Tommy loves him. And you know how hard it is to get him to sit down and pay attention for any amount of time!" Marsha said with a laugh as she returned to the living room holding two glasses of cold, bubbly Prosecco. The glasses were elaborately detailed at the bottom and sparkled in the sunlight coming from her bay window, which was slightly ajar. It was a beautiful 70-degree Saturday. Jill and Marsha were enjoying the gentle, fresh fall breeze that was blowing in.

"Thank you," Jill said as she accepted her glass. She sat at attention whenever she was with Marsha because her living room looked like it should be in a museum, cordoned off with red velvet ropes. It was full of framed art and expensive decorative vases that were mounted securely to prevent them from falling over. Everything was in its proper place and you could tell that the house was dusted very regularly—probably every day.

Jill appreciated the fact that whenever she and Joey came to visit with Marsha, she always pulled out the good China, cooked gourmet meals for them and gave them the royal treatment. It made Jill feel special. It also made her want to step up her game and return the favor whenever Marsha and her family came to visit. Marsha was an inspiration when it came to entertaining her guests.

"No worries, this Prosecco is only five percent alcohol. It's light and so delicious," Marsha said with a smile and a wink as they clinked the tops of their glasses together. She took a sip and then sat her glass down on one of her sterling silver coasters. Jill watched as Marsha turned around to grab a laundry basket full of warm clothes that she had just pulled out of the dryer. Everything she did made her look like the mom of the year. She started to carefully fold them as she continued talking up her son's tutor.

"...Jason has a dual degree in Psychology and Children's Education from the University of Chicago. I've gotten much better reports from Tommy's teacher since I hired him. He could probably help Joey a couple of times a month..."

Joey and Tommy were in the backyard playing a game of hide and go seek. Their games could go on for hours. Joey was "it" while Tommy stood with his eyes closed, facing the fence. He couldn't help peeking a few times to see the general direction where Joey was headed.

"No cheating!" Joey screamed as he scrambled around looking for the best place to hide in the Rogers' expansive backyard. They had about a quarter of an acre of land that included two full swing sets, a gravel-surfaced playground similar to the one Tommy had at school, a trampoline and a large, perfectly manicured vegetable garden. The entire area was protected by secure 10-foot fences so that Marsha could relax knowing that Tommy wouldn't be able to wander outside of the property.

Tommy was the same age as Joey and was very similar to him in appearance. They were both the same height, about 4' 7, and slim. They both had small chins and distinctively shaped noses. They could almost be twins if it weren't for the fact that Joey's hair was short and black, while Tommy's hair was longer and sandy blonde.

"...One time, Tommy asked me if he could go home with Jason. When I told him no, he went and hid in the back seat of Jason's car while he was in the bathroom," Marsha said with a chuckle.

"That's funny, Joey has done that with his father! He wants to go to work with him all of the time. And I constantly have to stop him from hiding his father's keys," Jill related and Marsha chuckled again.

"Yes, Tommy loves 'Mr. J.' That's what he calls Jason. It's so hard to find people who really understand the specific needs of a child with Williams Syndrome. He's a bit pricey for a tutor, but anything for our boys, right?" Marsha asked.

Jill glanced outside the window just in time to see Joey climbing into Marsha's garden and trying to hide himself between her tall, fully-ripened tomato plants.

"Joey, no!" Jill started to yell out through the open window, but Marsha stopped her with a hand on her shoulder as they both watched him.

"It's okay, even if he knocks one over I can just replant it later. Those plants are very hardy," Marsha said with a smile as she went back to folding. "Besides, the season is just about over. I'm going to have to finish harvesting and make some sauce."

Jill could not understand how Marsha could always be so calm, cool and collected all of the time. Nothing seemed to rattle her—even when Tommy had the occasional temper tantrum. Jill had never seen so much as a hair out of place on Marsha's head.

"Can I help you with that?" Jill asked.

"Absolutely not, you're my guest!" Marsha replied. "I know you probably had a crazy week. You just sit, relax and enjoy your sparkling wine. I have plenty more in the fridge."

Hearing that actually did make Jill feel a bit more relaxed, and she took another small sip from her glass. It was so nice to not have to feel guilty or responsible for anything, even if it was just for a few hours.

"This really is good," Jill agreed with a nod as she felt the bubbles rush to her nose.

"Great, I'm glad you like it because I'm going to send you home with a bottle," Marsha said matter-of-factly.

"Marsha. You are too good to me," Jill said.

Jill was a district manager at a well-known regional company that ran a chain of over 100 stores. She had started out working as a cashier at the company as a teen making $4.75 per hour and worked her way all the way up the ranks. She had been working ever since she received her first work permit at 14. She enjoyed the responsibilities of managing the company, but she couldn't help but feel guilty about the fact that she couldn't spend more time tending to Joey and 5-year-old Mia at home. They had a great part-time nanny who had been with them for years—she filled in whenever needed. Jill's bosses fully understood her family situation and allowed her to arrive late and leave early when it was necessary, which was a blessing, but sometimes she thought about leaving it all behind and becoming a full-time mom like Marsha. Money certainly wasn't an issue for Jill's family, but she was afraid of losing a part of herself if she were to give up her career.

Despite being a stay-at-home mom, Marsha still had her hand in a number of different entrepreneurial endeavors. She had written a small book about parenting special needs children that had sold more than a few copies on Amazon and had even been on display in a local Barnes and Noble store once. She was an expert knitter and jewelry maker who sold her wares on Etsy. She had earned an Associate's degree in Interior Design and a local real estate agency hired her from time to time to stage houses. She and her husband had a very comfortable middle-class lifestyle and lived in a quiet cul-de-sac located just outside of Springfield, Illinois.

"You'll probably get a chuckle out of this," Marsha said, keeping the conversation going. "Lately, Tommy likes to lock doors from the inside. He likes to see how frustrated his father gets trying to open the bathroom door when he really has to go. Tommy really gets a kick out of that."

Jill laughed. "Boys and their dads. Back in August, Joseph said that all he wanted for his birthday was a big, juicy T-bone steak. A couple of days later, an Amazon box showed up on our door with a $25 raw T-bone steak inside."

"What?" Marsha asked, looking confused.

"Apparently, Joey T got into the iPad when his father fell asleep using it and placed a 'one-click' Amazon order," Jill explained and they both started laughing. "How could I get mad? He loves his dad and I was happy to see how well he can spell and search online now. We've never seen him use that site before."

Suddenly, they heard Joey shriek as Tommy finally found him lurking in the garden. He chased Joey all around the yard trying to tag him. They were caught up in their own world together and just having a ball.

"Kids," Marsha commented as she watched them. "Wouldn't you like to do it all over again?"

"They've got it made. When did it end?" Jill asked as memories from her own childhood flooded in.

"Well, I think at about nine years old we started wanting to be grown up so badly that our wishes came true too quickly," Marsha said with a regretful smile. She paused for a moment as she got lost in her thoughts of being younger.

"Hmm. You may be right about that. Well, what a blessing that these two don't have that problem. In a way, they're forever young," Jill commented. "They'll always have that sense of innocence."

Marsha just sat quietly and focused on her work. She placed every shirt and sock neatly inside of the basket. There was an awkward silence that Jill desperately wanted to break.

"So, how about that last meeting. Crazy huh?" Jill said, trying to make it sound like it was small talk when it was really a topic that had been pressing on her mind for a while. She had been giving Joseph the cold shoulder ever since their first argument about Dr. Meron. She really didn't even know why it was bothering her so much.

"Yea, it's great, isn't it? We're so looking forward to it," Marsha said with a smile as she finished folding a t-shirt with such precision that you could put it on a display at a retail clothing store.

"Looking forward to what?" Jill asked with squinted eyes as she put her glass down.

"The appointment of course. Didn't you guys set yours?" Marsha asked without much of a second thought as she finally finished up and pushed the basket aside. She didn't notice the look of concern on Jill's face.

"Well, no…I…"

"No? What are you waiting for? Aren't you excited to hear more about the therapy?" Marsha asked with an incredulous smile. "Jack and I called him first thing the next day after the meeting. We have an appointment set."

"But aren't you concerned about…the side effects or…I mean, what do we even know about this doctor anyway?" Jill asked, not really knowing what to say.

"Well, how would we know about him unless we go talk to him? We have to be open to these things—especially something with this much potential to help Tommy. I looked up Dr. Meron's credentials online and I have his full resume. Do you want to see it?" Marsha asked as stood up from her seat and walked toward her home office.

Jill was stuck, amazed that Marsha was so eager to see Dr. Meron. She went over there feeling confident that she would have an ally—someone she trusted who could see her perspective on the matter. Marsha's life was so perfect already, why would she want to mess with anything?

Marsha came back with a folder containing the doctor's resume on a few sheets of textured, scented paper. Just then, she heard Tommy's voice shouting in the distance.

"Jason! Jason!" he said over and over as he jumped up and down. The excitement was contagious because Joey started jumping around too. Marsha and Jill looked out of the window and saw that Jason had entered the yard. He was a tall, broad-shouldered, brown-haired young guy who looked like he was just out of college. Marsha quickly glanced at the mirror next to the patio door to check her makeup and hair, then immediately headed outside to meet him.

"Marsha, I'm just going to head to the bathroom," Jill said, needing to pull herself together for a moment. She felt as if she had just gotten an unexpected gut-check from her friend. Was she overreacting about the potential dangers of the treatment program? Was she wrong to question its merits?

"Sure honey, you know where it is!" Marsha called out from the yard. By then, she was completely distracted by Jason's presence.

Jill grasped the folder in her hand tightly as she made her way to the guest bathroom down the hall. She turned the knob several times but it was locked. She knocked gently, but then remembered earlier when

Marsha told her how Tommy had taken on the curious habit of locking doors in the house from the inside.

"Good one Tommy," Jill said with a chuckle as she started back toward the living room. She realized that in all of the times that she had visited Marsha she'd never seen the upstairs or even been invited to see it. Glancing outside, she saw that Marsha and Jason were in a lively conversation that she didn't want to disturb. So she headed up the stairs to find another bathroom.

The first door she opened was a closet that was overstuffed with towels, linens and toilet tissue. She shut that quickly and then moved onto the next door. She turned the knob and peeked inside briefly. It wasn't the bathroom—it looked like Tommy's room, full of stuffed animals and SpongeBob Squarepants decorations. Jill was a little surprised by how unkempt and messy it was in there—bed unmade, clothes on the floor and scribblings all over the walls—Marsha was usually very organized and detail-oriented.

She opened the next door in the hall, but this time what she saw inside caught her attention enough to make her open the door all the way.

"What in the world?"

It appeared to be the master bedroom. It caught her attention because it looked like a storm had gone through it. Clothes were strewn everywhere, the bed sheets were pulled back and there were empty carryout containers on the dresser, nightstand and television stand. A glass was broken on the floor in front of the closet, which was ajar and leaking more clothes. It looked like a frat guy's college dorm room and smelled like expired takeout food. Jill couldn't believe her eyes—it was so bad that she wanted to start picking things up. Marsha was so meticulous about everything downstairs—she never so much as left a dish in her sink or a towel unfolded. How could the situation be so different in her bedroom?

At that point, Jill abandoned her plan to find the bathroom. She quickly closed the bedroom door and descended the stairs before Marsha came back into the house. She made it to the glass patio door and was relieved when she saw everyone still outside chatting. Pushing her way out, she took a deep breath as she tried to push what she'd just seen upstairs to the back of her mind.

Maybe that's not her *bedroom,* she reasoned. *Maybe she just has a messy guest?*

"Here she is!" Marsha said with a smile and gesture that could have put a Stepford wife to shame. Jill quieted her thoughts as she shook Jason's hand.

"It's nice to meet you, Jason," she said.

"Same here. Are you Joey's mom?" he asked with a welcoming smile.

"That's me," she said with a chuckle. Marsha frowned and quickly grabbed Jason to regain his attention.

"Joey is having some issues at school that I think you can help him with," Marsha said. She flirted, played with her hair and did whatever she could to keep his attention. Jill looked at her curiously and wondered if Jason was really as proficient a tutor as Marsha claimed or if she was excited about him for a different reason.

It was Saturday and an unseasonably warm fall day. Joseph had taken an early morning drive down to the lake for a long hike through the woods and a quick breakfast by the lakeside. He wanted to take some time to himself—his thoughts were consumed with Joey, Dr. Meron's proposed treatment, and the fact that his wife refused to speak to him about it. He felt uneasy, and it was getting to the point where it was affecting his work.

After his early morning hike, he went to Sophia's softball game, where she pitched a nearly perfect game—the other team had only three hits. Jill and Joey had gone to the Rogers' for the day and the younger girls were spending the weekend at their friends' houses. Grace was almost always missing in action on the weekends. So it was the perfect opportunity for Joseph to unwind and get his footing back before Monday.

Paul waved when he saw Joseph pull into the driveway. He was busy watering his newly planted mums. It was uncanny—it always seemed as if Paul managed to be outside when Joseph was either coming in or going out. Joseph nodded back in Paul's direction and then sighed as he grasped the steering wheel. He hesitated to turn the car off, wanting to pull back out.

Maybe if I just sit here for a while he'll go inside, he thought.

Joseph rolled up his window a bit and busied himself with his cellphone for a few minutes. He even checked a few voicemails, which he almost never did. Still, Paul continued to water his mums. Then he moved onto watering the lawn.

"Hey there Joe!" Paul called out when he saw Joseph looking in his direction again. There would be no avoiding this little rendezvous.

"Hey Paul," Joseph said as he finally climbed out of his car.

"Got anything exciting planned this weekend?" Paul asked as he approached.

"Not really. Mostly staying in. How about you?"

"Marge and I were supposed to take a trip in to see the grandkids, but she fell a bit under the weather," Paul answered. "Hey, how about we could go grab some lunch at The Lagoon?"

"No, I've got something to do Paul. Another time…" Joseph said as he started toward the front door. Just then, another car pulled into his driveway.

The truth was that Joseph had plans to see his fraternity brother Phil that weekend, but he wasn't keen to invite Paul. The last time Paul came over to hang out with Joseph and his friends, he had one too many drinks and was peer-pressured into running full speed into the pool to do a cannon ball. Instead of completing his planned cannon ball jump, he slipped on a wet spot, fell and aggravated a back injury. Joseph felt horrible when Jill felt compelled to go next door to apologize to Paul's wife for what had happened. Sometimes Paul tried too hard to fit in.

Phil jumped out of his car and ran to the trunk. He emerged holding a large cooler dripping with icy water. "Let's get the party started bro!"

Joseph turned a deep red as he laughed at his best friend's antics. He was always so full of energy and ready to have fun. Paul looked back and forth between the two with an awkward smile on his face.

"Thought you couldn't get here 'til after seven?" Joseph asked as Phil made his way up to the house. They slapped hands and gave each other a man hug.

"Yea, I know. But I heard your voice on the phone. You need me. I got here as soon as I could," Phil said as he put the cooler down. He nodded toward Paul in acknowledgment. "Now hurry up and open the door."

Joseph did as his 'big brother' told him. When Joseph and his frat brother Phil got together, it was as if they were transported right back to their college days in the 90s. They met the first day of rush week—Joseph was a freshman candidate and Phil was already a member. Phil was assigned to be his big brother during the process and it was a match made in heaven. Phil had a way of grounding Joseph and getting him back in touch with who he really was at heart: a down-to-earth guy who loved an adventure and had a wild side, but who also knew that appreciating and protecting his loved ones mattered more than anything. No matter how many milestones reached and successes achieved, Phil always helped keep Joseph in balance. Phil was the closest thing he had to a mentor, and that's why Joseph was eager to have him over for the weekend to talk about things.

"Uh, Paul?" Joseph called out when he noticed that Paul was quietly making his way back over to his side of the lawn.

"Yea?"

"We'll get together another time okay? Me, you, Jill and Marge?"

"Yea, sure neighbor. Talk to you soon," Paul said as waved weakly and went back into his house.

"I remember Paul. The cannon fall," Phil said as a devious smile started to grow on his face, but Joseph shook his head to stop his thoughts.

"Let's leave that unfortunate incident in the past."

They decided to take advantage of the sunny 70-degree day and lounge out by the pool to talk and catch up. Joseph didn't waste any time explaining what was going on—the decision that they were facing and Jill's unexpected resistance to finding out more about the treatment for Joey. His scheduled appointment with Dr. Meron was on Monday morning and he still planned to go alone, without Jill. He knew that he was playing with fire and needed someone to either put it out or stoke it and keep it blazing.

"You have to ask yourself if you can handle what's to come if you take that step," Phil said to him after processing all of that information. "You're a team, you're supposed to make a move like that together."

"But can I handle never knowing, if Jill causes us to miss this opportunity?" Joseph asked. "Would I ever be able to forgive her?"

Phil was quiet for a long moment before he spoke again. "Are you happy with your life Joe?"

"Of course," Joseph answered without hesitation.

"So why do you want to mess with it? Why would you potentially disrupt the 'flow'?"

"It's for Joey's sake. We don't know what he could be or do if he didn't have to struggle with the symptoms of Williams Syndrome. How can we rob him of that chance?"

"Have you asked Joey what he feels about it?" Phil asked.

"He doesn't fully understand what's involved. We're his parents— we have to make this decision for him. Look, I just want to know more about what is being offered at this point. Is that so horrible?"

"I don't think it's horrible, but talking to you, it seems as if you already have your mind made up," Phil said as he took a swig of his beer.

Joseph slunk back into his reclining beach chair. "Well, maybe I do. I'm going to see that guy."

"Your choice," Phil said and shrugged.

"Hey, it's easy to sit on the outside looking in and make judgments. Joey is doing okay, but he still has struggles. Doctor appointments every other week. There are things you don't see," Joseph said defensively.

"What part of what I said sounds like judgment? Hey, you know I love that kid— everything about him. But you're right, I'm not here every day. You're his father and you know best."

"Right. Exactly."

The conversation was clearly over but Joseph didn't look like he was really ready for it to end. Phil glanced over at his best friend's face with concern. He could tell that this conversation was just the tip of an iceberg.

CHAPTER 5
Her Sweet Baby Boy

Grace drove up to the drive-thru at the fast food restaurant closest to her high school with her boyfriend Scott in the passenger's seat. He had been tapping away at his phone intermittently since they first met up that afternoon. He convinced her to skip out after her lunch hour and take the rest of the day off from school. But first, a quick stop so that he could get a "proper lunch." He refused to eat cafeteria food.

"Welcome to The Burger Shack, can I take your order?" the cashier asked.

Scott immediately began running off his order. "A number 5, extra-large everything, another double cheeseburger, strawberry milkshake and an apple pie."

"Got it. Anything else?" the voice asked again.

"Just another strawberry milkshake please," Grace answered. She had already eaten lunch in the cafeteria.

"That'll be $14.49."

Scott settled back into his seat just as his phone was dinging again with a message. He was a tall, gaunt and lanky boy of 17 despite his voracious appetite. He was a senior and started for the school's lacrosse team, which made him a well-known jock and member of the school's popular crowd. Grace felt fortunate that he had chosen her to be his girlfriend during his last year of high school. Dating a senior like Scott instantly propelled her to the "A-list" among her peers.

They drove up to the cashier's window to pay and Scott never looked up from his phone.

"You got this, right babe?" he told her more than asked.

"Uh... yea, sure," Grace said as she hesitantly pulled out the debit card her parents had given her. She prayed that they wouldn't ever check the statement in detail because it was clear proof that she had been skipping school—a lot. She was starting to wonder if Scott's parents ever gave him money because he was always spending hers.

"Thanks babe," Scott said when the food arrived. He kissed her on the cheek and immediately started digging in. "So hungry. Mark's having a few people over. Wanna go?"

"Uh, sure," Grace said as she pulled out of the parking lot. "How do I get to his house again?"

"Turn left at the next light."

Mark was every father's nightmare, in the flesh. He had rugged good looks, untamed brown hair, effortless charm and an athletic body that he worked on regularly in the gym. He went through girls like newspaper issues—there was a new one just about every week that claimed he was her boyfriend. There was a rumor that he had caused three different girls to leave the school district due to the public embarrassment Mark caused them. Grace didn't like Mark one bit because she had seen the *real* him beneath his attractive outer appearance—he was an insufferable jerk with a narcissistic personality. But she tolerated him because he was one of Scott's best friends and teammates.

"So how long have you two love birds been going together now?" Mark leaned forward and asked Grace as Scott opened a can of warm beer.

"About seven months," Grace said with a satisfied nod.

"You must be a good one. I've never known this guy to settle down," Mark said as he gestured his head toward Scott.

Grace cringed at being referred to as a "good one," as if she were one of many, but she kept her thoughts to herself.

"Sure you don't want a beer?" Mark asked for the fifth time. He was used to girls taking one on the first or second offer. The two girls he had invited over were both holding beers.

"Positive. I can't stand the taste," Grace said, trying to relax. She looked over at Scott who was again tapping away at his phone.

"It's not about the taste sweetheart," Mark said with a laugh and slapped his leg. He was already tipsy and it was just 3 in the afternoon. He watched when Scott pulled Grace closer to him on the couch and a look of jealousy fell over his face.

"Hey, did Scott tell you he got into Loyola?" Mark asked out of the blue.

Scott shot him a look of disgust. "No, I didn't. That was supposed to be a surprise, dimwit."

"Oohhhh. My bad," Mark responded, looking satisfied again. "Well, the cat's out of the bag. He got a scholarship."

"You're going away? I thought you said you were going to a local college?" Grace lifted her head up to ask.

"I didn't know they were seriously considering me for the scholarship. I got in, and you know, plans change," Scott said nonchalantly.

"Don't worry, I'm sure he'll put you in his rotation freshman year," Mark joked and laughed heartily along with the other people in the room. But Grace wasn't amused in any way. Scott tried to wave him off, but Mark could be relentless.

"Put me in his 'rotation'?" Grace repeated and turned to Scott. "What is he talking about?"

"Please, a star athlete in college? The girls will be beating down his door," Mark explained.

"Don't listen to him, he's just jealous because he can't pull any A-level girls like you anymore. Only Bs or lower," Scott joked, taking a side jab at the girls who were laughing. But this time, Mark was the one that didn't find anything funny. His smile quickly turned into a frown because Scott had hit a chord. The truth was, Mark's jealousy of Scott ran deep. He had been demoted to second string on their lacrosse team because of a disciplinary action by the school and he still hadn't been accepted to any colleges, let alone on a scholarship. Scott was also right about the fact that many of the school's most attractive and smart girls wouldn't give Mark the time of day anymore, afraid that he might ruin their reputations.

"Hey Scott, who are you chatting on your phone? Is it Amanda? How's she doing?" Mark asked loudly. Scott winced and locked his cellphone instinctively. Mark's devilish grin returned.

Grace stood up from her seat, fuming by now. She had fallen right into Mark's trap. She didn't know if it was just insecurity or her women's intuition that caused her temper to flare. "Who's Amanda, Scott?"

"No one babe, he's just trying to get to me through you. He's jealous. Come on, let's get out of here," Scott said as he stood up and grabbed Grace's arm, but she yanked it away. She stormed out of the screen door and slammed it behind her.

"Hmm, I think I like her. She's spicy," Mark said with a smile as he sat back, again satisfied.

"You're a real tool, you know that? You know what I'm going to have to do now to get her to buy my new lacrosse gear?" Scott said as he crumpled up his empty can and threw it at Mark. "I need that before my visit to the college next weekend."

"Relax. I'm sure you've got other options," Mark said with a sneer.

"I'm sorry that your wife couldn't make it to this appointment, Mr. Todaro. I hope she'll be able to take off from work next time," Dr. Meron said, trying to sound sincere. But he suspected that there was more to Jill's absence than just a work conflict. It wasn't the first time that only one parent came to the initial consultation appointment because the other one was reluctant.

"Yes, I'm sure she'll be able to come next time," Joseph said with a quick nod.

"So before you get into your questions, let me first give you a detailed rundown of what my Williams Syndrome treatment entails. We'll start with a blood test, scans and thorough medical history for your son. The treatment plan involves a weekly injection of a serum that I've named WT42-580OF. I recommend that your child stays under inpatient observation for the first three weeks at my facility to monitor his vitals and progress under the program. After that, we'll evaluate his case to see if he should go home or continue to stay under our observation..."

Joseph listened intently to the doctor's explanation and took note of every important detail in his notebook. He didn't know when he was going to talk to Jill about it again, but when he did he wanted to be prepared.

"The earliest we could begin treatment on your son would be the last week of December. He would have to then take about two weeks off from school, but we can provide him with educational resources," the doctor concluded then paused. "So. Now would be the time for any questions."

"Has it been evaluated by the FDA?"

"Not yet, but that's in the works. We are still in the experimental phase for this serum, which would require you to sign a number of waivers before your son could be a part of the trials. This is the process that most new treatments go through before making it to the public," Dr. Meron explained. "I do have to inform you that we have a limited number of slots available. The serum is very expensive to make, but of course, there would be no cost to you in exchange for your participation."

"What about side effects? Anything serious to be concerned about here?"

"As you know, with any medication or experimental therapy there is always a risk of side effects. But I can tell you that up to this point, we haven't noticed any significant concerns," Dr. Meron explained.

"How many patients do you have on the treatment at this time?" Joseph asked.

"As of now, officially it's just one. Billy, the boy whose results I showed you at your Williams Syndrome meeting. But we're planning to add two new patients this month. We are quite optimistic that it will help them as well," Dr. Meron replied.

By the time he was leaving Dr. Meron's office, Joseph was feeling a mixture of relief and unease. He had asked each of the questions he had prepared and each one was answered promptly. He knew that Jill would have had a ton more, but this was a start. The doctor seemed very reassuring and confident, but there was still something nagging at Joseph's conscience. That little voice of caution that he had pushed to the back of his mind was trying to make its presence known again. He wrote it off as fear—fear of progress or fear of taking a risk, which was never something he wanted to give in to.

As he opened the door to the parking lot of the small medical building where Dr. Meron kept his office, he saw Ray Smith and his wife Mary Ellen coming toward him with their son Sammy between them. He hadn't seen Ray since the day he came to visit his office for friendly advice about the treatment.

Sammy was a fresh-faced, slightly chubby 14-year-old boy with short red hair who always greeted everyone with an ear-to-ear smile. He was just a few inches taller than Joey and had a bit of a struggle walking at times. He liked music and had learned to play a few chords on the guitar when he was younger. He was so good that he was regularly invited to play sing-along sets at Williams Syndrome walks and summer camps. Children with Williams Syndrome almost always had a special affinity for music that was more intense than the average person and in some cases, they took to musical instruments like bees to nectar. Sammy's father Ray, a veteran architectural designer, was also encouraging him to learn about building, construction, and architecture.

"Ray, Mary Ellen, how are you doing?" Joseph said with a nervous smile as he greeted them. A sudden wave of worry washed over him—he felt like he was caught red-handed doing something he shouldn't. He leaned down a bit and shook Sammy's hand like a proper gentleman—the same way he taught Joey to greet trusted strangers.

"Joseph. So glad to see you," Ray said happily. He was relieved to see that another familiar family was consulting with the doctor. "I see you decided to make the appointment after all."

"Yea. I just had a few questions that I needed answered," Joseph admitted. "What about you, your first appointment?"

"Actually no, it's our second time coming here. Today Sammy's being admitted to begin the treatments," Ray said self-assuredly. It was a complete 180-degree change from his unsure demeanor when he came to visit Joseph at his office.

"Really? Dr. Meron said that the first available treatment date was in December," Joseph inquired as he crossed his arms.

"Sammy's on a faster track because of his age. He has to get started right away."

"And you're comfortable with everything?"

"We are," Mary Ellen said as she glanced up at her husband and nodded. She put her arm around Sammy. "We've talked it over, and we're ready."

Joseph couldn't help but feel a twinge of jealousy at Mary Ellen's show of support and her willingness to let her husband make the final decision.

"Where's Jill?" Mary Ellen asked.

"Oh, uh, she's working," Joseph responded. He would have to wrap things up if he wanted to avoid any further questions. "Well guys, it was really nice to see you, but I have to head back. And good luck with everything. Keep us updated."

"Nice to see you too," Ray said with a smile as he shook Joseph's hand again. Joseph waved at Mary Ellen and Sammy, then they went their separate ways.

~

"I want to go home! Now!!"

Tamara ducked as a picture frame came flying at her head. It crashed into the wall and fell to pieces. "Billy, please. Just calm down, please."

"No, I won't! I don't want to be here anymore!!" Billy yelled. His voice had deepened a bit since he started the therapy and could really carry through the halls. "Get me out of here already!!"

Billy had entered Dr. Meron's research offices a small, sweet, bubbling 11-year-old kid with Williams Syndrome. He was now a rambunctious, demanding, and tantrum-prone 12-year-old who had grown to 5'4 inches tall. He was now considered tall for his age and could be a bit intimidating at times.

"Dr. Meron," Tamara pressed the intercom button and called for her boss. "You're needed in room 214 please."

She tried to calm Billy in the meantime and finally got him to sit down on his bed, but he was still fuming. He was upset that Tamara shut off his video game console and asked him to complete his homeschool assignment for the day. It seemed that all he wanted to do was play mind-numbing games and watch TV all day long instead of following the course plan they set for him.

When Dr. Meron finally made it to the room with an orderly behind him, Billy had regained his energy and immediately made a beeline for the door. He scratched and clawed to get out of the room, but was eventually restrained.

"Please take him to the calming quarters," Dr. Meron instructed. It was a sound-proof room that played classical music where Billy didn't have access to anything that could cause him or anyone else harm. There, a counselor would go in and sit with him until he finally calmed down. Sometimes, the process took hours.

"Doctor, I feel like we need to do something differently," Tamara said, feeling frustrated. She wasn't used to coming to work in a hostile environment. "He's starting to take an undesirable turn."

"You *feel* like? Are you a therapist or a scientist Dr. Goodwin? Please just go monitor him until the counselor arrives," Dr. Meron retorted angrily.

Tamara bit her lip to keep from responding and abruptly left the room. She was becoming more and more disillusioned as the days went on and wondered what she had gotten herself into. But she needed that research job to stay afloat. The student loans from her time in medical school loomed over her head like a dark cloud. Dr. Meron also provided her with a free apartment in an up and coming St. Louis neighborhood.

After he saw Tamara disappear down the hall, Dr. Meron sighed and leaned down to pick up the photo from the glass-faced picture frame that had shattered. He brushed away the remaining glass fragments and looked at the colorful image. It was a selfie photo of him sitting next to 8-year-old Billy, who was wearing a Cardinals baseball cap, at the last ballgame they attended together.

Jill made it a point to leave work early that day so that she could pick Joey up from school. She took him to his favorite place, Chuck E. Cheese, for an afternoon of pizza and games before it got too busy. She watched every move that Joey made, afraid that if she took her eye off of him for one moment he would disappear like he did in her dream. He went from game to game, winning, collecting tickets, and enjoying the freedom from having to compete with too many other kids.

By the time they arrived home, Joey was already sound asleep in the car. Jill picked him up gently and carried him into the house. She took her time taking him upstairs to his room. When she got there, she laid him down on the bed and pulled his Barney sheets up to his chest. She gazed at his little face and smiled as if she was seeing it for the first time.

For some reason, she didn't want to leave Joey's room yet. She walked around and started to pick up a little—some socks he had left by the closet, a plastic tumbler that still had a bit of orange juice inside. Then she saw the photo album that they had started for him when he was just a toddler. It was full of pictures of him as a baby, his first steps, and past holidays with the family.

Jill grabbed the album and sat down on the chair next to Joey's bed where she usually told him bedtime stories. She could hear him snoring gently, just like his dad. She started to flip through the pages of the album and with every sweet memory came a new tear. At a certain point, when the tears started to fall too rapidly on the pages, she looked up and gazed at her little Joey, who was now curled up in the fetal position still sleeping soundly. He had the most pleasant and relaxed smile on his face, which made her smile.

She finally had to admit to herself that she just didn't want Joey to grow up too fast and leave like he had left in her dream. The thought terrified her. She wanted him to stay right there where he was, just as he was: content, carefree, and childlike. Her sweet baby boy. But she also had to admit that what she wanted might not always be what was best for him.

CHAPTER 6
Things Are Looking Up

The kids had a half day at school, so Joseph and Jill decided to take them to Eckert's Farm to pick apples. With the exception of Halloween trick-or-treating, it was Joey and Mia's favorite thing to do in the fall. They enjoyed being free to run, hide and get lost among the apple trees. Jill manned the basket, which she planned to fill to the brim with the perfect mix of golden delicious and Fuji apples to make her first pie of the season. Joseph and Grace were mostly on picture duty—they both had a knack for capturing the best candid photos of the family. Sophia was the only family member who couldn't make it because she had to practice for her big game that weekend.

"Bet you can't catch me!" Joey tagged his sister Mia on the shoulder as soon as the apple wagon they were riding stopped. He immediately jumped off and started running into the fields. Mia wasn't as fast and limber, but she eventually managed to hop off of the wagon after him.

"Be careful guys! And no climbing the trees!" Jill called out to them. Joseph stepped down from the wagon first and then reached out his hand to help her and Grace down.

"Thank you, kind sir," Grace commented sarcastically in a faux British accent.

"It's my pleasure madam," Joseph responded in kind.

"Take note Grace, chivalry is still alive and kicking," Jill commented as she stood on her toes to give her husband a kiss on the cheek.

Without any explanation or fanfare, Jill and Joseph's relationship had gone back to normal. They were talking and laughing together again. Joseph wasn't sure what had changed, but he was definitely happy to have his wife's attention back. They still hadn't discussed anything having to do with Dr. Meron's treatment and Joseph didn't have any plans to until it was absolutely necessary. He would find the right time…eventually.

"Mom, Kat's already here," Grace said as she checked her cellphone. "I'm going to go find her. I'll be back later."

"Okay honey," Jill said as she and Joseph strolled in the direction where Joey and Mia had gone to play tag. She grabbed her husband's hand tenderly and gazed up at the tree branches, which were gently rustling in the wind.

"Beautiful day," she observed as she started to look more closely at the Fuji apples hanging within their reach.

"So glad it didn't rain. You can't really trust the forecast nowadays," Joseph said as he grabbed a perfect apple from the tree and tossed it into her basket.

"I'm kind of glad Grace's friend is here. I wanted to talk to you about something."

"Same here," Joseph said as he searched her face for a sign of what might be on her mind. "Let's sit down."

They found a bench in a picturesque area and sat close to each other for warmth. Joseph wrapped his arm around her, just like he did when they were first courting. He was quiet as he waited for her to start talking. She took her time, considering her thoughts before she spoke, and he continued to wait patiently.

"Well you know we went to see Marsha," she began. "Did you know that they've already signed Tommy up for that experimental Williams Syndrome treatment?"

"Did they?" Joseph asked, genuinely surprised. "Well, that was fast. Did she say when they're scheduled to start?"

"Not really, she became distracted," Jill said as she remembered how Marsha fawned over her son's tutor for the rest of the afternoon. "But she did make me think about some things."

"Like?"

"Like, maybe I've been a little too stubborn. And a bit unfair to you," Jill admitted. "I wanted to apologize to you for being so cold the past couple of weeks."

"There's no need to apologize. I should have been more understanding about your opinion in the matter."

"Yea, and about that. I've been thinking that my initial opinion may have been wrong. Maybe we should just hear this doctor out to see how and if he can help Joey," she said.

"Really?"

"Really. I want to know more; I have a lot of questions. I realized that I can't let my personal feelings get in the way of something that could possibly benefit our son," she said as she looked up into her husband's eyes. She felt the tears starting to come. "So what do you think, should we go see that doctor?"

Joseph looked back into her eyes and he was reminded of how much he loved her. She was so tough and resilient, but she also wasn't afraid to be vulnerable at the right time. Deep down, he wanted to tell her the whole truth—that he went against her wishes and had already gone to see Dr. Meron on his own—but he couldn't bear to spoil the moment. Instead, he simply wiped the moisture from her eye before a tear had a chance to fall.

"I'm on board. Let's do it," he said with a smile. "I love you, Jill."

"I love you too."

"This is going to be good."

"Yea, well let's just take it step-by-step and see."

"Grace, I've got to tell you something. But promise me you won't get mad at *me*, okay?" Kat said nervously.

Grace and her friend Kat were exploring the pumpkin patches together. Grace was testing out the new professional camera she had received for her birthday, playing with the zoom function. Ever since she was a little girl, she had thought about starting a career as a professional photographer—exploring the world and getting paid for it. Her parents supported her dream by getting her a new camera every year with the latest technology.

"Well, that depends," Grace said as she took a photo of one of the largest pumpkins she had ever seen.

"I'm serious. You know that saying, don't kill the messenger? Because all I am is the messenger right now. I'm your friend, so I have to tell you these things," Kat said.

Now she had Grace's full attention. "What is it, Kat? Spit it out."

"Okay, so you know Aaron has a bunch of friends that go to Central High," Kat started. "Well, he hung out with them last weekend and…"

"Yea, and?"

"…and he said he saw Scott there with some blonde girl," she rattled off quickly as she picked at her nails.

"What? Who? What were they doing together?"

"I have no idea who she was, but he did say that they were kissing and really close the whole time. But Aaron did say she wasn't *anywhere* near as cute as you," Kat said with a sympathetic look on her face. That look made Grace boil inside—she hated to be made a fool of in public. "I'm sorry Grace, I couldn't *not* tell you."

Grace didn't know what to say or do. This was the first time that she had a serious, long-term boyfriend and the first time that someone told her a guy might be cheating on her.

"Well, maybe they're just friends. He knows a lot of people," Grace reasoned, trying to remain cool, but she was so embarrassed. "Look, I've got to go find my parents."

Kat watched her friend pack her camera back up and put it into her tote bag. She could tell that there was a lot going on in Grace's mind.

"Are you okay?"

"Yea, yea. Fine," Grace said and waved her off as she walked back toward the apple orchard.

"I'll call you later?" Kat called after her, but there was no response.

❧

"What in the world is that?" Jill said as she approached the front door with sleeping Mia draped over her shoulder. There was a huge cardboard box covering the walk next to her flower garden.

It was dark and the end of a long, full day. After hours of running around the apple farm as well as dinner and dessert at their favorite restaurant, everyone was ready for bed. That is, everyone except for Grace, who jumped into her car as soon as they pulled into the driveway and drove off into the night.

"No idea. I didn't order anything recently," Joseph said. He was holding sleeping Joey. "I'll grab it in a minute."

After they put the kids to bed, Joseph went outside to grab the box, which was pretty heavy. He dragged it into the foyer and started to pull it open as Jill looked on.

Inside was a colorful box containing an 11-foot-tall inflatable dragon.

"What the…" Jill said as she crossed her arms and tried to look upset. "Joe, did you let him watch *Game of Thrones* again?"

Joseph just scratched his head, knowing that he was busted. Jill leaned down and grabbed the Amazon receipt from the box.

"Whoa, this thing cost $300!" she said and her mouth dropped open. Her shocked expression made him laugh. "You find this funny huh?"

"Hey, Joey One-Click strikes again," Joseph said with a shrug and they had a nice nice laugh together. He wrapped his arms around her neck and held onto her for a long time, relishing the moment.

Suddenly, things were starting to look up. Joseph felt relieved, hopeful and back on top of the world. But there were still some loose ends that he would have to tie up, and fast.

CHAPTER 7
Missing in Action

Sophia was so good at pitching her softball games in little league that she was already being scouted by high school coaches in the district. The coach at her junior high had scooped her up during the summer to train her and now she was the starting pitcher. At her young age, Sophia had nearly mastered the art of the underhand fast pitch and had a bright future in softball.

This was the game that qualified her team to enter the district championship and they were all excited. The tenseness that was in the air when the away team arrived on their school bus could be cut with a pair of scissors. Sophia was warming up on the sidelines wearing the custom t-shirt design that her dad had made for the whole team. Hers read "You Pitch Like a Girl" on the front, and on the back it said, "THANKS!" The rest of the team wore shirts with "You Hit Like a Girl" on the front.

Mia was already cheerleading on the sidelines as she usually did at her big sister's games. This time, she brought a pair of blue and white pompoms that Jill bought her online.

"Yeah Tigers!! Go Tigers!!" Mia screamed as she jumped as high as she could with her feet in the air.

"Yea! Go Tigers!" Joseph encouraged her with a few fist pumps. He was a proud dad that day. When he started throwing a ball around with 6-year-old Sophia, he never imagined that she would take to the sport so quickly and naturally. She had been the one to find out about little league softball for girls and asked to sign up. Five years later, here she was pitching a game that could put her middle school team on the map.

"Mia's a natural. I might have to sign her up for that cheerleading camp next summer," Jill commented with a smile. She glanced over at Joey, who was imitating his sister's pitching style by the bleachers.

"Yes, let's definitely do that," Joseph responded immediately. He wanted his kids to be involved in as many sports activities as possible. He knew how easy it was for them to get distracted in the age of social media.

"Look, it's Grace!" Mia yelled suddenly.

As soon as Joey saw his sister Grace coming down the walk toward the bleachers, he bolted in her direction. She had been scarce the past few days and he had missed her. Grace opened her arms and put on her biggest smile for him.

"Joey T!" she exclaimed as he jumped into her arms. She picked him up as high as she could off of the ground and swung him back and forth at her sides.

"Princess Grace!" Joey yelled happily when she finally set him down. "Where have you been??"

"My favorite little brother! I've been around, just a little busy," she said, feeling as if she might get emotional. She quickly hugged him to prevent him from seeing any tears. No matter how unhappy she felt some days, her brother always managed to make her feel special. He laughed as she flung him over her shoulder and walked the rest of the way to the benches. She managed to gather herself and stop any tears from falling before she reached her parents.

"Hey stranger," Jill said with a surprised look on her face as she hugged her daughter. It wasn't that often that Grace made it out to Saturday games because she was usually hanging out with her friends.

"Hey, didn't know if you were going to make it," Joseph said as he helped Joey down and gave his daughter a hug. "Haven't seen much of you lately."

"Yea I know, late nights studying with Carlie," Grace said casually. "So how does Sophie look?"

"Lookin' good," Joseph said as he sat Grace down next to him and held her close. He couldn't put his finger on it, but he could tell that something just wasn't quite right with his daughter. He felt as if he was losing touch with her and he didn't like it. She was his first born and they had always been very close.

The truth was that Grace had gotten into a big argument with Scott the night before and ended up spending the night in her car. He left her and went back to his friend's party without a second thought. Her cellphone had run out of power, her car charger wasn't working and she had no idea where she was. When she woke up the next morning, she remembered that it was the day of her sister's big game so she grabbed breakfast at a local fast food restaurant, charged up her phone and headed straight to the ballpark. She needed a positive distraction to prevent her from going off the deep end. She felt as if the social life she had worked so hard to build was slowly crumbling before her eyes.

When she finally confronted Scott about seeing a girl at another school, he flipped it back around and accused her of being insecure because she was the one cheating on him. He had a clever way of gas lighting her to make her believe that she was the one at fault.

Grace watched as her sister Sophia warmed up with a teammate. She remembered her own time as a member of a school sports team. She was accepted to the varsity volleyball team as a freshman in high school, but it started to interfere too much with her weekend activities. She decided to quit after-school sports at the end of her sophomore year, and soon after became more involved with the popular crew at her school. It wasn't long before she was also neglecting her studies.

Being in the right crowd was important to Grace for a number of reasons. The most pressing one was a childhood experience that left her feeling eager for acceptance. Her parents spent a lot of time and money planning an outdoor princess party for her eighth birthday at a local park. They even rented a pink limo for Grace and her friends to ride into the location with their parents following behind. The party accommodations were for over 50 children and their parents. The week before the party, she got into an argument with her best friend. That so-called friend went around their elementary school telling everyone she had a very contagious case of the "cooties." Just five kids from her school showed up to her party—two boys and three girls. Grace had to ride in the limo with her relatives instead. She never forgot the experience and it took a while for her to recover from it. Now, she did everything possible to avoid public embarrassment or ostracism. She just wanted to fit in and be popular.

By the time the umpire called the start of the game, the bleachers were packed full of parents and observers waiting for the first pitch, which Sophia would be delivering.

Sophia stepped up to the pitcher's mound in her bright white home uniform and leaned down to grab the rosin bag to powder her palm. Before the game was through, she would be completely covered in dirt from sliding into bases. She was highly competitive and would do whatever was necessary to get a win.

"Go, Sophie!" Joey jumped up and screamed as he clapped for his sister. The whole family agreed and a roar of support grew from the bleachers.

Sophia was nervous, but she sure didn't show it. She happened to glance over at the first basewoman and noticed Brendan, her persistent admirer, walking toward the home team bleachers with Tessa and two of his friends. He caught her eye and waved to her, but she kept her game face on and looked away.

The first batter up approached the plate and took a few practice swings. She was large for her age, and it was clear that she was considered the star player of the opposing team.

Sophia adjusted her cap as she looked at the batter squaring up, then focused her attention on her catcher. After a few moments in her pre-pitch pose, she brought her arm way back, whipped it around and released the ball quickly from her side. The pitch came with a high-pitched grunt that would have made Serena Williams proud. The batter didn't make a move as the ball sailed right over the plate.

"Strike!" the umpire called without hesitation.

"Yea!" Joseph and Jill yelled in unison. Joey jumped up and down on the bleachers with his fists in the air, cheering his sister on.

"Strike her out sis!" Grace said with a proud smile. She hadn't been to one of her games in a while and was amazed by the speed and accuracy of her pitch.

"Whoa! Did you see that?" one of Brendan's friends exclaimed in shock. Suddenly their interest increased and their eyes were focused on the game.

"Told you," Tessa said with a smile.

Brendan nodded and tried to look cool as he lounged with his buddies, but he was impressed as he watched Sophia strike three girls out in a row. The other team seemed a bit stunned by her pitches, and soon enough they began swinging at everything, just trying to make a hit. Only a few girls succeeded at that, but it wasn't enough to defeat the Tigers. They won handily, 7-0.

When the game was over, Brendan hung around after his friends had left. He insisted that they leave because he didn't want them to see him possibly get rejected again by Sophia. But he had to see her. He felt really bad about what had happened the last time they spoke—he didn't realize that he had been making fun of his crush's brother. He wanted to try to make it up to her and he knew that the longer he waited, the worse it would get. He had even talked to Sophia's best friend Tessa to learn more about her family and Joey.

"Hey Joey T!" Brendan said as he approached the area of the field where Sophia's family was congregated. He extended his hand for Joey to slap.

"Who are youuuu?" Joey asked, almost sarcastically, with his head turned to the side. He smiled at Brendan curiously yet cautiously.

"Uhh... I'm a friend of your sister Sophia's. Nice to meet you?" Brendan responded awkwardly. He looked over at Sophia, who was guzzling a bottle of Gatorade while talking to her dad and coach about the game.

Joey still looked at Brendan apprehensively, but he was too kind-hearted to leave him hanging. He slapped his hand quickly and then ran over to his sister.

"Who's that guy?" Joey asked as he pointed brazenly. Brendan felt like sinking into the ground—he would have done anything for an invisible cloak at that moment.

Sophia looked over at him and he half-waved. She half-rolled her eyes and finished drinking her Gatorade.

"Come on," she told Joey as she grabbed his hand and headed over to Brendan, whose heart started beating triple-time.

"Hey," she said. "Joey, this is Brendan. He goes to our school."

"You go to *my* school?" Joey said with a smile.

"Yup. Who's your teacher?"

"Mrs. Moldestad," Joey said immediately. "She's really nice."

"Joey goes to a class for kids who are extra special," Sophia said with a smile as she hugged her brother at her side. He hugged her back around her waist.

"That's pretty awesome!" Brendan said, loosening up. "Maybe I'll see you around school sometime?"

"Yea, cool!" Joey said, always happy to make a new friend. "I'll see you around school!"

"Joey T, can you go to Mom?" Sophia asked him.

"Can I have one of your Gatorades?" Joey, always the observer, had noticed how much Sophia drank the sports drink since she started playing for the school's team. He wondered if it was responsible for her great performance at the game.

"Take one of the blue ones," Sophia said and watched him as he ran to her duffel bag.

"You were so great," Brendan gushed. "I've never seen a girl pitch like that!"

"Yea, I've been working on my pitch all summer. Coach said by next year I could get it to over 45 miles per hour with more practice and strength training."

"Cool. Maybe we could go throw a ball around at the park sometime?" Brendan suggested. He had rehearsed exactly what he would say if he had this chance, so he was ready.

"Maybe. I'll let you know. Thanks for coming to my game Brendan."

"No problem. See you in school on Monday?"

"Sure," Sophia said with a nod and a wave as she headed back over to her family. Brendan watched her every step—so much so that he didn't realize that her father Joseph was shooting him an "if looks could kill" glare. When he did notice, Brendan nervously waved, turned, and walked away.

"Who's that kid?" Joseph immediately asked his daughter when she returned. His protective instincts were kicking in. He didn't want any boys distracting her from her goals in sports and school.

"Just some guy," Sophia brushed him off.

"It's Sophia's new booooyfriend," Joey said, teasingly.

"Quiet," Sophia snapped at him.

"He's really cute," Grace commented as she reached over to give her sister a hug. "I've gotta go, sis. Great job today."

"Thanks sis," Sophia said and her face lit up. She looked up to her sister in so many ways and quietly wanted her approval. It had been a while since Grace had seen her pitch a game.

"Hey, are you okay honey?" Jill asked Grace before she had a chance to walk away. She grabbed her hand in a motherly way. "You look a little under the weather."

"Yea, I'm fine. Just a little tired. I'll see you guys later," Grace said and faked a smile.

"Drive safe hon," Joseph said, still concerned. Grace could be very guarded and layered. Getting her to open up was like trying to break into a Fort Knox vault. He chalked it up to the moodiness of teenagers and vowed to keep a closer eye on her.

Jill had noticed a major change happening in Grace over the past couple of weeks and she didn't like it one bit. She decided to take her out for one of their "mother-daughter" lunches soon to find out what was going on.

Though it was only 5 p.m., Debra's bedroom was completely dark except for the small flat screen television lit up with images from *The Sound of Music*. But she wasn't watching it. The blinds and curtains were drawn tightly. It had been a week since John removed the 60-inch flat screen that he mounted to the wall on the first day that they moved into their house. He took it to his mother's basement.

John took Patty for the day to his mother's house, where he was staying. It was the first time he had seen his daughter since he left after threatening Debra with divorce. However, he still managed to make it to all of his sons' football games on the weekends. He barely spoke to his wife when he came to the door at 11 am, even though she pleaded with him to stay and talk for a while. She told him that she had changed her mind about Dr. Meron and that she would never contact him again. John just ignored her, grabbed Patty and her things, and walked back to his truck.

Debra finally had what she thought she wanted—a peaceful house and a day to herself. But every moment was more miserable because she had the sinking feeling that her family was falling apart and it was all her fault. Her anxiety was slowly turning into a bout of depression. She had to literally drag herself out of bed in the morning to tend to Patty. She hadn't home-schooled her daughter for over a week and canceled most of her speech therapy sessions. The house was a complete mess because Debra no longer had the energy to clean up after her daughter. Her days mostly consisted of sitting on the couch in the living room or on the stool in her kitchen and staring into space while Patty ran around the house getting into various shenanigans. She quickly learned that since the entire house was childproofed, there really wasn't any way that Patty could hurt herself. The worst case scenario was that she would cause a mess, then Debra would have to get up the energy to clean. She also realized that by the time 7 p.m. rolled around, Patty was so exhausted by her activities that she fell right asleep. As soon as her daughter was in her bed, Debra turned on the baby monitor, retreated to her own bedroom and drew the blinds.

Debra glanced over at the empty side of the bed where John normally slept. It was still made with the blankets tucked under his pillow. She would lean over to sniff it every now and again for comfort. She had to deal with his absence before due to his trucking job, but at least she knew he would be back. Now, she wasn't so sure.

It was getting to the point where even her favorite movie was no longer satisfying to her. Every time she looked at the happy, gleeful Governess Maria, dancing and singing with the children, she grew more and more resentful.

Why can't my life be like that? What is wrong with me?

She heard a strange tune that sounded like it was coming from the television at first, but when the tune began to clash with the sounds coming from the TV she realized it was her cellphone ringing. She had almost forgotten what it sounded like to receive a call from someone.

She sat up on the bed and looked around for her phone, which was on the dresser. She hurriedly went to pick it up after muting the TV and saw that it was John's mother calling.

"Yes, Anne?" Debra said into the speakerphone, trying to sound upbeat.

"Debra, thank God. Look, I need you to come get Patricia," Anne said without even bothering to say hello. She sounded agitated.

"Why, what's going on?"

"She's been throwing a screaming tantrum for the past two hours. That's what's going on! She tossed my pill tray and I had to spend the whole afternoon reorganizing them. She's into everything. I just can't take her, I'm done," Anne said with finality. "Please come get her now."

"Isn't John there?" Debra asked. "Can't he bring her back?"

"No, John isn't here. He had some business to handle. Can you be here within the next half hour?"

"Uhhh. Yea Anne, I'll be there. Sorry about this," she said, though she wasn't quite sure why she was apologizing. John had requested the time with Patty.

If he had business to handle, why would he take her? she thought.

As soon as Debra ended the call she started pulling her hair into a ponytail. She was thankful that she had been too lazy to get back up and get her bottle of wine from the refrigerator. If she had arrived at Anne's house with a trace of alcohol on her breath, John would divorce her for sure and she would never hear the end of it.

As she was driving to Anne's house, her thoughts volleyed back and forth between feeling embarrassed by Patty's behavior and being angry with John. She couldn't believe that he had just left his daughter there—Patty didn't really know her grandmother other than occasional visits.

How could he just leave her at his mother's house when he was supposed to be looking after her? He barely sees her at all, and now when he has a day with her he leaves?

When she finally pulled up to Anne's house, her angered thoughts about John had just about won her over. She was starting to feel resentful as she rang the doorbell. Anne snatched the door open as if she had been standing there the whole time.

"Thank God. Can you please go get her?" she said as she pointed to the back room. Debra could hear Patty screaming and then she heard a crash.

"Patty!" Debra called out her name as she went to see what had happened. Anne trailed close behind.

"Oh no!" Anne shouted as she ran to the broken pieces on the ground. "Not my mosaic vase!"

"That's not nice Patty! Bad girl," Debra scolded her as she scooped her onto her hip. Patty calmed down and put her thumb in her mouth.

"That's all? Bad girl? I got this vase at QVC Debra. It's a one of a kind!" Anne said angrily.

"I'm sorry Anne, I will pay for it," Debra offered as she started back toward the front door.

"Did you just hear me? I said that it's one of a kind. It's irreplaceable!"

"Then I will get you something very similar, I promise," Debra said as she opened the door to leave.

"You have got to get that child under control. Until then, I can't have her at my house anymore," Anne said.

Debra paused and turned back to look at her mother-in-law. "Your *grandchild* has been diagnosed with attention deficit disorder, so yes, sometimes she is a bit much to handle. Or did your *son* forget to tell you that? Did you also forget that your *grandchild* has Williams Syndrome?"

"My son tells me everything," Anne said with her nose turned up.

"So then why didn't your son tell you that Patty has a serious phobia of insects? That huge photo of the bee on a flower there may have triggered her!"

Anne looked back at the photo, which was featured over her fireplace mantle. "Well, you don't have to get nasty Debra. I didn't know she was afraid of bees."

"Goodbye Anne," Debra said as she closed the door behind her. She paused and took a deep breath in. When she released it, she realized that her heart was beating more rapidly and for the first time in a while, she felt a burst of energy. It felt good to give Anne a piece of her mind. She was always criticizing Debra and John's relationship in some way.

Debra looked over at Patty and saw that she was smiling. Patty had this curious look on her face as if she knew something that Debra didn't. For the first time in weeks, Debra cracked a smile. She chuckled and gave Patty a peck on the cheek.

"We're going to be okay, Peppermint Patty. Let's go home."

John's father was a "rolling stone." He had been married three times and had multiple children outside of his marriages. John didn't even know who his dad was until his mother finally got a court-ordered paternity test when he was eight years old.

As protective as he was of his mother, he also resented her for a number of reasons. One reason was that she chose to have him out of wedlock with a married man, so he had to grow up without a father in his life. But the biggest reason was her dependency on him— John had been working since he was 12 years old doing odd jobs to help his mother cover her bills. His mother hadn't worked a day in her life. He wasn't able to go to college because he had to hold multiple jobs between the ages of 16 and 30 to pay his mother's rent along with his own. When he finally got a job in trucking that paid six figures, his mother wanted a house. When he married Debra, he took on the weight of two mortgages along with medical bills for his daughter Patricia's condition. His whole life had been spent taking care of women. And he was starting to wonder if it was a worthwhile life.

He was initially attracted to Debra because she was kind, sweet, ambitious, and strong, but she still chose to defer to him as her husband. He didn't feel pressured or minimized by her. So after just seven months of dating, they got married. The first decade of their marriage went reasonably well, but after Patricia was born and diagnosed with Williams Syndrome, a lot changed in Debra. She started to become needy and idle, making excuses for why she couldn't keep up with her work-at-home medical coding job. Eventually, she quit it altogether. Suddenly, she started to seem more and more like his mother—completely dependent on him. And to top that off, now she was going behind his back and making decisions without his consent.

John loved his wife, but there was no way that he could handle another unrepentant, domineering woman in his life telling him what to do. He decided that he would rather cut his ties with Debra now than to allow that to happen.

"Daddyyy. How much longer do I have to stay here?" Sammy whined.

"We're going to talk to the doctor about that today Sammy," Ray answered. It had been over two weeks since Sammy entered Dr. Meron's in-patient treatment program and everyone was getting antsy. Mary Ellen came to visit Sammy every day, hoping that she would see some positive change in him. But instead, Sammy only seemed sadder and more agitated each day.

"What is taking him so long?" Mary Ellen asked, annoyed. Dr. Meron had been so responsive to them before they brought Sammy into the program, but ever since they checked him in, the doctor was almost impossible to reach. Mary Ellen tried to call him at least three times a day, but was always directed to voicemail or Tamara.

Finally, they heard the door knob turn, indicating that someone was coming into the room to consult with them. It was all very clinical—the room where Sammy spent most of his time had white walls, an uncomfortable twin-sized bed and a two-way mirror that made them feel like someone was always observing them. Dr. Meron had a camera trained on the room 24 hours a day—they said it was to ensure Sammy's safety, but it felt more like he was the caged subject of a scientific experiment. Ray and Mary Ellen were becoming more and more uncomfortable with the arrangements, but they tried to stay focused on the benefits that Sammy would enjoy.

"Mr. and Mrs. Smith," Tamara said as she walked into the room with a smile plastered across her face. "It's nice to see you both again."

"Where is Dr. Meron?" Ray asked.

"I'm sorry, but Dr. Meron was called away to an urgent meeting in Chicago yesterday. But I have all of the information that you need," Tamara tried to assure them. She walked over and handed Sammy an iPad to keep him occupied. He immediately started toying with the program she had open for him.

"You've got to be kidding me," Mary Ellen said as she shot up from her seat. "We don't get to speak to him for weeks and then he can't even make our appointment?"

"Why didn't someone call us? We could have waited another day!" Ray exclaimed.

"Mr. and Mrs. Smith. I understand how you feel, and that you're anxious about the progress of your son. But I assure you that anything that Dr. Meron knows, I also know. I spend hours every day with Sammy," Tamara said as she flashed a smile in his direction. Sammy smiled back at the sound of his name.

Mary Ellen reluctantly settled back down on the bed and folded her arms in protest. Ray reached over to rub her on the back to calm her down. Her nerves were shot.

"So..." Tamara said as she started to flip through the notes on her clipboard. "Sammy has received two injections to date, and while it's too early to note any significant changes, his vitals have remained normal throughout his stay."

"How long will be it before we see any changes in his appearance? His learning abilities?" Mary Ellen asked.

"Please understand that we can't accurately estimate that. Each child is unique and will respond differently to the treatment. We're hoping to see noticeable progress in about two months," Tamara answered.

"Okay. So can we take him home?" Ray asked.

"That's what I really wanted to talk to you about today. Based on Sammy's special case and his age, we want to keep him here for at least another month."

"Another month?" Mary Ellen repeated in an agitated tone. Ray began rubbing his eyes in frustration.

"He doesn't like it here," Ray said. "He wants to come home."

"I understand that. But Dr. Meron wants to keep a very close eye on him as this is an important case for his research," Tamara tried to explain in a soft tone.

"Dr. Meron should be here," Mary Ellen snapped back. "And he's more than a case for your study. He's our son."

"Of course Mrs. Smith," Tamara said as she bowed her head, a little embarrassed. She spent so much time in that scientific environment that she sometimes spoke carelessly about the children as subjects. "I just want to let you know that this is the best place for Sammy right now. We need him under close observation."

Ray sighed and Mary Ellen looked over at him with her wide doe-eyes. He could tell that she was very concerned, but also knew that he was the only one who could calm her down and assuage her fears.

"Don't worry Mary Ellen, they're doctors. This is common and we knew that this would be a possibility. Sammy's in good hands," Ray assured her. "Okay Dr. Goodwin. But can you please have Dr. Meron call us as soon as he's back in town?"

"Certainly," Tamara said with a smile as she glanced over at Sammy, who was now completely engrossed with the iPad. "How are you doing over there Sammy?"

"I'm doing fine, thank you for asking!" Sammy said confidently and politely, but he didn't look away from his iPad.

Ray and Mary Ellen kissed and hugged their son, then quietly left the room with Tamara. After showing them to the front door, she went back to check on Sammy.

"Where are Mommy and Daddy?" he wanted to know. He had been so fixated on the app that he didn't realize that they were leaving for the day.

"They're headed home for today. We're going to keep you with us for a while," Tamara said as she started to put a blood pressure reader around his arm.

"Noooo, I'm supposed to go home with *them*," Sammy complained as he tried to take the blood pressure sleeve off of his arm. "I'm going with them!"

"They'll be back tomorrow Sammy, please relax."

"Nooooo," Sammy said and jumped up from the bed. "I want to go home!! I want to go home now!!"

Sammy's fit quickly devolved into a full-on tantrum, causing Tamara to call for help to have him taken to the calming room.

As Tamara watched Sammy in the calming room through the two-way mirror, she was relieved that his parents didn't see him acting this way. But she was also angry with Dr. Meron for leaving her to deal with this situation on her own. The families trusted him as the face of the therapy, but more and more he was missing in action. He was being invited to colleges and universities to speak about his research, attending conferences, and talking to representatives from drug companies. His focus now seemed to be more on taking the treatment to the next level and monetizing it, but Tamara felt that he was moving things along way too fast. There were still things they didn't know and potential issues that needed to be explored.

CHAPTER 8
A Prayer for Grace

"This place is so beautiful and romantic. I feel like I'm on a first date," Jill said gleefully as she clinked glasses with Joseph. "This place has five stars on Yelp, you know."

"Yup, I know. Only the best for you," Joseph said with a smile as he sipped his champagne. It had been a while since they went out to eat as a couple without other couples. They had been getting along so well that Joseph wanted to do anything possible to keep her happy.

"Ooo. I'm going to try the roasted chicken with shallots and butternut squash. That sounds so delicious," Jill said as she pointed her freshly manicured fingernail to the line on the menu. He had taken her to the salon earlier to have her nails done and a shoulder massage.

"You already know what I'm going for..." Joseph said after barely glancing at the menu.

"Big juicy steakkk!" they both said in unison with a laugh, remembering the huge steak that Joey had ordered for his dad.

They enjoyed their meal and had a very long conversation about the kids. They talked at length about Grace and what could be causing her mood swings. They agreed that they would send Sophia to the best softball summer camp they could find in the area that next year. They also discussed which primary school Mia would attend for kindergarten. Since her fifth birthday fell in early September, she would have to wait one more year before officially enrolling. They also talked about Joey and having him see Marsha's tutor, Jason. Jill had already shared Marsha's "dirty" little secret; how Marsha's upstairs bedrooms were in complete disarray. Joseph shrugged it off, saying that Marsha was probably just really busy.

Though they talked about everything under the sun, there was one pink elephant in the room that wasn't mentioned—a pink elephant that only Joseph could see. They had an "initial" appointment scheduled with Dr. Meron soon, but Jill still had no idea that Joseph had already gone to see him. Every time they talked about the appointment, he felt a pang of regret that he hadn't been more patient. He knew that if Jill ever found out that he had gone behind her back, it wouldn't be good.

After dinner, they slowly strolled back to their SUV, hand in hand. When they arrived back at the car and Joseph took the driver's seat, he paused before turning on the ignition. He looked down at the wheel, appearing to be in deep thought.

"What's wrong honey?" Jill asked, looking at him. There was another long pause.

"Jill, there's something that I need to tell you..." he started to say. He had a sudden urge to just rip off the bandage and get it over with. He had to tell her about his visit with Dr. Meron.

"Sure, what's up?"

Joseph tore his gaze from the wheel and their eyes met. His wife's eyes were clear and honest—they sparkled even in the darkness of the parking lot. In all of the time they were together, he had never caught his wife in even a little white lie. She was genuine, trustworthy, and open with him. In that moment, he just couldn't bring himself to crush her with the revelation that he had been keeping something from her.

"Uh, um...well...I think I'm going to take some time off of work soon," he said, thinking on his feet. "I've been feeling a bit stressed out lately, snapping at Amy. It's probably because of everything that's going on with Joey and Grace."

"That sounds like a great idea hon," Jill said as she patted him reassuringly on the knee. "Maybe I'll see if I can do the same."

Jack sat in his car down at the entrance to the cul-de-sac where he lived. He had a perfect vantage point where he could see his home and all of the lights that were still on. It was after 11 p.m. and he had been at the office for as long as he could without falling asleep at his desk. The last time he did that, Marsha threw a fit for a week. She hated waking up the next morning and not having him there in the house. She showed up to his office that day, Tommy in tow, accusing Jack and any woman in proximity to his office of having an affair. Jack was lucky to have kept his job after that episode. He quickly learned that Marsha didn't care too much what time he came in the house, as long as he came in every night before she woke up the next morning. He had always known his wife could become a bit unhinged at times, but it was starting to get worse.

Finally, after about 10 more minutes of waiting in his car, Jack saw the light in the upstairs master bedroom go out. He sighed and waited another 20 minutes before putting his car into gear.

He slowly crept up to the house at five miles per hour and parked on the street. Opening the garage door would definitely wake Marsha up. She was usually asleep minutes after hitting the pillow.

Jack sighed as he took the key out of ignition. He finally felt that he could relax after over 12 hours spent at the office. He slowly made his way out of his car, up the driveway and through the side entrance to the house.

Jack was a big guy with a big appetite, so his first order of business was to grab a bite to eat. He quietly made his way to the kitchen and left the light off as he raided the refrigerator.

He found a leftover rotisserie chicken and put it in the microwave. He returned to the fridge and found a cold beer at the back.

"This must be my night," he said with a big sigh as he sat down at the center kitchen island and carefully cracked open the can.

Jack sat in the darkness of the kitchen and ate the entire chicken in a half an hour. All that was left was bones when he finished. He had taken to stress-eating as a way to cope with the dramas of his home and work life, but it wasn't doing any favors to his waist line.

Jack had an arrangement with his company to work seven days per week. He told his wife that the schedule was unavoidable, but the truth was that Jack actually *wanted* to go to work every day. It was an unusual request for a salaried position, but his boss was happy to have him there as much as possible to help keep their demanding projects on track. His job was difficult, but he preferred the stress of the office over the stress of going home. Some days, Jack would just go into the office on a Sunday for a few hours in the morning and then explore the town where he worked the rest of the day. It was his favorite thing to do.

Jack and Marsha had gone to see Dr. Meron together and Tommy was approved to join his trials. Tommy would begin treatments in a month and they were hoping to see significant changes in his appearance, size, and health by the following summer. They had a follow-up appointment with Dr. Meron in the morning, so after another 30 minutes of sipping his beer, he finally decided it was time to go to bed. By now, Marsha would be fast asleep—as soon as her head hit the pillow she was out like a light until 6:30 am to see Tommy off to school.

Jack tiptoed up the stairs and paused on every creak to listen for any sounds from the upstairs rooms. It was eerily quiet. His first stop was at Tommy's room. He peeked inside and saw Tommy lying on his side, fast asleep, with his headphones on. Marsha made him listen to ambient music, audio books, and positive affirmations each night in hopes that it would help improve his confidence, speech, and reading abilities. There were also other reasons why she kept his ears covered.

Finally, Jack made it to the master bedroom that he shared with Marsha. There was resistance as he tried to push the door open because of all of the clothes and junk on the floor. He quietly stepped around and started picking up a few things to throw in the trash and the hamper as he normally did before going to bed.

As he grabbed a few items from next to the bed, he realized that Marsha wasn't under the covers. He went to the other side of the bed and there Marsha sat, on the floor, in the darkness. A sliver of moonlight shone on her from the window. She looked up at Jack with an icy cold glare that sent a shiver down his spine. He could tell that something was wrong.

"How nice of you to finally show up to your home," she taunted. "Is there any food left in my refrigerator?"

"Marsha, why are you sitting in the dark?" Jack said nervously as he reached out his hand for her to get up. She just continued to stare at him. Jack could now see that her eyes were red and her eyeliner was running down her face as if she had been crying for hours. She hadn't washed her face or taken down her hair.

"Get that hand out of my face," she said as she smacked it away. "You know, you really disgust me. How fat are you trying to get Jack? Like, blimp fat or planet fat?"

Jack had learned to ignore her random pot shots about his weight as a way to de-escalate these episodes. The more he protested, the more she took pleasure in trying to break him down. He glanced over and saw that both lamps had been swatted off the nightstands.

"What happened honey?" he said as he went over to pick up the closest lamp, which had a broken light bulb. "Are you okay?"

"Don't feign concern with me, Jack," Marsha said as she grabbed hold of the bed behind her and began pulling herself up. When Jack tried to place the lamp back on the nightstand, she swatted it back down.

"Leave it there! Leave it right there!" she screamed and pointed.

"Marsha, you'll wake Tommy, please calm down."

"There goes that phony concern again. You don't care about me or Tommy," Marsha said as she pulled her shirt off and tossed it haphazardly in the corner. Jack was about to turn to reach down for it, but she turned and stopped him with a look.

"Don't you dare touch it. Leave it *right there*!" she commanded. Jack stopped in his tracks. He was starting to get nervous because Marsha seemed more agitated than usual. "That's where I want it to be!"

"Maybe you should get some sleep honey," Jack encouraged as he started to turn back the covers. There was a takeout container between the sheets with food still in it.

"So now you think you can tell me what time to go to bed? I'll go to bed whenever I want to, just like you shovel food into your mouth whenever you want!" Marsha said as she put on her silk robe, agitated and shaking from anger.

When Jack saw her go into the master bathroom and close the door, he started to pull the sheets off the bed. The smell from the food box was so bad that it was starting to turn his stomach. Marsha opened the bathroom door and peered out just in time to see him putting the sheets in the laundry basket.

"You know what Jack, get out," Marsha said. She walked to the bedroom door and flung it open. "Out! Out! Out! Out of my room!"

Jack frowned and tried to look dismayed, but it was a welcome invitation. He grabbed one of the pillows from the bed and quickly left the room. Marsha slammed the door shut, went back into the bathroom and slammed that door shut as well. She paced back and forth for a while before sitting down on the closed toilet seat. She knew that she was overreacting, but she was having a hard time controlling her feelings. She was feeling hurt, stressed, and rejected.

She grabbed her cellphone out of her robe pocket and scrolled back through her recent conversation with Jason, Tommy's tutor. For the second time in a week, he had turned down her invitation to meet for lunch or dinner. She scrolled back to earlier conversations that could only be interpreted as flirting and tried to figure out where it all went wrong. When she once again saw his last two-word text, "Can't sorry," she threw her cellphone at the wall with full force and then broke down in tears.

When Jack opened the linen closet upstairs, sheets and covers fell on the floor all around him. The closet was overstuffed with linens from Marsha's many unnecessary trips to her favorite home stores. She was obsessed with making her home look picture perfect on the outside, but it was a clever facade for what was really going on at the Rogers' house.

It took Jack a while to organize the overstuffed linen closet enough to get the door to close again. He took a throw blanket downstairs with him and headed to the basement, where his favorite old recliner sat. Marsha refused to have it in the living room anymore and he managed to sneak it downstairs when she wasn't looking. She never went to the basement.

After settling into his chair and switching on the television, he tried to get comfortable. He settled on an old episode of Andy Griffith—ironically, it was the episode when Andy played the role of a marriage counselor for a feuding couple. Within moments, he was laughing. But when the episode ended, thoughts of his troubles returned. He pulled the covers away and headed back upstairs to the kitchen.

The next day, Jack was awakened by the sound of Tommy playing loudly upstairs. "Tommy, time for breakfast!" Marsha called out in a sing-songy voice.

When Jack came upstairs, the sun was shining through the patio doors, indicating that it would be a beautiful fall day. He smelled bacon cooking—his favorite scent. He made his way to the kitchen and saw Marsha flipping pancakes while Tommy sat at the table playing with his plastic utensils.

"Right on time," Marsha said with a smile as she placed a large plate of flapjacks at the center of the table. She looked perfectly coiffed with her hair in a tight bun. She was wearing high heels and a belted dress that perfectly complimented her figure. "Bacon is cominggg."

Jack slowly sat down in his seat at the table and watched his wife. She seemed completely normal as she went between tending to the bacon and pouring two tall glasses of orange juice for them. When she heard the coffee machine beep, she grabbed her favorite mug and began pouring herself a cup.

"As soon as we finish breakfast, we'll go. So please clean yourself up quickly," Marsha said to Jack as she placed the bacon on the table. "Dig in guys."

During the ride, Marsha monopolized the conversation with excited thoughts of what they would discuss with Dr. Meron. Jack remained quiet the whole time, wondering if he was still in real life or if he was now in the Twilight Zone. He was starting to wonder if he was the one who was losing his mind.

Jack knew that Marsha had a bit of a volatile personality before he married her, but it had gotten much worse ever since Tommy was diagnosed with Williams Syndrome as a toddler. It was like she was trying to punish herself for something, but mostly she ended up punishing her husband. He didn't know what to do except try to avoid her as much as possible. Unfortunately, that also meant spending very little time with his son. He was becoming more concerned about Marsha's "night and day" behavior and how it would ultimately affect their family.

Jill took a half day off of work so that she could go up to Grace's school and take her to an impromptu "mother-daughter" lunch. She knew Grace's entire school schedule, including the breaks between classes. She knew that Grace's lunch hour started precisely at 12:45 p.m., so she arrived at the school by noon to play it safe. For some reason, Grace didn't answer any of her mother's calls from earlier in the day.

At 12:05 p.m. Jill glanced up from her phone just in time to see someone familiar exit the high school building along with a tall male student. It was Grace and her boyfriend, Scott. Jill looked at the time on her phone again and immediately knew that her daughter was supposed to be in class.

Grace and Scott were arguing the whole way to her car. She seemed distressed and he seemed annoyed. Jill watched them as they got in and darted out of the parking lot. She quickly turned on her car and followed them.

Jill continued to follow Grace for hours as if she was a private detective. She watched as they went to the mall and came out an hour later holding bags from the Sports Authority and Lids. It prompted her to check her online banking statement—she saw pending charges from Grace's card for over $150 from those stores. She bit her lip and took a deep breath to stop herself from jumping out of the car right then and there. She wanted to see where else they were going.

After the mall, Grace went to a private suburban street, parked and spent over two hours there with Scott. By the time 3:30 p.m. rolled around, her high school would have been letting out. Jill was amazed to learn that her daughter had just skipped half of her classes. Instead of confronting Grace directly, she made a U-turn and headed back to the school so that she could talk to the guidance counselor.

By the time she arrived back home, Jill was fuming and her head was spinning with the information she had attained about Grace's activities over the past months. After taking Joey and Mia to their play room to watch television, she went into the kitchen and grasped the sink for balance.

Earlier she learned that Grace was behind in almost all of her classes, mostly due to poor attendance. They had been consistently sliding since the previous semester. The guidance counselor told her that she hadn't been looking into any colleges and if her current grades persisted it was unlikely she would be accepted to any desirable schools. After some research at their bank, Jill also learned that Grace had made over a thousand dollars in charges from the family's account over the past month—mostly at times when school was in session.

Her cellphone buzzed in her purse and she immediately went for it. It was Grace, finally calling her back over five hours later.

"Hey Mom!" Grace said sweetly. She was completely clueless about what her mom had discovered.

"Grace. I'm only going to say this one time. Come home, *right* now," Jill said in a shaky voice, trying to keep her cool. Her tone scared Grace.

"Why mom? What's wro--" Grace tried to say before her mom hung up the phone.

Less than an hour later, Grace slowly pulled into the driveway. Joseph left earlier than usual from work and came home when he heard how hysterical his wife was on the phone. He pulled the blinds back to look for his daughter. He felt torn between feeling sorry for what she was walking into and betrayed by her unexpected behavior. They'd never had any major problems from Grace—until today.

Finally, after a few minutes sitting in her car to gather her thoughts, Grace emerged and cautiously trudged towards the front door. She had her school bag slung across her torso, full of textbooks that she hadn't cracked open in weeks. Joseph could tell by her expression that she was worried.

Jill was sitting on the couch with her back to the door, trying her best not to launch out of her seat. She thought of how hard she worked from the age of 14 to keep her grades up and earn enough money to be able to go to college. She also thought of the 529 savings account that she and Joseph had set up for Grace when she was just a toddler that was now fully funded for four years at a top university. Her thoughts were all over the place. She even started to think about the article she'd read recently about millennials and their prospects when they chose not to go to college.

Joseph opened the door before his daughter had a chance to put her key in. They exchanged looks and Grace immediately knew that her worries were justified. Something was up. She saw her mother sitting on the couch and reluctantly went over.

"Mom, what's wrong?" Grace said meekly, keeping a safe distance.

"Didn't I ask you to come *right* home, Grace? It's been an hour," Jill said as she rubbed her forehead in frustration.

"Sorry. I was over at Carlie's studying for an exam," Grace replied while shifting around on her feet.

"Oh really, what exam would that be?"

"Um. Biology."

"Really? So tell me...what is anabolism?" Jill asked as she turned to look her daughter in the eye.

"Well, we...haven't gotten to that yet," Grace answered.

"So then what was the last thing you and Carlie just studied?"

Grace just looked down at the ground.

"Well, I learned today that you haven't been to biology class in over a week!" Jill said with a raised voice as she stood up. She was holding a packet of paperwork that the school's guidance office printed up for her.

Grace was still quiet. She knew that she had finally been caught.

"What's gotten into you, Grace? Do you really think that you can miss this many classes and still graduate from high school?" Jill wanted to know.

"It's not that many classes."

"You've missed over half of your classes last spring and this semester!" Jill said as she started to flip through the pages.

"We need to know what's going on with you, Grace. This is really serious," Joseph added.

"I knowww Dad," she whined.

"Apparently you don't!" Jill almost screamed. "You've been hanging out with that boy. That's more serious to you than school?"

"He's my boyfriend, mom. Of course I'm going to hang out with him a lot," Grace said as she flopped down on the love seat.

"You see your boyfriend at school and on the weekends. You don't play hooky with him to go to the mall and buy him sneakers!"

"How do you know what I do with him??" Grace asked as she looked at her mother curiously.

"Because I followed you today. I followed you around the whole time you were skipping class Grace," Jill revealed as she glared down at her daughter.

"Wow, seriously? So you're stalking me now?"

"Don't try to turn this around on me!" Jill said. Her ears had turned beet red. "You're in the wrong here."

"What am I wrong about exactly? I'm almost 17. Maybe school just isn't for me!" Grace said in protest.

"School is not *for* you?" Jill said incredulously. "Did you know that college graduates make an average of a million dollars more in their lifetimes than high school graduates? And let's not even talk about the prospect for high school dropouts!"

"Money isn't everything Mom. Love matters more. Scott and I are in love and we want to get married one day."

This revelation got Joseph's attention. "Wait, you want to do what?"

"We've talked about it Dad. He's going to Loyola on a scholarship next year and I want to go out there with him," Grace told him, becoming increasingly bold with her declarations. She had been found out—she might as well lay all of her cards on the table. Jill put her hands up in surrender and walked away for a moment when she heard this.

"Let's just get this straight. You think an 18-year-old athlete is going to take you to college with him and marry you or something?" Joseph asked.

"You don't know Scott, Dad, he cares about me! You've never even given him a chance!"

"If he really cared about what's good for you, he would want you to finish high school!" Jill yelled.

"Scott cares about me more than anyone I know, including you!" Grace retorted.

From there, the discussion went from a tense conversation to a three-way shouting match. It ended with Grace storming out of the house and screeching off down the street.

Joey had been watching the entire argument between Grace and his parents from the doorway. He was careful to close the door to the playroom so that Mia didn't hear what was going on. He couldn't stand it when anyone argued in his home or around him. It was more than his general aversion to loud sounds—there was a vibration of energy in the air that he didn't like when the people he loved weren't getting along. He felt it very strongly. Joey wanted a lot of things—his Barney night light, trips to Chuck E. Cheese, and unlimited access to Cheerios and pizza—but most of all he wanted his family to be happy and for his home to be peaceful.

Joey had seen a change in Grace before his parents did. He was very intuitive. He was a great watcher and listener—even when no one thought he was paying any attention. He was always observing everyone around him; their behaviors, nuances, and body language. He just didn't always react immediately to what he saw.

Grace began changing right after she started dating Scott. Joey heard her on the phone in her bedroom arguing with her boyfriend on several occasions. She quit playing volleyball even though she loved it. Joey used to do pass-set-drill sets with her before her games.

He noticed that his sister seemed sadder. She wasn't as confident in herself and would make negative comments about her appearance. She would barely eat her breakfast in the morning. Grace had the most beautiful, bright white smile but she rarely smiled at anyone anymore.

Joey wanted to help her—he was on a mission to make his sister happy again. He had a knack for taking even the most complex problem and reducing it down to a simple solution. He would make Grace a peanut butter and jelly sandwich for lunch and slip it into her tote bag in the morning. He would buy her favorite candy bars at school and leave them in front of her bedroom door. He looked up to his big sister and wanted her to feel special.

One question nagged at him after his sister left the house...

Why would Grace think Scott loves her more than we do?

Joey went back into the playroom and closed the door. Mia was laying down on her side watching Nickelodeon on full blast. Joey quietly got down on his knees in front of a table and whispered a short prayer.

God, please let Grace do better in school. Please let her know that we love her more than Scott. Please let her be happy again. Amen.

He stood back up and went over to the closet where he had hidden his father's iPad. He put in the password, which he had learned easily after watching him a few times, and opened the Amazon app. He knew just what his sister needed to be herself again.

CHAPTER 9
Family Dinner

Joseph called Dr. Meron from work the day before he and Jill were scheduled to come in for their "first" appointment. He asked the doctor not to reveal the fact that they had met in person before about Joey and that he was pre-approved to join the trial.

Dr. Meron was happy to comply and looked forward to meeting them both.

On the day of the appointment, Jill asked so many questions that she almost had Dr. Meron stumped in some cases. As Joseph expected, she came with a notebook full of points and sub-points that needed to be addressed. She asked each one frankly and didn't care if she was being repetitive or taking up too much of the doctor's time.

At one point in the discussion, Dr. Meron slipped and alluded to his previous meeting with Joseph.

"Well as I told you before Mr. Todaro, we only have a few slots available for the initial trials..." he started to say.

"When did you tell him that?" Jill asked with a wrinkled brow as she looked at Joseph.

"Uh…I called before the appointment today. I had a few preliminary questions that couldn't wait," Joseph said as his heart skipped a beat.

"Oh. Okay," Jill said with a nod and went back to her list.

Finally, after about two and a half hours of conversation, Jill felt satisfied with the information she had gathered and written into her notebook. Dr. Meron joked about her thoroughness, but quietly he was a little nervous about the fact that she had taken so many notes of his answers.

"Well you sure kept him on his toes," Joseph said with a smile as they left the facility. He placed his hand on the small of her back as he guided her to the car.

"Did you hear what he said when I asked about the potential long-term effects of this treatment?" Jill asked.

"That they won't know anything for at least five to 10 years. But that's a risk with any medication, right?"

"True, but do you really want our son to be one of the first to possibly experience those negative effects in 10 years or so?"

There was quiet in the car for a while as Joseph pulled onto the freeway and pondered her question. He thought about where Joey would be in 10 years at the age of 23. He hoped that his son would be graduating from college or working at the family business. He hoped that he would have a serious girlfriend who loved and accepted him for who he was. Joseph knew there was a lot they didn't know about the treatment, but what if it helped him to better achieve those goals in the future?

"This all scares me too Jill," he finally said. "But it's a matter of fate. You heard the doctor—Joey's the ideal age for this treatment because his body and mind are still developing, and it just so happens that Dr. Meron's trials are happening right now. At this moment in time. We have to jump on this opportunity."

"'Jump on the opportunity.' I keep hearing that phrase," Jill said as she rested her head back on the car seat. "I don't have a problem taking risks, but something just doesn't feel right to me Joe."

"Have you talked to Marsha more about it? You trust her judgment when it comes to Williams Syndrome research, right?"

"I guess. But Marsha has been acting a bit strange lately," Jill said. "And Joey's been seeing the tutor she raved about, but I don't see that much of an improvement yet. Plus he's really expensive."

"Hmm. Well, give it some time."

The next few minutes were mostly quiet as Jill looked over the notes she had taken. She rested her head back and after a few more minutes of riding in silence, she had nodded off in the car.

It was family karaoke night at Mullen's Tavern.

Joey was being called to the stage to sing by the emcee. He turned and flashed a wide smile at his mother before taking off toward the front.

He suddenly bounced backward and hit the floor. He tried to go to the stage again where the emcee continued to call his name, but he bounced right back again.

"Mommy!" Joey yelled out in distress. She went over to grab him up from the floor and tried to help him get to the stage. But she was unable to take another step forward as well. She tried several times in vain to move forward.

Joey looked up at his mom as if to say "why?"

Jill slowly opened her eyes, waking from the disturbing dream. She remembered that she was still in the car.

"You okay? You've been asleep the whole ride," Joseph told her as he pulled onto their street.

"Yea. Fine," she said groggily as she rubbed her forehead.

When Joseph and Jill finally arrived home, all they wanted to do was relax in the den together and watch television before the kids got home from school. As they walked up to the front porch, they noticed a tiny package from Amazon sitting on the doorstep. They were starting to get more and more of these unexpected deliveries over the past few months.

"You?" she asked him as she leaned down to grab it.

"No, I don't think so," Joseph answered as they entered the house.

"I know what this is," she said with a smile as she pulled open the tiny box. Inside was a Gatorade Dash button. "Joey. For Sophia."

"Joey One-Click," Joseph said with a chuckle. "I think it's time for us to change the settings on Amazon."

"No. Let's hold off on that for now. I think this could get interesting," Jill said with a curious smile as she placed the button high up on the refrigerator.

It was a tradition for the Todaro family to get together the week before

Halloween for a day of pumpkin picking at Eckert's Farms and then a big dinner at the family restaurant. Joey was excited to hear that his favorite uncle, James, was coming that year. James was Joseph's younger brother and a bit of a character. One moment you would want to wring his neck and the next you would laugh yourself to tears, wanting to give him a big hug.

Joey was always excited to see his Uncle James because James was the only adult who was as excited as he was about going to Sky Zone, a trampoline park that allowed the kids to jump, flip, and slam dunk basketballs for hours. Most of the time the adults watched as the kids jumped around, but Uncle James would immediately take his shoes off and join in.

"Dad, can we go to Sky Zone tomorrow with Uncle James?" Joey asked as he tugged on his father's sleeve.

"Uh, I don't know, maybe Joey. Your uncle might be busy tomorrow."

"No, I'm not," James said with his eyes aglow. Joseph gave him a look. He had been looking forward to spending some down time at home that weekend—not surrounded by screaming kids jumping all over the place.

"Still, I'm not sure. That's a big maybe buddy," Joseph told Joey, hoping the issue would be closed but knowing that wasn't likely.

"I think they have Ultimate Dodgeball on Saturdays Uncle James," Joey said, turning his attention to his uncle.

"No way, cool!" James said enthusiastically as he bit sloppily into his pulled pork sandwich.

"And Mom and Grace can go to SkyRobics..." Joey continued to talk his idea into existence as Joseph exchanged glances with Jill. This would likely go on for hours.

Just then, Grace showed up and to everyone's surprise, she brought Scott along with her. The sight of him caused Jill's apple cider to go down the wrong pipe and she went into a coughing fit.

"You okay honey?" Joseph asked as he patted her back.

"What…Grace," Jill tried to say in between coughs.

"Princess Grace!" Joey shouted when he saw his sister.

"Uh, Grace, come here for a moment," Joseph told his daughter before she had a chance to sit down. Scott went up to a nearby table where other guests were sitting and took an extra chair without asking if it was taken.

"What's up Dad?" she asked as he led her to the front lobby of the restaurant.

"You didn't tell us you were bringing him. We reserved this table just for the family. You know it's our tradition."

"Why is it a problem? I consider Scott to be a part of *my* family now," Grace proclaimed.

"Grace, come on, you're starting to get a bit ridiculous. You've known this guy for what, a few months?"

"Seven months. And his name is Scott, Dad."

"That isn't long enough to call someone 'family.' And you know how your mom feels about him right now."

"She doesn't even know him. She's met him like twice!"

"She doesn't like how he's been distracting you from your studies and neither do I. And Grace, to be honest, you don't really know him that well either."

"I know he's a good guy."

"Maybe, but I don't think he's good for *you* Grace."

"How can you say that if you don't even really know him?"

"Call it 'father's intuition.' And I'm a guy, I know guys Grace. I know guys like *him*," Joseph told her. "I just want what's best for you Princess. You deserve better."

Grace shook her head. "So, do you want us to leave Dad?"

Joseph looked into his daughter's perfectly round brown eyes and sighed. He knew that he would eventually have to go through this type of situation with his first daughter and a boyfriend, but he had hoped it would be delayed by a few more years.

"Of course not Grace. But please, next time give us a little notice."

When they returned to the table, Uncle James was giving Scott the third degree and it didn't seem like they were hitting it off.

"What position do you play?" James asked.

"Midfielder," Scott answered shortly as he grabbed a biscuit from the basket in the middle of the table.

"Oh, so you're the backup guy. You probably don't have much of a record to talk about then. I was an attacker in high school. That's a man's position," James said right before spooning a load of buttery mashed potatoes into his mouth. In just a few minutes he had made the decision that he didn't like Scott one bit.

Scott looked at him with dismay, starting to get defensive. "I'm not a backup. I had my fair share of goals last semester."

"How many? I bet you don't even know," James said with a chuckle.

"Uncle James!" Grace protested as she plopped down into the seat next to Scott. He didn't make any attempt to pull it back for her.

"What? It's just sports talk Gracie," James responded innocently as he threw his hands up in surrender. "It's not my fault he can't cut it as an attacker."

"I've subbed in as attacker before," Scott said, starting to turn red with embarrassment.

"What for the JV squad?" James shot back.

"You know what? No more 'sports talk.' What do you feel like eating Scott?" Grace said, trying to change the subject as she motioned to the waitress for a menu. She knew how confrontational and relentless her Uncle James could be.

"I dunno, whatever," Scott said as he relaxed back in his chair and pulled out his cellphone.

"Did you bring some money for you and your date middie?" James asked him, and Grace looked at her father with a look that said: "please help."

"Dinner's on us," Joseph said to them both. "Get what you want."

Joseph, Jill, and James watched Scott and Grace closely over the next half an hour. Scott sat back and relaxed as Grace went over the menu, reading off the various entrees to him. He finally decided on the fried chicken dinner and she chose a salad. Their dinners came right before everyone else received their desserts. Scott inhaled his food and Grace barely ate a few bites. The dinner table was mostly quiet because the energy had changed as soon as Scott came to the table.

"Princess Grace, are you coming with us to Sky Zone tomorrow?" Joey asked with ice cream and chocolate syrup on his upper lip. "You can be on my dodgeball team!"

"Uh, sorry buddy. I can't tomorrow," Grace said as she continued to pick at her salad. "Maybe another time."

"Hey, I love that place!" Scott exclaimed. "The SkyJam's awesome."

"Yea!" Joey said, standing up. He hoped that it would lead to Grace changing her mind.

"It's not a sure thing that we're going yet Joey T," Joseph said and motioned to him to sit down. He did so, reluctantly.

"Why aren't you eating Grace?" Jill asked her daughter.

"I've already gone over my calories for the day Mom," she answered and finally just pushed her plate away.

"You're on a diet now? I didn't know that," Jill said with her usual motherly look of concern. The only thing she had noticed Grace losing was her zest for life and the brightness that was usually in her eyes.

"Not on a diet. I'm just watching what I eat," Grace said as she picked up her cellphone and pulled a lock of her brown hair tightly behind her ear. It was a nervous habit.

"So how have you been doing in school, Scott?" Joseph asked.

"Okay, I guess. Last year, finally," he answered without looking up from his plate.

"Are you on track to graduate in May?" Jill asked.

"Yea."

"Do you think graduating from high school is important Scott?" Jill interjected.

"Yea, of course," he answered with a scoff as if it was a stupid question.

"Well, according to Grace it isn't," Jill immediately said. "Last I heard, she plans to drop out and follow you to college so that you two can get married and live happily ever after."

"What? *Married?*" James asked his brother in a loud whisper. Joseph waved him off.

"Mom!" Grace protested. "This isn't the time or place. Please stop!"

"Wait. *This* kid is going to college!?" James again asked his brother as he pointed at Scott with his spoon. "And Grace wants to marry him??"

Scott just looked over at Grace for a moment and then back at his plate, feeling overwhelmed. Joey and his younger sisters were quiet as they watched the conversation go back and forth like they were watching a tennis match.

"When would be the right time? You're barely home anymore," Jill responded. "We don't get to see you because you're always with him!"

"Grace, I love you, you know that. But there is no way I'm letting my beautiful niece go to a movie with this clown let alone *marry* him!" Uncle James said frankly.

"Yo, seriously. What is your problem dude?" Scott finally responded to James with a flippant attitude.

"You. Being with my niece. Invading my family time, that's my problem, '*yo*,'" James said as he got up and started to make an aggressive movement towards him. Joseph stood at the same time to restrain his hot-headed brother. He wanted to jump across the table to strangle Scott as much as James did, but he had his kids and family to think about. James was still a bachelor in his late thirties, always doing whatever he wanted no matter the consequences. Families at nearby tables were watching and the room was getting quieter.

"You know what? We're gonna get out of here," Grace said as she stood up and pulled Scott up from his seat. "Come on, let's go."

"My pleasure," Scott said tauntingly.

"Princess Grace, please don't go," Joey pleaded. "Come home with us! I have something for you!"

"Sorry Joey T, but I'll see you soon. I promise," Grace said as she waved to her brother and forced a smile.

"It's a really good thing you have Grace there to protect you," James said as he watched them leave.

"Grace, call me later," Joseph called out to his daughter as she left the table. "We really have to talk."

"Okay Dad," she said, looking embarrassed as she disappeared around the corner with Scott close behind.

After Grace and Scott left, everyone settled down and there was quiet for a while. James sat down and finished his dessert right down to the last bite as if nothing had occurred. Joseph called for the check and everyone glanced around the table as if they were searching for something to talk about. Finally, Joey was the one to break the silence.

"So I guess they're not coming with us to Sky Zone tomorrow?" he asked the table.

Joseph looked at him and shook his head. Jill laughed, and soon everyone at the table was laughing. As usual, it was Joey T to the rescue at a tense moment.

Despite their amusement, both Joseph and Jill's level of concern for their daughter had gone up sharply. Scott was that guy—the one who could take her away from her potential and towards a life filled with trouble. They would have to have a family meeting soon to help get her back on track.

CHAPTER 10
Happy Halloween

When Billy first started Dr. Meron's treatments, his blue eyes were bright and "stellate," which meant they had a lacy pattern that made them look starry. It was a common feature of children who were diagnosed with Williams Syndrome. Looking into their eyes was almost like looking into the universe with a planet at the center.

Dr. Meron finally received enough funding from his private donors to buy new testing equipment, which included a refractor. This tool, used by ophthalmologists to do eye exams, allowed him to take a close look at Billy's eye pattern and confirm that it had changed.

"It seems to have taken on a streamed pattern. Nearly solid," Dr. Meron said to Tamara as she took notes. "I think we're going to have to get an ophthalmologist in here to evaluate this further."

"Should I just call someone local? If so, we're going to have to tell him about our research and get some type of confidentiality agreement," Tamara said.

"No, I have a colleague from Columbia," Dr. Meron said as he turned the machine off. "I'll email you his number."

"Can I go back to my room now?" Billy asked with his arms crossed.

"Don't you want to go outside for a while Billy, get some sun? Maybe go shopping for your Halloween outfit and some candy?" Tamara asked him.

"No. I'm not getting dressed up for Halloween, that's lame," Billy said and rolled his eyes. "I'm at level 12 and my team is waiting. So can I go?"

"Okay son, go on," Dr. Meron said and gestured with his head for the door. Billy immediately stood up and hurriedly left the room.

"Dr. Meron, do you have a moment? I wanted to talk to you about the upcoming holidays and what your plans were for Billy," Tamara said.

Dr. Meron didn't respond as he continued to write in his portfolio. Tamara took his silence as an invitation to continue.

"Halloween will be here soon and I thought it would be a good idea to take Billy out to nearby neighborhoods for trick or treating? Just to see how he does in a social environment."

"You heard what he said, he doesn't want to get dressed up for Halloween," Dr. Meron said.

"Right. But don't you think that's a little out of the ordinary for a 12-year-old boy? He used to love that sort of thing."

"Tamara, this treatment was designed in part to help Williams Syndrome children mature at a faster rate. This isn't so out of the ordinary, he just has different interests now."

"Very true doctor. At the same time, his social skills seem to be suffering and he's becoming very isolated. All that he ever wants to do is watch television and play violent video games," Tamara continued.

"Like a normal teenage boy. I don't see a problem here," Dr. Meron said as he got up from his chair to leave. "We'll have a small Halloween party in the common room with all of our current participants. Invite their parents and get some candy."

"Okay doctor," Tamara relented. "Will you be there?"

"I'll be out of town this weekend. Call me if there are any issues or *important* developments. And please try to schedule that eye appointment for next Wednesday," Dr. Meron said as he left and closed the door behind him.

Debra stuffed one more handful of spinach into her Nutribullet cup, tightened the top, put it on the base and set it in motion. When it was finished processing her strawberry, banana, and spinach smoothie, she grabbed a straw and headed back into the small room that she used as a home office before quitting her at-home medical billing job. Over the past week, she had cleaned it from top to bottom and rearranged everything to her liking.

Her favorite motivational audiobook played in the background, telling her how she could heal her life. In less than a month, she had listened to and read over 15 self-help books.

After taking a long sip of her cold smoothie, Debra opened her laptop and went back to her search for affordable college courses. Before she got married to John, her goal was to go to college for accounting. She had always been very good with numbers in high school, getting

As in all of her math classes. But her family didn't have the money to send her to college and she soon became distracted with other things. She took low-paying office jobs in the medical field and transportation industry before she married John. They had the same break time at the trucking company where they worked and soon started taking lunches together. It wasn't long before they were engaged.

Despite the many detours that Debra took in her life, she still had a passion for accounting and the money that came with this type of career. She wanted to get in touch with her true self again. She wanted to be self-sufficient, explore, and make her own money. Time away from John and her new audiobook obsession helped renew her perspective.

It had been weeks since she had heard from John. At first, she felt like she was suffocating and became very depressed, but soon she started to look at his absence as a blessing in disguise. It was a chance for her change her life for the better because she had been miserable long before John decided to leave. She still loved John dearly, but one thing she learned from her father long ago was that you can't force a man to love you back—he either does or he doesn't.

Let him go. If he's yours he'll come right back to you.

"Mom!"

Debra put her audiobook on pause when she heard her oldest son calling her.

"I'm in here, Zac!" she called back. He found her and kissed her on the forehead.

"Hey Mom, I'm about to head out. Patty's in her room, she's watching Doc McStuffins again," Zac said. "Dad's outside."

"Okay honey, you be safe out there today. No helmet, no hitting," Debra said as she turned back to her laptop and tied her long unkempt hair up into a bun. Zac paused and turned back around.

"Aren't you going to come to the door?" he asked. His mother always jumped to attention when she heard that his dad was outside and waved to him.

"Uh, no sweetie. I'm pretty busy right now. Tell your dad I said hi," Debra said, flashing a smile at her son.

"Okay, Mom. Love you," Zac said.

"I love you more," Debra replied.

John watched the front door as Zac came outside. There was no sign of Debra as his son closed and locked the door behind him.

"Your mom's home?" John asked Zac when he climbed into the passenger seat of his truck.

"Yea, she's in her office doing something," Zac told him as he put on his seatbelt. "She said hi."

John nodded slowly as he pulled backward out of the driveway. He had become accustomed to seeing her at the door whenever he came by. He wondered what she was doing in her office, which was in a complete state of disarray the last time he saw it.

Debra hit a stroke of luck when she happened to find Doc McStuffins on her streaming TV service. She soon learned that as soon as Doc McStuffins came on the screen, Patty fell into an open-mouthed trance. So whenever Debra needed a few hours to herself, she just turned on Patty's favorite show and there was peace. It was also educational and helping Patty with her lessons.

After about a half an hour of research, Debra was missing her little girl. She headed upstairs to Patty's room where she found her daughter sitting cross-legged on the floor in front of her television.

"Hey Peppermint Patty!"

She was too close to the screen, so Debra moved her back about a foot and sat Patty between her legs. She hugged her daughter and kissed her on the side of her head playfully. They both watched the program together for the rest of the afternoon.

For the first time in a long time, Debra was feeling good about herself and about the future. Even though she was concerned about what the upcoming holidays would be like without her whole family together in the same house, she still looked forward to what the new year would bring.

Joey T was a pretty big deal in the school's drama department. When he was in the sixth grade, they asked him to play Romeo's best friend Mercutio in a production of "Romeo and Juliet." He remembered every line and ended up being the star of the show. He was confident and natural on stage—he enjoyed the attention. The drama department had decided that they would be doing a rendition of *It's a Wonderful Life* for the school's upcoming holiday play. Joey was cast as Clarence the Angel.

His upbeat and bubbly personality was perfect for the role.

"Where's Joey T?" Mrs. Rayburn, the drama teacher, called out.

"He's coming!" Suzy, the girl playing Zuzu, said. They were about to rehearse the scene after George Bailey jumped in to save the angel. A boy named Roger was playing George, and another named Tim was asked to play the role of the bridge maintenance man.

"I'm here!" Joey T shouted as he ran to center stage. He was dressed in a long white robe and pretended to float around the stage. Suzy giggled at him from the side of the stage. She enjoyed watching Joey in action.

"Okay, last scene for today," Mrs. Rayburn said as she looked over her script. "Let's start with your line, Tim. Action!"

"Hey, how'd ya happen to fall in?" Tim asked.

"I didn't fall in, I jumped in to save George," Joey said as he flipped through the pages of his book, pretending to dry it out.

"You what? Save me?" Roger, the actor playing George asked. He and Tim were both reading from their script. Joey was one of the only actors who already knew most of his lines.

"Yup. You didn't go through with it, did ya?" Joey asked.

"Go through with what?" Roger asked again.

"Taking your own life by throwing yourself off that bridge," Joey said.

"Hey, that's illegal around here!" Tim exclaimed.

"It's illegal where I come from too," Joey said.

"And where's that?" Tim said as he took a sip from the cup he was holding as a prop.

"Heaven," Joey answered matter-of-factly. Tim spat his drink all over the floor and some of it landed on Roger's shoes.

"Oh gross!" Roger exclaimed, breaking character. Everyone watching backstage laughed.

"Okay, and scene!" Mrs. Rayburn called out. "Very good guys, but I need you to study those scripts more closely before the next time we meet. I want you to give it a try without the paper. See you all next week. Enjoy your Halloween weekend!"

Joey immediately started taking his robe off and ran backstage.

"Hey Joey T!" He heard a female voice calling his name and whipped back around. It was his co-star, Suzy.

"Hey, Suzy!" Joey said with a huge smile. Suzy looked a lot like the girl who played Zuzu in the movie. She was small, had short curly strawberry blonde hair, and was two years behind Joey in school.

"Look at what I found in my desk," she said as she pulled something out of her pocket. It was a button with Joey's picture at the center that identified the wearer as a "Joey T Fan."

Joey was a little surprised when he saw the custom button that his father designed for him when he started middle school. They had hundreds made and distributed them to everyone they knew in town.

"You are a really good actor," Suzy complimented him as she put the button back into her dress pocket. "I'm a Joey T fan now!"

"Thanks, Suzy," Joey said, blushing.

"How did you remember all of those lines that quickly?" Suzy asked.

"I just practice a lot. And my mom and sister Mia help me. Plus I've seen *It's a Wonderful Life* a bajillion times," he told her.

"I have too, but I still forget what to say sometimes. We should practice our lines together before the play," Suzy suggested as they began walking backstage. "So what are you doing for Halloween Joey?"

"Trick or treating. Do you wanna come?" Joey asked.

"I'm going to my grandparent's neighborhood for trick or treating," she replied. "But you can come to my house after school next week to practice saying our lines if you want?"

"Sure!"

"Okay. See ya, Joey!" Suzy said with a wave as she ran backstage.

Mia had just finished having her face powdered and sparkles applied to her face and hair. She was the perfect mini fairy godmother for Halloween with her white dress and a wand that made a fairy dust noise when she waved it. She pranced around the house, happily practicing her fairy godmother routine on her tippy toes. As she descended the stairs and turned the corner to find her father, Joey jumped out suddenly wearing a scary rabbit mask.

"Raaarrrhhhhhh" he growled. Mia went running and screaming into her father's legs. Joey took the mask off and laughed. He was dressed up as Steve Urkel that year, complete with thick red-rimmed glasses, red suspenders, high-water jeans, and thick white socks.

"Did I do thaaattt?" he said in a nasally tone then snorted, imitating Urkel. It was only the first of hundreds of times he would say it throughout the rest of the night.

"Joey," Joseph scolded him with a wink and Joey disappeared to the back room. He had invested a lot of time in teaching his son the art of a good prank. His costume was Willy Wonka from the classic movie.

Halloween was a pretty big deal at the Todaro house. They had a ghoulish display covering the front of their house, including music, ghosts, and goblins that popped out whenever someone stepped up on the porch. They set up a video feed so that they could watch the front porch footage from inside on a 60-inch television.

Joseph leaned down to take a better look at his daughter's costume. She relaxed, composed herself and spun around, doing her best fairy godmother impression.

"Wow, you are the best ballerina ever Miss Mia!" Joseph raved.

"I'm Cinderella's fairy godmother Daddy!" Mia said as she waved her wand one more time.

Just then, Grace came in dressed in all black—a black blouse and black jeans. She was wearing a long black wig with two white stripes like Lily Munster.

"Graceeeee," Mia said as she glided across the floor toward her with her wand extended. She waved her magical wand all around Grace as the fairy dust sound played continuously. Grace leaned down and gave her little sister a big kiss on the cheek.

"You look so amazing Mia," she told her.

"Hey Princess, is that your costume?" Joseph asked Grace as he grabbed her gently and kissed her on the forehead.

"I guess. Just forgot something upstairs, Dad," she said and quietly slunk her way upstairs. She hadn't spoken much more than a sentence a day to her parents since their recent family dinner. She passed her mother in the hallway upstairs and gave her the cold shoulder. Jill just shook her head and followed Grace into her room. She was dressed up as Jane Austen, one of her favorite authors.

"Grace, your Dad and I need you to be here for a family meeting on Wednesday at 8 p.m. Can you put a reminder in your phone?" Jill asked.

"I think I'll be busy Wednesday," she said without ever looking up. She shuffled through her desk drawer and found her new portable travel charger.

"It'll only take about an hour. You can go back to your friends afterward if you want," Jill said as she crossed her arms.

"I might be busy studying or something. You know, since school is so important and all," Grace mumbled under her breath as she hurried past her mother, not waiting for a response. She ran downstairs and straight to the door without saying another word.

"Princess Grace, wait!" Joey yelled when he saw her opening the door to leave. He ran back to his playroom to get the gift he bought for his sister.

Joseph watched his daughter leave on the 60-inch screen. She jumped a little when the ghost and goblin popped out on the porch again, but went right to her car.

Joey ran outside and called out to his sister one more time, but she was already pulling off down the street. He was clutching the pink and green volleyball he bought for her. He had drawn a picture of him and his sister passing the ball on the back along with the words, "For Princess Grace, I hope this makes you smile again! Love Joey T."

CHAPTER 11
Out on a Limb

Ray's son Sammy had been in the treatment facility for over six weeks. In all that time they only spoke to Dr. Meron again in person once. That conversation between Ray, his wife Mary Ellen, and the doctor went sour very quickly. There was still no sign of any change in Sammy's behavior, reading ability, speech, height, health, or appearance. That day, Dr. Meron convinced them to keep Sammy in the program thanks mostly to Tamara's mediating skills.

But more recently, Sammy had to be transported to a local hospital to be treated for elevated blood pressure which alarmed the doctors there. Like many other children with Williams Syndrome, Sammy had problems with hypertension that required regular monitoring by a heart doctor. ER doctors were unfamiliar with the treatment that Sammy was receiving and what impact it may have been happening on his overall health, but they administered a new type of medication that brought his blood pressure back to normal. After an overnight stay, he was back at Dr. Meron's facility under close monitoring.

After the latest episode, Dr. Meron promised to see the Smiths in person again. He couldn't allow situations like this, where local hospitals were calling him for confidential information regarding his research, to potentially derail the trials. He had been considering whether or not he should continue to allow Sammy to be a part of the program.

"The Smiths are in your office Doctor," Tamara told him when he arrived. "Do you want me to attend?"

"No Tamara, I will call you if I need you," the doctor said. "Were you able to set that appointment with my colleague Dr. Thomas?"

"Yes. He couldn't make it this week, but said that he can come up on Monday at 2 p.m.," Tamara told him. "I went ahead and booked it. His schedule seems to be very busy."

"That will work," Dr. Meron said as he headed toward his office. When he arrived at the door he paused for a moment to get his thoughts together. He knew that either way this conversation went, the Smiths were not likely to be happy. But they had signed a lot of paperwork that prevented them from talking about the treatments or seeking any legal action in the future. He took one more deep breath, and then went in.

"Hello Mr. and Mrs. Smith," he said sternly as he sat down at his desk and opened Sammy's file folder.

"Doctor," Ray responded with a nod. He and his wife were a bucket full of nerves by that point. They had been called to the hospital hours after Sammy was admitted there because the facility was his listed point of contact.

"Well, I think it's pretty clear why we're here today. I was as upset as you are to hear that Sammy was required to check into a local hospital yesterday for an elevated blood pressure," Dr. Meron started. "We administered his medication as usual, but for some reason it was not responding, which is why we had to take him to Houghton Memorial. He's now safe, fine, and back in our care."

"Why didn't someone call us immediately when he was taken there?" Mary Ellen wanted to know.

"I think that most likely our staff was busy trying to ensure that Sammy was receiving the care that he needed at that time," Dr. Meron tried to explain. "And I do apologize for that. But we need to discuss Sammy's participation in the initial trials."

"Can he come home while receiving the treatment? I think that we could do a better job of watching him and monitoring his readings," Ray said. "I've already talked to my boss about taking family medical leave."

"Well…" Dr. Meron started to say as he shifted in his seat and sat back. "The thing is, I'm not sure that it's a wise idea for Sammy to continue the treatment at this time."

"What? Why not?" Ray asked, looking confused.

"I'm concerned that my formula may be interfering somehow with Sammy's medications and I'm not willing to take that risk," Dr. Meron explained. His reasoning wasn't wholly honest—the truth was that he wasn't willing to take the risk of having to stop his trials for a patient who wasn't likely to respond to the treatment.

"Sammy is also on diabetic medication, which could also be a concern in the future," Dr. Meron continued. He looked down at his desk as he tapped his pen, waiting for Ray and Mary Ellen to adjust to what he was telling him.

"So…what are you saying exactly? That you just want to drop him now? After all this time?" Mary Ellen finally asked. "You told us you could help him!"

"Mrs. Smith. Please understand that this is in the best interest of your son. We discussed the various conditions and risks associated with the treatment. I believe this is the best decision for Sammy."

"You can't do this. He's going to be 15 soon," Mary Ellen said as tears started to form at the corner of her eyes. Ray began rubbing her back for comfort.

"There's no guarantee that even after the next few weeks there would be a significant difference in his case, Mrs. Smith. Not one that would justify the potential of this happening again," Dr. Meron said. "I'm very sorry."

Ray wiped away a tear of his own. He stood up and grabbed his wife's hand, feeling defeated and conned. "No, you're not."

"As I told you when we first met, I am working on a formula that will help teens and adults who are living with Williams Syndrome. I can put you at the top of the list for when those trials are active. You'd be the first to receive a call," Dr. Meron said. Mary Ellen was now sobbing quietly as she held onto her husband for support.

"No. Delete our files. Delete our phone number. This was all a mistake. Everything," Ray said as he hugged his wife and began to lead her out of the room.

"Mr. and Mrs. Smith, I—"

"Just give us our son!" Ray Smith turned back and yelled at him.

"What room is he in right now?"

When they arrived at Sammy's room, they looked in the two-sided mirror and saw him sitting on the side of his bed smiling as he fiddled around with an iPad. He still had the hospital band on his wrist. Ray and Mary Ellen composed themselves before they entered his room.

"Hey Sammy!" Ray said enthusiastically as he sat down next to him. His wife knelt down in front of him and tried to hold back tears. "What are you playing there?"

Ray assumed that it was a regular kid's game, but he was a little surprised when he saw him solving a puzzle. The game celebrated with him each time he made a correct choice.

"Guess what Sammy? We're going home today!" Ray told him.

"Yay!" Sammy exclaimed. "Can I take my game with me, Daddy?"

"Hello, Mr. and Mrs. Smith! How are you?" Tamara said as she entered the room. Mary Ellen didn't look up or say anything to her.

"Are those his discharge papers?" Ray asked shortly as he stood up to face her. "We want to get out of here as quickly as possible."

"Discharge papers? Who told you he was being discharged?" Tamara asked.

"You know, I don't know what kind of operation you all have going on in here, playing around with our heads, but I'm through with it. Just give me the sign-off papers, we're leaving with Sammy," Ray said and sat back down next to his son.

Tamara didn't argue with them—she could tell that they were in a state of distress. She just left Sammy's room and went straight to Dr.

Meron's office.

"Come in," Dr. Meron said from behind the door, hearing her knock.

"Doctor," Tamara said as she closed the door behind her. "The Smiths are saying Sammy's been discharged from the program?"

"That is correct. Please draw up the discharge papers and make sure they have all of his things," Dr. Meron answered without ever looking up from his desk. Tamara was starting to get ticked off by his nonchalant demeanor. Despite their advanced knowledge in science and medicine, doctors like him usually had little to no training in effective communication skills.

"We still have 10 weeks left in his treatment plan. How could you take him off the program so soon?" she asked.

"Dr. Goodwin. I am not required to consult you or explain my final decisions on my patients, but it is clear that Sammy's trip to the hospital yesterday cannot happen again. Not if we're to continue with our trials uninterrupted. You should have called me first."

"I called you four times. You didn't call back until eight hours later. Should I have waited that long before getting him help? His blood pressure reading was extremely high and we couldn't normalize it with his medication," Tamara tried to say calmly.

"Regardless of what happened, he is simply not a good candidate for this initial trial. We should not have accepted him considering his health concerns," Dr. Meron said. "That was my mistake."

"You mean you shouldn't have given this family false hope," Tamara said. The words flew out of her mouth before she could stop them. Dr. Meron looked up at her. He was shocked by her frankness.

"Draw up the discharge papers, Dr. Goodwin. Immediately," he said.

Tamara nodded and turned to open his office door. She paused for a moment and looked down at the $500 burgundy-toned Louboutin pumps that she'd just treated herself to from the stipend she was receiving. The amount of her stipend increased when Dr. Meron received new private funding that month. Her pulse raced as she searched her thoughts for a moment. She thought of the look of terror on the Smith's faces when they met her at the hospital. Then she thought of the look of disappointment in Ray Smith's eyes when she entered Sammy's room just minutes before. She finally mustered up the courage to speak to her boss again.

"Dr. Meron, I know that this is your program. And I respect that. But please remember that these are my patients too. They're counting on me too. I hope that you'll be able to respect and understand that," Tamara said, then closed the door before he had a chance to respond.

With Thanksgiving and the holidays coming up soon, Jill decided to take a few cooking classes to learn new dishes. She had signed up for a fall appetizer class at their favorite local farm with Grace as her plus one, but now that Grace was barely even speaking to her it was highly unlikely that she'd want to attend. Grace hadn't even attended the family meeting that Jill and Joseph scheduled. Jill was starting to feel a bit overwhelmed and wondering if some type of an intervention would soon be necessary.

The cooking class was pretty full and buzzing with the sounds of ladies talking about their plans for Thanksgiving. Jill hung her purse on the hook in front of the countertop where she was sitting. She glanced around to see if there was anyone there that she knew.

"Hello Jill," a voice said from behind her. She jerked her head around and saw Marsha standing there, just a little bit too close, looking at her with a strange look on her face. Marsha's hair was sloppily pulled into a ponytail. Jill had never seen her without her hair done in a style. She wore a large over-sized shirt that had a stain on it. Her eye makeup was messy and her eyes looked red and dull as if she had been crying for days.

"Marsha! It's so nice to see you," Jill said, trying to hide her shocked expression, as she stood up to give her friend a hug. "How did you know about this cooking class? It's over an hour away from you guys."

"I saw you post about it on Facebook a few days ago," Marsha explained as she sat in the seat right next to Jill.

"Oh. Well, it's nice to see you, it's been a while," Jill said, feeling a bit of tension in the air. "So, how was Tommy's Halloween?"

"It was great, just great," Marsha said with very little enthusiasm. "He dressed up as the Kung Fu Panda."

"Cute," Jill said with a smile as she picked up her cellphone to answer a text message.

"Who's that?" Marsha asked curiously, trying to look at the screen.

"Just Joseph. I left him a huge piece of apple pie on the counter from a party at my office," she said as she looked at his 'thank you' text and photo.

"So Jill. How are things going with Joey and Jason? Has he seen him lately?" Marsha wanted to know.

"Yes. He sees Jason about once every 10 days or so. I think the drive is a little bit of a stress on him, though," Jill answered.

"Okay ladies," the instructor called out to the room. "Thank you so much for attending our fall appetizer cooking class. We have a lot of great new ideas to explore today. Let's start off by putting on our aprons…"

Marsha brought the tutor Jason's name up throughout the entire class. It became so uncomfortable that Jill started actively bringing up Jack's name to make him the point of conversation. She even tried turning the discussion to Dr. Meron's program and Tommy. But every time, Marsha would direct the conversation right back to Jason. It was like trying to get a dog away from his bone.

"...nowadays, it seems as if Jason is spending more time at your house than mine," Marsha said with a nervous chuckle as she side-glanced at Jill to see her expression. Jill just continued to smear herb cream cheese on her toasted crostini bread slices.

"Not really," Jill said without much of a thought. "You know, you should bring Jack to one of these cooking classes. He would love it."

"Yea, probably a little too much," Marsha said with a scoff. "They might not have any food left for the next class!"

Marsha started laughing but Jill just looked at her friend curiously. She secretly hated it when Marsha talked about Jack like that because it had gone way past playful ribbing. Jack was very insecure about his weight gain, yet he refused to see a doctor about how it was affecting his health.

"So, when was the last time you spoke to Jason?" Marsha asked.

"It's been a while. You know what Marsha, I have to go to the bathroom. I'll be right back," Jill said as she grabbed her purse from the hook. In her hurry to get away from Marsha for a while, she forgot her phone on the counter.

Marsha watched Jill head toward the bathroom, wondering if she had something to hide. As she continued to prepare her own crostini bite, her eyes darted over to the cellphone that Jill left on the counter. She glanced around to see if anyone nearby was watching, and then quickly swiped her finger across the screen. A password was required.

"What are you doing Marsha?" Jill asked, looking at her friend curiously. She had come back for her phone.

"Oh, nothing," Marsha said nervously but pretended not to be bothered. "I thought it was mine."

By the time Jill and Marsha parted ways, Jill was eager to get away. She felt as if she had just rendezvoused with an entirely different person. It was something straight out of an episode of Star Trek. She had never seen Marsha behave so strangely and not look put together. Jill wanted to help her friend through whatever she was going through, but she already had enough drama going on in her own life with Grace and deciding if Joey would participate in Dr. Meron's treatment program.

Jill's list of priorities was full, so whatever Marsha was going through at the moment, it would definitely have to wait.

"I just want to know if we're any closer to making a decision," Joseph said. He and Jill sat across from each other at the kitchen island over a cup of coffee. It was Sunday and they finally had a quiet opportunity to discuss Dr. Meron's trials.

"I know you're eager to do this honey, but I really need to look over the paperwork he gave us more thoroughly. Some of the terms seem a bit...oppressive," Jill said. "It's mostly geared toward protecting Dr. Meron and his research, but not that much on protecting our child."

Joseph sighed. He had wondered many times why his wife didn't pursue a legal career. She would have made a great contract negotiator, reading every word of every agreement they'd ever signed from their mortgages right down to the terms and conditions on their cellphone plans.

"I understand, and you're right," Joseph said with a nod. "But I'm concerned that there won't be a slot left by the time we call him. He said that they're also seeking participants from other states now."

There was a knock on the door and the doorbell rang. They exchanged looks to see if either of them was expecting someone, but they both shrugged. Joseph turned on the front door camera app to see who it was as he went to the door. A young boy stood there holding a bat and glove.

"Hello Mr. Todaro," Brendan said formally when the door swung open.

"And you are?" Joseph asked as he crossed his arms.

"Brendan. Brendan Romero. Nice to meet you," he said with an extended hand, which Joseph reluctantly shook. "Uh... Sophia invited me over. We're supposed to play ball at the park today."

"Oh. Okay. She didn't tell us that," Joseph said, examining the boy from head to toe as he invited him in to sit on the couch. "Sophia!"

Minutes later, Sophia came bounding down the stairs dressed in her workout t-shirt with her cleats hung over her shoulder, confirming Brendan's story. He had been to all of her games since the district qualifier and they were hanging out together in school more.

"You didn't tell us you were having company today," Joseph said as he caught her at the bottom of the stairs.

"He's just a friend Dad, relax," Sophia said with an eye roll as she went past him. "We're just going to the park down the street. Come on Brendan."

"Can I go too, Sophie?? Pleeeeease??" they heard a voice call out as they headed for the door. Joey ran up to them to stop them from leaving.

"Hey, Joey T!" Brendan said and slapped hands with him.

"Hi, Brendan!" Joey T said with a smile, hoping they would let him come along. He had seen Brendan in passing in school and Brendan always went out of his way to say hello now. "Could I come to the park with you guys?"

"Maybe next time Joey, okay?" Sophia said as she held her hand out to give him a high-five. His smile disappeared. He looked disappointed but nodded his head and slapped her hand anyway.

"Okay."

"Actually, I was kinda hoping Joey could come along too," Brendan spoke up as he gestured to his bat. "With three people we could hit the ball around some more. Practice some tag plays."

Joseph looked over at Brendan, a little surprised. Joey started to smile and move from side to side, gearing up to go get his baseball glove.

"Okay Joey, but you have to stay with us the whole time. Hurry up and get your stuff, we'll meet you out front," Sophia said as they opened the door. Brendan stepped out onto the porch.

"Sophia, hold on," her dad said and pulled out his wallet. He handed her a $20 bill. "Just in case the snack stand is open over there."

"Thanks, Dad."

"What's that kid's name again?" he asked.

"Brendan. He's been to my games," Sophia told him. "We're in the same classes at school and he's on the baseball team."

"Hmmm, okay. He seems like a good kid, but please be back before dark."

"I will."

"And if he wants, he can stay for dinner. Mom's making her famous chicken casserole."

"Okay Dad," Sophia said with another eye-roll and a smile as she headed outside to talk to Brendan.

When Joey came back downstairs, he was dressed in his favorite Cardinals jersey and matching hat. He also had his bat, ball, and glove. Before heading out of the door, he ran to the kitchen. Jill watched as he jumped high and tapped the Gatorade dash button. She chuckled as he ran outside.

Joseph watched from the door as Sophia, Brendan, and Joey walked down the street as a group toward the neighborhood park, chatting away. The look of pure joy on Joey's face said it all.

Dr. Damarus Thomas was a revered ophthalmologist who made millions after inventing a device that helped older people with vision problems see their electronic devices more clearly. He and Dr. Meron had both graduated from Columbia University medical school the same year. While Dr. Thomas' career seemed to take off right away, Dr. Meron's floundered for a long while. They were colleagues and had worked together professionally in the past, but they were also competitive "frenemies."

Dr. Thomas lived and practiced in St. Louis, which wasn't that far from Dr. Meron's Illinois office. He was a little surprised by the invitation to come to Dr. Meron's research facility to examine one of his patients because they hadn't spoken for years. But Dr. Thomas was curious to learn more about what his old classmate was working on.

"Howard, how are you?" Dr. Thomas said when Dr. Meron finally came out to meet him in the waiting room. They stood and shook hands.

"So glad you could make it out here Damarus. I really would appreciate your feedback on one of my patients," Dr. Meron replied. "My research is still in the early trial phase and I know that I can count on your discretion."

"Of course," Dr. Thomas said with a nod as they walked to an examination room. "Tell me more about your patient."

Dr. Meron opened the door where Billy and Tamara were seated. Tamara nodded at the doctor who she had spoken to on the phone several times. She had received him when he arrived and sat him in the waiting room because Dr. Meron wanted to make a dramatic entrance.

"It's Billy," Dr. Meron said as he invited Dr. Thomas inside.

"Your son Billy?" Dr. Thomas asked, shocked by the revelation. "What is he being treated for?"

"He was diagnosed with Williams Syndrome when he was eight months old—right around the time Jane passed," Dr. Meron said, remaining stoic. He had learned long ago how to separate his personal problems and feelings from his work. Right now, he was discussing Billy as a patient, not his son. His work was his life now.

Dr. Thomas was visibly taken aback. "I never knew."

"Williams Syndrome has been the focus of my research for the past eight years. I've created an injectable serum that replicates some of the lost genetic matter that causes the symptoms," Dr. Meron explained. "It's a form of DNA repair. Sort of a gene-editing process."

"How is that even possible?" Dr. Thomas said as he sat down in front of Billy to look at his eyes.

"This is what Billy looked like approximately one year ago," Dr. Meron said as he handed him a photo. "He had severe speech, reading, and learning delays. Today, he's reading on a ninth-grade level."

"That's amazing," Dr. Thomas said as he took the picture.

"These are magnified photos of his eyes one year ago. As you can see, there's a noticeable change there," Tamara said as she handed him two other photos.

Dr. Meron gave her a stern look. He didn't ask her to provide a magnified photo of Billy's eyes—he just wanted to get Dr. Thomas' professional okay that Billy's eyes were normal.

"Interesting," Dr. Thomas said as he looked over the photos. "His eyes have a completely different pattern now. Let me take a closer look."

At the end of the exam, the two doctors went into Dr. Meron's office to chat. There was a look of concern on Dr. Thomas' face when they sat down.

"Howard, I'm not sure where to start. I'm overwhelmed," Dr. Thomas began.

"I know. It's a pretty big deal."

"Well, yea, but that's not it. First, it's not usual for the pattern of a child's eyes to change that dramatically that quickly. His eyesight seems fine, but it's hard to explain," Dr. Thomas said, taking a moment to carefully choose his next words. "It's more than just a change of pattern, his eyes are completely different. It's almost as if they belong to someone else."

Dr. Meron frowned. "Well, clearly they don't."

"I know, but it's concerning to me. And they approved this serum of yours for clinical testing?"

"That's pending," Dr. Meron said as he crossed his fingers on the desk in front of him.

"Pending? Please tell me you received your approval before giving this serum to Billy?"

Dr. Meron stood up defiantly and walked to his window. "He's my son. I'm responsible for him and I make the decisions for him. We're days away from getting a final approval for new participants."

"I can't believe this," Dr. Thomas said, standing up to leave. "I can't be here. This is unethical, and now you've involved me!"

"You should be so lucky to be involved in this! WT42-580OF will revolutionize how we approach the treatment of genetic disorders for both children and adults for years in the future!"

"I was never here Howard. And for the record, I do *not* support this," Dr. Thomas said with finality before exiting. Dr. Meron seethed quietly in his chair for a while after his colleague left.

"He's just jealous," he finally reasoned to himself. "It's to be expected."

"Okay, my love, we will be back later this week to check on you," Marsha said as she leaned down to talk to Tommy. She combed her fingers through his hair a few more times to keep it out of his face.

"Okay, Mommy, I love you! You can go now," he said and then put on his headphones. Lately, his mom wasn't paying as much attention to what he was doing on his phone, so he figured out how to download a bunch of his favorite movies and songs. Marsha and Jack would definitely be surprised when they saw the charges.

It was Tommy's first day in Dr. Meron's treatment center. He would be there for at least the next two weeks under observation as he received the injections. Dr. Meron considered him to be an ideal candidate.

Jack wasn't able to take off from work that day, but promised to visit Tommy that weekend. Marsha didn't protest because she had some "business" to attend to that day. After giving Tommy one more big kiss on the forehead, she left him in Tamara's hands.

"Bye bye honey, I love you!" she said with a smile and tears welling up in her eyes. She fought them back because she couldn't afford to have her makeup streak.

That day, she dressed up in the new figure-flattering wrap dress and thigh-high boots that she recently purchased. She went to the hair and nail salon early that morning to ensure that her look was perfection. She looked modelesque as she strutted to her white Lexus.

She drove for over a half an hour listening to club music for energy and confidence. She wanted to feel young again. Her destination: Jason's house. She knew his address from the resume he sent to her when applying for the tutoring position. She just hoped that he hadn't moved.

After looking for parking on Jason's block for a few minutes, she finally found one right in front of his apartment building. She glanced in the rearview mirror once more to make sure that her hair was perfectly in place and makeup flawless. It was.

Marsha sauntered her way to the lobby of Jason's apartment building and caught the door just as someone was exiting. She took the elevator to the 11th floor and checked her dress in the mirrored walls.

She was nervous as she stood in front of Jason's door, but took a deep breath and knocked confidently. She knocked again but there was no answer. After 15 minutes of waiting and knocking, she realized that he just wasn't home at the moment. She figured he might still be at work, even though it was after six by that time.

After over an hour of waiting on the window sill near Jason's apartment, there still was no sign of him. She decided it would be best to wait outside in her car since it was right in front of his building.

At around 10:30 p.m., Marsha was awakened by the sound of laughing and loud talking. She regained an awareness of where she was and looked at herself in the rearview mirror. Her hair had been mushed against the window, giving it a flat appearance on one side. Her fake eyelash was curled downward as if it might come off at any moment. As she tried to fix herself up, she heard more laughing and turned to look at the front of Jason's building.

Jason and a young woman were standing there, chatting and laughing as they enjoyed the perfect fall night. Marsha was crushed as she watched him lean down to give her a long, deep kiss. After what seemed like an eternity, Jason released his date and pulled her into the lobby. Marsha jumped out of her car and called after him.

"Jason!" she shouted. Her foot had fallen asleep, so she ended up tumbling to the ground. Jason turned just in time to see her getting up.

"Mrs. Rogers? Is that you?" Jason said as he rushed over to help her.

"Hi, how are you, Jason?" Marsha said, trying to look elegant as she climbed to her feet.

"What are you doing here?" Jason asked, putting two and two together in his head.

"I came to see you! It's so hard to get in touch with you these days," Marsha said with a sweet smile, trying to fix her hair. "I was starting to get concerned about you."

"I've just been busy," Jason explained, knowing deep down that this was more than just a friendly, professional check-in.

Against his better judgment, Jason had gone to lunch with Marsha Rogers one afternoon. She dropped Tommy off at the sitter's. At the "date," Marsha had more than a few drinks and tried to kiss him. She had always been very flirtatious, but he was surprised by her forwardness. He realized then that they had officially crossed the line and he was trying to find a way to separate himself from the situation. He now saw that disappearing wasn't going to cut it for Marsha. She had been texting and calling him almost every day. She was acting like a teenage girl.

"Well I understand that, but Tommy misses you. We both miss you," Marsha said as she stepped toward him. He took a step back, glancing at his date. She was watching the two, looking confused.

"Mrs. Rogers..."

"Marsha."

"...I really like your son and I love the work that we do together, but I'm afraid I'm not going to be able to tutor him anymore."

"What? No! Why not?" Marsha asked.

"It's just not amenable to my schedule at the moment. I have too much on my plate."

"Too much on your plate? But you still have time to tutor Jill's son? She told me you were at their house just recently!"

"I may have to end that arrangement as well. I'm being considered for a new position at my old school," Jason said. "Look, I really have to go, my girlfriend is waiting. I'm fine, really. Please have a safe drive home, Mrs. Rogers."

"Wait, no Jason. You can't just cut us off like that," Marsha said as she followed him. "We need you."

"I'm sorry Mrs. Rogers," Jason said as he quickly closed the auto-lock door inside of the lobby so that she couldn't follow them. "Please drive safe."

"But Jason," she pleaded as she watched him wait at the elevator with his date. The elevator wait was unusually long, and the two tried not to look back at Marsha as she stood there like a sad puppy in the window, knocking lightly and trying to get Jason's attention.

Finally, the elevator opened and a few people came off.

"Hey, don't let that lady inside," Jason said to them before they boarded the elevator.

When Marsha tried to slide her way inside, the last guy closed the door behind him tightly. That's when she decided it was time to throw a fit.

"Let me in! I need to talk to someone!" Marsha commanded.

"Whoa, relax lady," he said with his hands in his pockets as he continued to walk down the street with his friends.

"Don't tell me to relax!" Marsha yelled back at him. "I'll show you relaxed!"

She jerked at the glass door, trying to force it open. When it didn't give even a little bit, that just made Marsha even madder. She went outside to the sidewalk and started kicking random cars, including her own. She found Jason's car a few yards down the street and punched the hood so hard that it left a dent. When someone finally spotted her and threatened to call the police, she ran to her car and jumped in. Her hand was throbbing with pain as she screeched off down the street.

CHAPTER 12
Reaching Out

Tamara spent the entire morning in her office with the door closed. She usually left it open so that anyone would feel comfortable coming in for a chat. She also wanted to be the first to know if there was an issue with one of the children. But lately, the energy in Dr. Meron's facility was becoming toxic.

The 10 children who were now receiving treatment were becoming more and more detached, resisting any suggestions or advice from her. Billy had learned that if he threw a tantrum, it would allow him to play video games in peace for hours in the calming room without being interrupted with school work. Dr. Meron still had him scheduled for injections even though Tamara advised that it was time to end them and allow him to adjust naturally.

Dr. Meron was still out of the office most of the time, leaving Tamara to tend to a growing list of patients. As soon as she resolved one situation, another one popped up. She was starting to feel like the administrator of a day care for troubled kids rather than a scientist doing medical research.

There was a beep from her phone.

"Dr. Goodwin," Dr. Meron said through the intercom. "Can you please come to my office."

"Sure thing," Tamara said through clenched teeth and grabbed her clipboard. On the way to Dr. Meron's office, she passed Tommy Rogers' room and looked in. He was quietly staring at the wall, seeming to look into space. He looked bored. It was a bit unusual because Tommy's favorite thing to do was put his headphones on and watch videos.

When she arrived at Dr. Meron's office, his door was open and there were five other people in the room with him—all of them wearing lab jackets.

"Dr. Goodwin, please come in," Dr. Meron invited her and then closed the door behind her. "These are my new team members. They will be helping us manage cases over the next year."

He went down the line naming each person, their background, and the role that they would play. Everyone in the group seemed pleasant, except for one.

"This is Dr. Manuel Richards. He will be taking over as lead researcher starting Monday," Dr. Meron revealed. "I'd like you to assist him in the same way that you've assisted me—particularly when I'm out of town."

"Lead researcher? That's my position," Tamara asked, visibly shocked at the revelation.

"Yes, I know, but I'd like you to play a new role, focusing mainly on weekly test-taking and educational programs."

"I'll need every current patient's file on my desk by 2 p.m.," Dr. Richards said bluntly without saying hello. He and Dr. Meron had the same smug expression and body language. "Also a transfer of administrator privileges on the server."

"Yes, that's correct," Dr. Meron said with a nod. "I suggest that you all meet among yourselves to get better acquainted and to learn from Dr. Goodwin. I believe this arrangement will be very effective."

Tamara looked dumbfounded and was speechless as Dr. Meron walked over to open the door and let them out. The other new team members left the room, but she stayed behind and finally found her voice again when Dr. Meron sat at his desk.

"You're giving him my position?"

"Well yes, but your current stipend and arrangements will remain the same. I still think of you as a highly valuable member of this team," Dr. Meron said in a patronizing tone.

"But he doesn't know a thing about all the research we've done over the past few years. How could he be promoted over me without one day on the job?"

"You're going to get him up to date Dr. Goodwin. Dr. Richards has extensive experience with experimental treatments like ours. I believe he'll be able to get us on track," Dr. Meron said.

"So you think that we're off track?"

"Not necessarily, but I am concerned about some of the situations we've had in the past couple of months, such as Sammy Smith's visit to the ER. I'm still receiving voicemails from some very inquisitive doctors at that hospital."

"That couldn't be avoided, Doctor," Tamara explained. "I couldn't jeopardize the child's life. What if it had been Billy?"

Dr. Meron looked up at her sternly. "But it wasn't Billy. Please don't bring my son up just to make a point."

After a short pause in the conversation, he stood up once again and went over to open his office door.

"This is going to be a very hectic day for us all, Dr. Goodwin. If there isn't anything else, I'd really like you to get back to work," he said.

Tamara sighed heavily, unsure of what to say again and left hurriedly. On the way back to her own office, she passed Tommy's room again and found him still staring into space. She decided to put aside her own distress and go chat with him.

"Hey Tommy," Tamara said gently as she entered the room. "How are you doing today?"

Tommy looked over at her curiously as if he had just been shaken from a dream. "My mommy didn't come this morning."

"Oh, sweetie. She might have just been busy today but I'm sure she'll come tomorrow. I'll give her a call."

"You promise?"

Tamara paused and looked at Tommy for a moment. She normally would have promised him immediately, but something stopped her. She remembered the looks of disappointment on the Smiths' faces when they found out that she and Dr. Meron couldn't help their son Sammy. They were devastated and turned cold. She didn't want to see that look on anyone's face again in life.

The truth was that Tamara was starting to realize that she had made promises to a lot of parents that she wasn't sure she could live up to. And the idea of becoming a tool of not just one, but now two arrogant doctors was a little too much for her to bear.

~

"To be or not to be... that is the question!" Joey recited with his hand at his heart. Suzy sat and watched him put on a short performance of one of Shakespeare's classics. Joey and his mom had practiced various soliloquies together for years—it was part of why he did so well in school plays. Though he didn't fully understand what the words meant, he had them word for word.

"Who said that?" Suzy finally said after giving him a round of applause.

"Prince Hamlet," Joey answered as he sat down across from her. It was a mild fall day, so they were outside enjoying the sun and playing in the leaves.

"What's that on your eyes?" Suzy inquired as she moved closer to look at the green of Joey's eyes. "It looks like little lightning bolts."

"Really?"

"Yea, it's pretty cool," she said with a smile.

"Thanks!"

True to her word, Suzy had asked her parents if Joey could come over to practice lines for their upcoming play. Jill reluctantly agreed but wanted to accompany him to the play date. She and Suzy's mom, Alison, watched them together from the patio.

"When did you and your husband know?" Alison asked after taking a sip from her pumpkin-flavored coffee. "I mean, when was Joey diagnosed with Williams Syndrome?"

"At about nine months old," Jill answered. "He had open heart surgery at 10 months old. It was a very hard time and we were terrified—his father slept under his crib the night before."

"10 months old?" Alison exclaimed. "I can't imagine what you guys went through."

"Yes, but by the grace of God we got through it," Jill said as she sipped her coffee.

"Amen to that," Alison said with a nod as she looked back over to the children. By that time, they were doing everything except for practicing lines—Joey had gathered a pile of leaves for them to jump into. "They really get along nicely. A natural pair."

"I see that. I have to admit, I was a bit jealous when Joey told me he didn't want to practice his lines with me this week," Jill said with a smile.

Alison laughed. "It's all Suzy's been talking about recently. We're new to the area and she doesn't have a lot of friends yet. Some of her classmates tease her because she's so small. She tried out for the school play in hopes of meeting new kids."

"I see. I know how that can be—Joey had some of the same challenges when he first went to school."

"Maybe we could do this more? I'd love to have you guys over this weekend. We're going to be firing up the pit, barbecuing, and making s'mores."

Jill nodded and looked pleased with the idea on the outside, but something tugged at her on the inside. Joey had never had a girl as a play date other than his sisters. The whole time they were at Suzy's house, Joey hadn't spoken to his mom or looked her way for over an hour.

She remembered the dream she had where Joey grew up and disappeared. She checked herself, immediately realizing that her fears of losing him to the world were responsible for why she felt some resistance to allowing him to hang out with Suzy. Like any mother, she liked her Joey T just the way he was, but she also knew that it wasn't fair to try to keep him all to herself. He was growing up in his own way and at his own pace.

"What happened to your hand?"

Jack was a little surprised to see his wife Marsha sitting at the kitchen island at 6:30 in the morning. Ever since Tommy was checked into the treatment facility, she had been sleeping late—sometimes as late as two o'clock in the afternoon. By the time he arrived back home from work, she was back in bed. On this particular morning, she looked like she hadn't slept at all.

As soon as Marsha heard Jack's voice, she crumbled up the paper that she was writing on. Her other hand was wrapped with a white bandage.

"Nothing, it's fine," she said as she stood up from her seat with the paper still tightly clenched in her fist. She moved past him quickly before he could ask any more questions.

"Have a good day at work," she said as sweetly as she could before going up the stairs to her bedroom. Jack noticed that she tossed the paper in the wastebasket near the staircase before going upstairs.

He tried to put it to the back of his mind, but after drinking his orange juice and having two frozen breakfast meals, curiosity got the best of him. He grabbed the paper out of the trash and opened it back up. It was scribbled in her very best handwriting.

Dear Jason,

I am so sorry for what happened recently. I have just been a little stressed and now I'm distressed that you won't answer any of my calls, texts or emails. I'm worried about Tommy and afraid that not having you in his life would hurt him. He adores you, almost like a father or big brother, and I have come to feel the same way. Most of the time I feel as if I'm doing this all on my

The letter ended abruptly and Jack was left feeling shattered.

"Like a father to him? He has a father," he mumbled under his breath.

He sat down on the step and read the letter over and over. He read between the lines and realized that this was more than just an appeal for Tommy's sake. As contentious as their relationship had been over the years, he never imagined that Marsha would or could ever be unfaithful to him. He knew that they needed counseling to get along, but he thought that simply limiting the time they spent together would fix things. Clearly, it hadn't.

"I don't know what to do with her anymore mom," Jill said as she rested her head on her mother's shoulder. "She's completely out of hand. Totally rebellious."

"Well, that just might run in the family, Jill. You were no piece of cake yourself!" her mom, Teresa, said with a chuckle as she gently caressed Jill's hair. Whenever Jill was experiencing a crisis or had questions she found difficult to answer, she came to visit her parents. Her mom was a wise and caring woman who had served on her city council for over 20 years before retiring. She was an example to all of her girls of how a woman could pursue a meaningful career while still having a balanced life as a wife and mother.

"Mom, I wasn't *that* bad," Jill protested.

"Don't take it as an indictment, my love," Teresa said with a smile. "I was the same way. And we both turned out okay, didn't we?"

"Well, yes, but it was different when we were young. There were checks and balances," Jill reasoned. "Nowadays kids just have unlimited power and means to do whatever they want."

"That may be true," Teresa said as she leaned her daughter back up to face her. "But there's something else that we had in common that kept us on the right path."

"What's that?"

"A loving and supportive family," Teresa explained as she looked into her daughter's big brown eyes. "When people go astray, it's because they don't have that. Grace was blessed with a great family, and she will be okay. You have to know that."

"But what am I supposed to do in the meanwhile?" Jill wondered aloud.

"Jill, you don't always have to *do* something. Sometimes all that we can do for our children is pray, love them, and be there for them in the most important ways."

"I feel as if I should stay on top of her, you know? She needs guidance. This boy just isn't right for her."

"But that 'guidance' usually turns into arguments between you two, doesn't it?" Teresa asked.

Jill sighed. "Yes."

"Don't you know by now that the more you fight with a rebellious person, the more rebellious they become?" Teresa asked. "They will do anything to prove you wrong. Just love her through this time in her life."

"You're right as usual, Mom."

"I know I am, that's why you come to me for advice," Teresa said as she patted her daughter's knee and headed to the kitchen to make tea.

"Mom, there's something else I wanted to talk to you about," Jill said as she followed her. "Is Dad around?"

"You know where he is, his den as usual. Marv!" Teresa called out to him. A few minutes later, he appeared. He was a distinguished-looking, tall, white-haired man who was always called upon to play Santa Claus at holiday family functions.

"Jilly Bean!" he said with a look of pure joy on his face. He was always happy to see his youngest daughter.

"Daddy!" They hugged and Jill felt any anxiety melt away. She knew it was time to have this discussion regarding Joey with her parents.

For the next 20 minutes, Jill explained everything that had transpired over the past few months since the Williams Syndrome meeting when they first learned about Dr. Meron's revolutionary treatment. She had hesitated to tell her parents anything about it at first, but now decision time was coming soon and she needed some solid advice. Dr. Meron told them that the deadline for making a decision for the first round of trials was that month, and that there might not be another opening for years.

"They showed us the results of their first case, a boy named Billy, and he seems to be doing great," Jill told them. "But it's almost too good to be true. And I'm afraid of how it might affect Joey. What do you think?"

"Well first off, tell us what the real issue is here Jill," Teresa said, reading her daughter like a book. "We can't give you our best opinion without 100 percent honesty."

Jill paused and looked at her parents, who were both looking at her like she was sitting in the principal's office. She knew that she wouldn't be able to get anything past them at this point. She looked down at the table and there was a long, uncomfortable pause.

"I'm afraid that my beautiful baby boy isn't going to need me anymore," Jill finally said and broke down in tears. "He's always needed me, and now I feel that slipping away. I love him just the way he is and I feel like I'm being pressured by everyone to change that!"

Teresa got up and comforted her daughter. Marv reached across the table and grabbed her hand.

"It sounds like this has been weighing heavily on your mind for a while," Marv said, hating to see his daughter cry. "Don't worry Jilly Bean, we're going to figure this thing out."

"Yes we are, we're going to talk this through, even if it takes all night," her mom said as she sat down next to her at the table.

CHAPTER 13
Choices and Consequences

"Let's go, Soph, let's hit it out of the park this time!" Joseph yelled out to his daughter from the stands and whistled loudly. He, Jill, Mia, and Joey arrived early to get front row seats to the game, which was packed with bystanders due to the notoriety the team was getting in the school newspaper. They were 15-1 for the season and today's game was against the one team they'd lost to—the Lady Bengals.

Sophia's softball team was heavily favored to make it to the state championship game. They only needed to win one out of the next two games to qualify. This was a big day for everyone and Sophia had been nervous the entire week. Brendan was over at the house almost every day helping her with her school work because practices were taking up so much of her time.

"We're dynamite, we're dynamite, we're tick tick tick tick tick tick tick tick BOOM dynamite (clap clap) BOOM BOOM dynamite!" Sophia's teammates chanted as she walked up to the plate and did a few practice swings.

The opposing pitcher was a year older and had similar skills to Sophia. At their last game, the Lady Bengals won by just one run and Sophia's team was devastated by the loss. They were eager to return the favor. It was now the bottom of the 8th inning and the Bengals were again leading by one run.

As Sophia squared up at the plate, Joey jumped up from his seat and started to do a few moves that he called his "victory dance." The family and other onlookers cheered even louder, sending a roar of energy across the field.

The first pitch was a strike that Sophia watched sail over the plate.

"Okay, that's a good look, Sophia. If you see another one, swing away!" Brendan called out to her from behind the fence.

The next pitch was a little inside, putting the count at 1:1. Sophia knew that she had the best chance out of anyone to bring the runner on base home to tie things up, so she resolved to pummel the next pitch no matter what. As the ball flew her way, she took a step forward and was stunned when the fastball hit her on the hip instead. She grabbed her hip in pain and leaned forward.

"Hey!" Joseph stood up and yelled. Jill held him back as Sophia's coach came over to check on her. She waved him off and began limping her way to first base. The crowd applauded, but the excitement had been drained from the air.

Unfortunately, the next two batters struck out, leaving the Bengals in the lead. Sophia's pitching was shaky during the last inning as she tried to hide the discomfort in her hip. The final score was 3:1, Bengals.

After the game, Sophia was so hurt by the loss that she pulled her hat down low over her eyes and refused to look up at anyone as they came over to pat her on the back. She fought back tears with all of the power she had left within.

"It's okay Sophie, you'll get 'em next time. Still got another shot at the big game," her dad tried to reassure her, but she was inconsolable. Brendan stood nearby, wondering if he should try to say something. But he could tell that she wasn't in the mood to chat.

Joey came right over and leaned down in front of his sister, holding a cold bottle of lemon-lime Gatorade—her favorite flavor.

"Here you go Sophie," he said as he handed his sister the bottle and smiled up at her. "We have to get ready for the next game!"

Sophia looked down at her brother and couldn't help but smile back through an eye full of tears. She brushed one away before it had a chance to fall on her shirt.

"Thanks, Joey," she said. She took a long sip of Gatorade and then started packing up her things. Her coach called the entire team over for a final pow-wow.

"We'll meet you at the car, honey," Jill told her. Joey and Mia decided to hang behind and wait for their sister on the field with Brendan. As soon as he had the chance, Joey immediately started running the bases and sliding into home plate.

"So I had a long conversation with my parents," Jill told Joseph when they were finally out of earshot of the kids. She had thought long and hard about what she was about to tell him.

"Oh, yea? What did you guys talk about?" Joseph asked as he draped her arm around her shoulder.

"About Grace. About Joey. About a lot of things," she replied with a sigh. "I'll tell you more in the car."

Jill ran down her entire visit with her parents, from her mother's advice about how to help Grace, to her decision to finally tell them about the treatment they were considering for Joey.

"They have this way of seeing through me like no one else can," Jill said, but then corrected herself when she saw the look on Joseph's face. "Well, except for you of course."

"No, I get what you mean. Go ahead," he said.

"Well, they got me to admit some truths about why I've been resistant to signing Joey up for those treatments. And while they didn't explicitly condone the therapy, they made me realize that I have to make a decision one way or another."

Joseph nodded and allowed her to continue.

"I say we go forward with it, but that we do so with caution. I have to talk to Dr. Meron about some of the paperwork he wants us to sign. I need to be sure that we'll be able to pull Joey out of his program at any time for any reason. And also that his name and case information will not be publicly disclosed."

Joseph smiled and nodded, looking relieved. "I totally agree. After thinking about it more, I'm glad we waited and really gave this a lot of thought."

He reached over to embrace her and they had a long, warm hug that lasted several minutes. Before long, they heard a tap on the trunk—it was Sophia with her gear.

"Everything will be okay," Joseph reassured his wife before letting the kids into the car. "You'll see."

For the first time in months, John got out of his truck and walked up to the front door of his house to ring the doorbell. He was there to pick his son up for football practice, but instead of beeping the horn as he usually did, he decided he wanted to see inside of the house.

Debra hadn't called or texted him in weeks and he was starting to get concerned about it. He thought that taking a long no-contact break from her would get her to appreciate him more. But instead, it was starting to seem like she was getting a little too comfortable with the arrangement.

"Hey Dad," his younger son Jeremy said as he opened the door. "Did you call? My fault, I didn't hear the phone ring."

"No, no," John said as he came inside and started looking around. "I just wanted to come in and check on things."

"Oh, okay. Let me go grab my stuff—we'll be down in two minutes," Jeremy said.

John went to the back of the house where Debra's office was, thinking that she would be there, but she wasn't. It was curiously quiet, which was unusual because Patty was almost always playing and running around the house getting into things. He went over to her desk and saw a few colorful college brochures. He was surprised by how clean and tidy it was in there.

John casually went upstairs to look for Debra there, but the bedroom was empty.

Jeremy and Zac came out of their shared bedroom holding all of their football gear.

"Where's your mother and Patty?" John finally asked them, trying to sound nonchalant.

"Oh, she went to some orientation thing at a college and took Patty with her," Zac said.

"But her car's in the driveway? How did she get there?" John asked.

"She took a cab. The car wasn't turning on because the battery's old, and she was in a hurry to get Patty to the sitter's," Zac explained.

"The sitter's? She's leaving Patty with a stranger?"

"It's some lady she found online who takes care of special kids like Patty," Zac said. "Could we hit the road, Dad? Coach'll have the whole team running extra laps if we're even one minute late."

John looked at them, speechless for a moment. Then he nodded and reached into his pockets for his keys. "Yeah, let's go."

After dropping Zac and Jeremy off at practice, John sat in the parking lot near their school trapped by his thoughts. After a few minutes, he picked up his cellphone to send Debra a text message. The entire text thread between him and his wife had been almost entirely one-sided until that day—scrolling through all of them made him feel a little bad. He was also starting to feel like he was losing his grip on the situation and his family.

Debra had been trying to lose 10 pounds ever since the birth of her daughter—most of it was excess flab from around her waist. After going on a smoothie and juicing fast for two weeks, the extra weight was gone and she was now fitting into a pair of jeans that she bought before she was married. The red marks and pimples on her face cleared up as well. Debra looked and felt like she was 10 years younger—she was amazed that this level of change was possible after just a few months.

Going to the college orientation that day made her feel like she was a high school girl filled with wonder again. The campus was bustling with young people who were just getting started on their futures. She was now going to be one of them. As she leisurely strolled back to the main street where she was meeting her driver, she took in a deep breath, closed her eyes, and listened to the leaves rustling on the ground around her. For the first time in a long time, she felt as if she was in the right place at the right time. She wanted to stay there for a while.

But her moment was interrupted by the buzz of her cellphone in her purse. She grabbed it quickly and hastened her steps a bit, thinking that it was the Uber driver giving her an update. She stopped in her tracks when she saw that it was John texting her.

I need to speak with you, it said. *It's urgent.*

She wrinkled her brow as she read the words over again. She wanted to call him immediately, excited to hear from him, but something caused her to hesitate from pushing the button just yet. She put her phone back into her purse and continued on her way. When the Uber driver pulled up, her phone buzzed again.

Why did you take our daughter to a stranger today?

When she read the second message from him, she was happy that she hadn't called him. He was just calling to start an argument and that was not how she wanted to end this beautiful day. She got into the car and sent him a quick text.

Can't talk right now. Maybe tomorrow.

Right after sending it, she called the sitter to let her know that she was on the way and then put her phone on mute. There was a time when John would have been her number one priority no matter what was going on, but her priorities had clearly changed.

For some reason, Joseph was having a hard time sleeping at night. It started when Jill agreed to allow Joey to join Dr. Meron's treatment program. He felt guilty about still withholding the fact that he and Dr. Meron met without her. Though he was excited about the possibilities of how the new serum would help Joey, part of him wished that she would have just said no and let him off the hook. But now they were in it—the call had been made and the date was set to admit Joey into the treatment center in late December.

That same old question was starting to nag at him as well:

Is this for him or for you?

Now, after much reflection over the matter and talking to voices of reason, including his wife's, he was starting to wonder if his enthusiasm was coming from the right place.

It was midnight on a Friday, and Joseph was having yet another sleepless night full of anxious thoughts. He finally shuffled his way downstairs in the darkness to the kitchen to make a cup of calming tea and get a quick snack. When he switched on the light in the kitchen, he jumped back when he saw his daughter Grace sitting near the door, looking out the window with a bag of chips in her hand. She had a dark blue hoodie on with the hood pulled over her head as if she was trying to hide.

"Hi, Dad," she said solemnly, trying to force a smile.

"Princess Grace, what are you doing down here? I would have thought you'd be out with your friends on a Friday," he said as he walked over to her and gave her a fatherly hug and kiss on the head.

"Yea, not tonight," she said flatly. "I was a little tired."

The truth was that Scott called her just an hour before and told her he had plans with his friends. She was already dressed and ready to go pick him up when he canceled on her.

"Why are you sitting in the dark?" he asked as he pulled a mug and tea bag out of the cupboard. "Why not go to bed?"

"I don't know, I was just thinking about some stuff," she answered and started to get up. "I'm going to bed now. Goodnight, Dad."

"Grace, wait," he said, standing in her path. "Can we just talk for a little while? About anything you want. I feel like we don't really get to talk that much anymore."

Grace looked up into her Dad's eyes and agreed with a slight nod. They both sat down at the kitchen island. There was a pause as Joseph gave his daughter a good once over. She looked different—stressed, thinner in the face, and vulnerable. Grace had always been a very confident and happy child, which made it very difficult for Joseph to see her this way.

"So, your mom told me that you're doing a little better at school," he said. "She went to see your guidance counselor the other day."

"Yea, I figured it was best if I start going to classes more. Try to get my grades up," she said. The whole truth was that Scott ridiculed her when he found out she was failing most of her classes and might not graduate from high school.

"Well that's great Grace, I'm really proud of you," Joseph said. "I also just want to let you know that no matter what you're going through, no matter who you decide to date, and no matter how you do in school, your mom and I will always love you. We'll always be there for you."

Grace looked down at her hands and started picking her nails. "I know Dad."

"Let me tell you a story," Joseph said after taking a sip of his tea. "And this is just between us, okay?"

"Okay."

"After my second year in college, I went abroad for the summer and spent two months in Italy. I met this free-spirited young lady named Alessandra who taught me how to be wild and unpredictable. I had so much fun with her that I called home and told my parents that I wasn't coming back for school in the fall."

"No way," Grace laughed. "I know Grandpa wasn't happy."

"He threatened to cut off my funding, but I was defiant. I tried to get employment in the little town where I was staying, but that was almost impossible. When my cash ran out, so did Alessandra. I was homeless for over a week before I finally had to call Grandma and Grandpa."

"What did they say?"

"They didn't say anything. They didn't say 'I told you so,' though I'm sure my father was tempted to. They just paid for my plane ticket home and gave me a big hug at the airport," he explained. "For a while after that, I felt so defeated and stupid."

Grace listened intently.

"But not long after that, I met your mother and I never looked at another woman the same way. When I think of how I almost missed out on this life with you guys over a fleeting thing, I almost want to kick myself," Joseph said as he shook his head.

"How did you know that Mom was the one for you?" Grace asked.

"Well, for one, she was, and is, smart. She has taught me lessons that have been invaluable over the years and helped me build my business. Also, she wasn't afraid to speak up and challenge me, where most of the girls I dated in high school and college didn't want to ruffle any feathers," Joseph explained.

Grace looked down at her fingernails again.

"Your Mom has been a pillar of strength for me and for the entire family. These are the things that differentiate someone who's just a pretty face like Alessandra and a truly beautiful woman who you want to spend your whole life with," Joseph said, choosing his words carefully.

"That's so nice, Dad," Grace said with a genuine smile.

"But there's more to it though, Grace," Joseph said, feeling as if he was finally getting through to her.

"What's that?"

"Even if you're a wonderful woman like your mother you could get yourself tied up with a guy who just can't appreciate those special qualities," he told her. "All that he'll do is waste your time."

"'Waste Her Time.' That's a hashtag on Twitter you know," Grace said with a laugh.

"I have no idea what that means, but okay," Joseph said, enjoying a laugh with his eldest daughter. "I don't want you to let anyone waste your time. You are a lot like your mother. You deserve to be treated with respect, acknowledgment, and love. Please just always remember that, okay?"

"Yes Dad, I will," Grace said and stood up from the table to give her father a hug.

"I love you so much," Joseph told his daughter.

"I love you too."

Jill never procrastinated when it came to holiday shopping. In fact, she usually got started as soon as November arrived. This year, she had a new shopping buddy that made the experience even more fun—Suzy's mom Alison. They turned out to be quite the team when it came to finding the best stores to shop and deals to take advantage of. Jill was making more of an effort to help Joey explore new things and people, so she started bringing him to Suzy's house more often. On one visit they looked through some circulars together and the rest was history.

"Adam is going to love this instant tent," she said as the store employee helped load her SUV. "He goes camping at least 10 times a year."

"Definitely. You should tell him to call my husband the next time he goes," Jill suggested.

"Most certainly," Alison agreed. "It was so nice to have a day of kid-free shopping. Please thank your sitter for me."

"I will," Jill said. "Hey Alison, would you mind if I were to stop by someone's house for a few minutes before we head back home? We're in her area."

"Of course not."

Marsha Rogers had been Jill's usual shopping buddy, but this year was different. Something was going on with Marsha that Jill couldn't understand. They hadn't spoken for a long while. Their shopping trip brought them to within 15 minutes of Marsha's house, so Jill wanted to give her a call.

Jill called Marsha's cellphone and landline number twice each, getting voicemail every time. She decided, against her better judgment, to go by the house and ring Marsha's doorbell.

When Marsha came to the door, she peered her head outside and looked them up and down.

"Hi Marsha, I was in the neighborhood and thought I'd drop by. How are you doing?" Jill said with a smile.

"Who's that?" Marsha asked unenthusiastically as she glared at Alison.

"Oh, um. This is Alison Gilles. She's the mom of one of Joey's friends," Jill said. "Alison, this is Marsha Rogers. We were just doing some shopping out here."

"Nice to meet you, Marsha," Alison said, offering her hand. Marsha just looked at it, refusing to open the door all of the way.

"So first you steal my son's tutor, and now you replace me with a new shopping partner," Marsha said with an agitated nod. Jill was a little taken aback by her rudeness and was starting to think it wasn't a good idea to come.

"I've been trying to call you Marsha, but you don't answer the phone," Jill said. "Are you okay?"

"I'm fine, thanks for asking. Just very busy right now," Marsha said, trying to sound more upbeat. "Why don't you all get back to your shopping and have a good day!"

Marsha closed the door before they had a chance to respond. Jill and Alison just looked at each other for a moment, then made their way back to Alison's SUV.

"That was kinda weird," Alison commented.

Marsha went upstairs to her bedroom to watch them leave through the window. Deep down, she wanted desperately to talk to her friend Jill, but seeing her with Alison reminded her of how Jason left her behind for another woman. She had sent him several letters that were all returned to sender.

She didn't know why she was so fixated on Jason, but for some reason, she just couldn't let him go. Or the *idea* of him. He reminded her of a life that she once wanted to live. He brought a freshness and newness to her now humdrum life that she wanted to hold onto. Now she was losing her passion for everything else; even neglecting to make regular visits to Tommy at Dr. Meron's facility. She barely made it out of the house once a week.

After Jill and Alison finally pulled off, Marsha climbed back into her bed and pulled the covers up to her chin. This was her new normal.

CHAPTER 14
Standing Up for What's Right

Ray Smith had taken time off from work so that he and his wife could visit Sammy at the treatment center every day. Ever since Sammy was unceremoniously released from Dr. Meron's treatment program, Ray didn't have a reason to stay home anymore, but he did anyway.

Mary Ellen quickly went back to her usual routine of cleaning up the house, doing laundry, cooking three meals a day, and looking after Sammy. But Ray could tell that she wasn't her usual self. She had been crushed by the news that the revolutionary treatment they were so excited about wouldn't be able to help her son. When she wasn't busy with household chores, she was holed up in her bedroom watching television alone. To Ray, it was starting to feel like she was actively avoiding him. He felt that he had somehow failed her and Sammy—that maybe he should have done more to get Dr. Meron to keep Sammy in his trials. Mary Ellen depended on her husband to make everything work—that was how their marriage had always worked.

"Daddy, look!" Sammy said as he put the finishing touch on his Lego block creation. He loved building and making things with his hands.

"Great job Sammy!" Ray said, mustering up as much enthusiasm as he could. He glanced over at the young architect kit that he had hoped to open up with Sammy when he finished the course of treatments. Now, he wasn't sure if Sammy was ready to work on a project that challenging.

"Can you take a picture?" Sammy asked.

"Oh. Oh, of course, son," Ray said as he searched the couch and the table for his cellphone. When he couldn't find it he started to get frustrated.

"Where is my phone…" he mumbled under his breath as he stood up to look around the living room. After five more minutes of fruitless searching in the kitchen, he stopped and kicked the bottom cabinet. He put both of his elbows on the kitchen counter and gently rested his head in his hands in defeat, quietly sobbing.

"Daddy," Sammy said as he tugged on his father's shirt. "What's wrong?"

Ray remained quiet and kept his face covered, not wanting Sammy to see his tears.

"Daddy," Sammy persisted. "Here, I found your phone. Look."

Sammy set the cellphone down on the counter next to his father and gently patted his shoulder. "It's going to be okay, Daddy. Please don't be sad."

Ray peeked down at his cellphone through two fingers and then glanced at his son. Looking at Sammy's bright, starry eyes brought him back to earth. He wiped the tears away, leaned down, and gave Sammy a big hug.

"You're right son, it *is* going to be okay," Ray said, regaining his composure. "We're all going to be fine."

Joseph sat in his swiveling desk chair, watching the rain drops bead up on the large glass window pane in his office. It had been cold, gloomy, and rainy for most of the week.

Although the sun hadn't made an appearance in a while, things were mostly quiet and peaceful on the home front for Joseph and his family. He had regained communication with Grace. Mia joined a ballet class to keep her busy as she waited to enroll in kindergarten. After the devastating loss to the Lady Bengals, Sophia and her team managed to come back and qualify for the state softball playoff games. Joey was busy getting ready for his role in the school play and had a new friend in Suzy. And Jill was now excited to enroll Joey in Dr. Meron's program.

But as ideal as everything seemed to be at home, Joseph couldn't shake a sinking feeling that had been bothering him ever since Jill had a change of heart. It was a feeling that something wasn't quite right—that he was about to make a big mistake, or that he had already made a huge mistake. That feeling washed over him at work, when he was eating and even when he was sleeping. He usually had good dreams, but lately, he was having the occasional nightmare.

He was also starting to worry about everything. He worried about how the treatment might affect Joey in 10 years. He also wondered if the treatment would help at all. He worried about how to explain Joey's absence from the house to his sisters. And of course, he worried about Jill somehow learning that he had been planning to go forward with or without her approval.

He used to begrudgingly attend the Williams Syndrome meetings for parents because it was at Jill's request. But now he was really longing for the experience of being around others who could relate to what he was going through. The next meeting was coming up soon and he couldn't wait to attend to see what the other parents were up to. Never before did he realize the value of that group as a way to connect with others—they were their own micro-community and support system. He was particularly interested in finding out how Ray Smith and his son, Sammy, were doing since they were among the first to opt into Dr. Meron's program.

Finally, after nearly an hour of contemplation, Joseph picked up the phone. He knew that whatever was causing him to feel troubled could only be resolved in one way: by talking to his wife.

"Hey, honey, what's up?" Jill picked up on the first ring. Hearing her voice calmed Joseph's nerves a bit. She sounded happy.

"Hey, just thinking about you," Joseph said. "What are you up to?"

"Well, it's that time of year, you know. We're all trying to get a head start on all of these holiday orders."

"Same here. Do you think you could get away for lunch? Madriagno's?"

"Oh, what I would do for their chicken Caesar salad right now," Jill said, thinking about how great it would be to relax over a meal in their favorite dimly lit restaurant. "But I just can't right now. Anne Marie would hate me if I skipped out and left her with all of this work."

"Okay, I understand," Joseph said, rubbing his temples.

"Are you okay honey?" Jill asked. She could tell when her husband was going through something.

"Uh yea, I just really wanted to talk about some things."

"Well, we could do that later for dinner. Want to go out then? I should be home by 6:30."

"It's probably going to be a late night. But it's fine, let's just make it another time," Joseph said, waving the whole idea off. He reasoned that if it was meant for him to spill out his thoughts to his wife right now, the Universe would have aligned to make that happen.

"Okay. Well, I hope everything's okay. Love you."

"I love you too. I gotta get going," Joseph said hurriedly. "See you at home."

"One more thing, Joe. I just wanted to thank you for keeping me on my toes. I'm glad you forced me to look more closely at the treatment program," Jill admitted. "This could be a really great thing for Joey."

"Right, of course," Joseph said with a quiet sigh. "Well, I'll see you at home later."

When Joseph hung up the phone, he immediately started to look over his date calendar so that he wouldn't be consumed by negative thoughts again. After looking a couple of months into the future, he then went back a few months. Looking over the dates, he realized that problems had been brewing in his home ever since the day he first laid eyes on Dr. Meron. As he glanced over at the family photo on his desk, he wondered if that was a coincidence or a sign of more problems to come.

With the school play coming, Joey and his participating classmates were allowed to spend an early period during school rehearsing in the auditorium a couple of days per week. The opening date of the play was right before Christmas, and tickets were already sold out. Joey's family had bought two rows worth of tickets.

When Mrs. Rayburn dismissed them from afternoon rehearsals, Joey and Suzy made a beeline for the cafeteria so that they could be the first on line for lunch. In his eagerness to get his hands on his favorite meal—chicken nuggets and French fries—Joey forgot to take the angel robe off. He stood out in the heavy cafeteria crowd as he made his way to the lunch line.

"I'm going to get some Jell-O too," Joey said to Suzy as they stood on the line waiting. They were full of energy after practicing on stage.

"What in the heck are you wearing?" someone said from behind Joey. Then a chorus of laughter went up. Joey turned around and saw Mitch, one of the school's notorious bullies, standing there among his friends. Mitch was very short and skinny, but his quick wit made him one of the most feared boys in school.

"I'm playing Clarence, the Angel," Joey replied innocently, not understanding why it was so funny. "In the school play."

"What? More like the tooth fairy," Mitch shot back and laughed again with his friends. He aggressively grabbed Joey's robe and tugged on it, trying to pull it off. Joey frowned and pulled away sharply, realizing that this wasn't a positive encounter.

"Keep your hands off of him, you blockhead!" Suzy yelled.

"Ooooo," Mitch taunted her. "I'm shakin' in my boots."

"You should be!" she shot back.

"Back off, Mitch," a voice said from behind the small crowd of kids that was forming. Sophia's friend Brendan and his friends had just entered the cafeteria after playing handball outside and saw what was going on.

"Nobody was talking to you," Mitch said defiantly. His smile quickly turned into a frown when he saw Brendan fist bump Joey in solidarity. Brendan's friends gathered nearby. They didn't know Joey, but if he was cool with Brendan he was cool with them too. They also didn't like Mitch.

"Well, he's talking to *you*," Brendan's best friend spoke up. He was one of the largest kids in his class and had an intimidating presence. "Beat it, Mitch."

Mitch looked around at the kids who were observing and began to turn red from embarrassment. He originally thought he'd picked an easy target, but now he was starting to feel like he was the one with a bull's eye on his shirt.

"What's it to you all anyway?" Mitch continued defiantly, not wanting to look defeated.

"What's it to you? Why do you have to pick on people all the time?" Brendan asked. A few voices in the crowd agreed—no one had ever really stood up to Mitch and they were tired of his bullying. "What's your problem, man?"

"My problem is that he looks ridiculous in this thing!" Mitch said with a laugh as he again went to pull Joey's robe.

"Hey, don't touch my robe!" Joey exclaimed as he swatted Mitch's hand away.

"Look I'm not going to tell you this again Mitch. Joey T's with us and you'd better just leave him alone," Brendan said with finality. "Come on guys."

They all went with Joey so that he could get his chicken nuggets and fries. A few kids clapped—a few laughed and pointed at Mitch. Suzy tauntingly stuck her tongue out at him before running to catch up with her new friend.

Jack grasped the railing as he struggled to lift his foot up to the top of the last step. When it was finally solidly positioned, he dragged his other foot up to meet it. He immediately bent down to rest his hand on his knee, huffing and puffing to catch his breath. Climbing stairs was never that easy for him, but it had become increasingly difficult over the past few weeks.

Ever since Jack read the note that his wife had written to their son Tommy's tutor, he had been binge-eating even more than before. He would buy large stuffed deep dish pizzas and eat them within minutes. He would often browse his food delivery app and order a full spread of deli food including pastrami, roast beef, and salami sandwiches, macaroni salad and platters full of sliced cheddar, Swiss, and provolone cheeses. It was enough food to feed his whole department, but he managed to finish most of it off before leaving the office at night.

Jack had been a little overweight as a boy and almost always went back for second or third helpings at the dinner table, but playing school sports kept him reasonably fit. When he met Marsha, he was 6'2 230 pounds—the size of a football player. But with each year of married life, he gained at least five to 10 pounds. Now he was tipping the scales at 315 pounds and it was taking a toll on his health.

He knew that what he had was a food addiction because he would eat even when he wasn't really hungry. Eating calmed his anxiety and gave him a euphoric feeling.

Whenever he was having problems at home or at work, he would immediately reach for a takeout menu or head to the refrigerator.

On this particular day, Jack received an urgent phone call from Dr. Meron's treatment facility regarding his son. Tommy was having frequent, sometimes violent tantrums, which was way out of the ordinary for him. He was usually a very mild and calm child who spent most of his time listening to music and watching videos. Tamara Goodwin called to inform Jack that Tommy's mother hadn't been to visit in over a week and she thought it might be the source of his distress.

After finally catching his breath, Jack pressed the buzzer to be let into the facility. A few minutes later, Tamara met him at the door.

"Hello, Mr. Rogers, it's good to see you again," Tamara said as she shook his sweaty hand. "Are you okay?"

"Yea, yea I'm fine," Jack said as he wiped the sweat away from his brow. "What's this you say that my wife hasn't been here in over a week?"

Tamara began to walk him toward Tommy's room. "Well, at first she was coming just about every day, then it was less frequently. Now it's just been a phone call or two over the past week."

"Our agreement was that she'd be here every day," Jack told her as he followed her through the halls. "I work seven days a week—I had to leave the office and drive over an hour to get here."

"Yes, I know Mr. Rogers, and I'm really sorry about that," Tamara said with sincerity as she stood in front of Tommy's door. "But this was urgent, and we haven't been able to get in touch with your wife today. We had hoped to be able to release him to your care soon, but now we're thinking about extending his in-patient stay."

She opened the door carefully and they both peered inside. Tommy was sitting on the floor in a corner of the room, rocking back and forth, clutching his knees. He was clearly agitated.

"Hi son," Jack said as he went to pull up a chair near his son. "What's going on buddy?"

Tommy just kept rocking back and forth, never looking up at his father.

“Dr. Tamara tells me you’ve been a little upset. Do you miss your mom?” Jack asked. There was no response from Tommy. He seemed to be in his own world.

“Tommy, son,” Jack said as he reached over to touch his son’s shoulder.

“No!” Tommy shrieked as he smacked his hand away. “I want Mommy!”

“Tommy! It’s me, your dad,” Jack said, feeling a bit embarrassed. When he tried to reach for his son again, Tommy jumped up and started slapping and smacking Jack uncontrollably.

“Leave me alone! Leave me alone!” he screamed over and over again. Tamara picked up her walkie-talkie and called for help as Jack finally gained control of Tommy and held him tightly in his arms. A couple of lab workers arrived in a matter of seconds along with Dr. Meron’s new protege, Dr. Richards.

“What is going on here?” Dr. Richards wanted to know when he saw Jack clutching his screaming son.

“I called Mr. Rogers in to see Tommy. He’s been acting—”

“Did I authorize you to do that Tamara?” Dr. Richards said, cutting her off in his usual condescending tone.

“No, but I—”

“Please take the patient and his father to the calming room,” Dr. Richards said to the workers. He waited until they had left and closed the door before speaking again.

"Listen Tamara, from now on, you are to get authorization from me *first* before making any phone calls. I thought I made that clear with you at the last staff meeting."

Tamara was put off by his tone and decided that instead of apologizing, she would stand her ground.

"Firstly, Dr. Richards, I would prefer it if you called me by my professional name, Dr. Goodwin, since we're in a professional setting," she began. "Secondly, I called Mr. Rogers because I believed Tommy needed to see a familiar face. He hasn't seen his mother in over a week."

"You see, this is precisely why Dr. Meron brought me in," Dr. Richards said as he shook his head disapprovingly. "Are you truly aware of the sensitivity of this research? The level of confidentiality that's needed here?"

"That confidentiality doesn't extend to the parents," Tamara told him. "The parents deserve to know what's going on with their children."

"The parents don't need to be included in every situation that happens here, Tama— Dr. Goodwin. Dr. Meron is still trying to keep the doctors at that local hospital from inquiring more into our research after they treated Sammy Rogers," Dr. Richards told her.

Tamara nodded and sighed. She couldn't believe that she was still being made to feel guilty about getting Sammy the urgent care that he needed.

"We must take every step possible to calm each patient and resolve the situation before needing to call anyone for any type of urgent visit. Are we clear?"

Tamara opened her mouth to say something more, but then hesitated. She knew that she was already on thin ice with Dr. Meron and one more bad report could mean her job. It would be at least four to six months before she could find a similar research position with fair pay and she was already falling behind in her bills. So instead of protesting, she took a deep breath instead and managed a smile.

"Yes Dr. Richards, we're very clear."

"Good. Please escort Mr. Rogers out and assure him that all is well. Tommy will be just fine," Dr. Richards said curtly before leaving the room.

"How do you know that? You don't know anything about what's going on here," Tamara said under her breath as she flopped down on the bed. She was helplessly torn between her obligation to her profession and her obligation to the families they were supposed to be helping. It was very clear to her now that Dr. Meron and his newly appointed team were only concerned about continuing their research, at any cost.

CHAPTER 15
"Pitcher" Perfect

John was sitting in his mother's basement flipping through the channels aimlessly. Every time he saw a commercial for Thanksgiving dinner with a smiling family, whether it was biscuits baking or a turkey being pulled out of the oven, he cringed and turned the channel immediately.

Work usually kept him busy, but his trucking company had to cancel a few of his hauls for the week at the last minute. He was stuck in the house for two straight days. He hadn't been able to get in touch with Debra for more than a few minutes in the past week because she was always busy working or taking Patty somewhere. He tried to play it cool and wait for her to call, but days went by with no contact. He was starting to get worried that she might be seeing someone else.

"Johnnnn," his mother called from upstairs. "Johnnnny!"

The sound of his mother's voice was like nails on a chalkboard. Hearing her call his name was like listening to an emergency horn blaring in the background. Ever since he had been staying at his mother's house, she had been ordering him around like he was some kind of cabana boy. And to make things worse, she still treated and talked to him like he was 12 years old.

"What, Ma!?" he yelled back, putting the television on mute.

"The garbage needs to go out tonight!" she yelled back.

John stared at the wall for a while, wondering how his mother managed to do anything without him there. Finally, after a moment of reflection, he mustered the energy to get up and trudge his way up the stairs. His mother, Anne, started grilling him as soon as he appeared in the kitchen.

"Why do you lock that basement door? I hope you're not doing any funny business down there."

John rolled his eyes and just continued to pull the bag out of the trashcan.

"Don't forget the bags in the bathroom and laundry room. The cat litter bag is full," she told him as she watched his every move. He stopped and looked at her.

"You couldn't go get those, Ma?"

"I got them the last time," she said as she shuffled across the kitchen floor with her glass of wine in hand. "Besides, it's the least you can do, sitting down there watching TV and doing whatever else all day."

John dropped the trash bag in the middle of the floor. "Really? It's the least I can do? Did you forget who pays the mortgage here Mom?"

"Hey, hey. Watch your tone with me. I'm still your mother," Anne snapped back. "Just get the trash out please, I'm going to bed."

John took several deep breaths, trying to calm himself down. Arguing with his mother was a fruitless endeavor. The only way to deal with the situation was to avoid her as much as possible because she could be a toxic person. He waited to hear her bedroom door shut before going around the house to pick up the rest of the trash.

When he finally went back to his spot in the basement after taking the garbage to the street, he glanced down at his phone and saw the indicator light blinking. He had a new text message from Debra.

Got your message. All is well, found a great new sitter for Patty. Good nite.

John immediately called her before she had a chance to turn her phone off. After four long rings, he was about to give up, but she finally picked up on the fifth ring.

"Hi," she said softly into the phone.

"Hi, how are you?" John asked, feeling relieved at the sound of her voice.

"I'm doing well, how about you?"

"Doing great."

"Did you see my text?" Debra asked.

"Yea. You found Patty a sitter? That's good to hear, I'd like to meet her," he said.

"Of course. She has experience watching after children who have special needs like Patty. She's great."

"So does this mean you'll be going to that school?"

"Yup, I start in the spring," she confirmed.

"Congratulations, I know you've been wanting to do that accounting program for a while," he said, genuinely feeling proud of his wife. He couldn't remember the last time he had a phone conversation with her that lasted more than 15 seconds. It reminded him of when they were courting—they would talk their entire lunch hour about their goals and dreams.

"Thank you, John, that means a lot," Debra said. "Um, I hate to change the subject so abruptly, but I have to tell you this before I forget."

"What? What's going on?"

"I know that this is a soft spot between us, but we really need to sit down at some point and talk about the treatment that Dr. Meron is proposing for Patty. I heard that they are closing the trials soon, and there's no telling when they'll open up again.

"You know how I feel about that Debra," John started.

"I know, but, we at least have to have a conversation about it John," Debra said sternly. There was a long pause as they both considered what to say next. Debra was tired, so she decided to drop the matter for the moment.

"Well John, it was nice to catch up with you, but I really have to get some rest tonight. I've been running around since 6 a.m. this morning and have to get up around the same time tomorrow."

"Right. Same here," he said as he cleared his throat. "Tell Zac I'll be at his practice tomorrow."

"Will do, good night," she said, then quickly ended the call.

John put the phone to his heart and leaned his head back on the recliner.

"Why didn't I ask her about Thanksgiving plans?" he whispered

to himself.

The last thing he wanted was to have to spend that important day without his family, but as the holiday approached he was starting to realize that that was exactly what was going to happen. Sitting alone in that basement, missing his family, he was starting to understand exactly what it meant to be separated.

For the first time in a long time, Jack took a few days off from work so that he could spend more time at home and find out what was going on with his wife and son. After seeing the wild way that his son Tommy reacted at Dr. Meron's facility, he knew that he could no longer bury his head in the sand. He took a half day on Friday and then the rest of the weekend off.

When he arrived home mid-afternoon on Friday, the house was completely quiet as if no one was home. Marsha's car was in the driveway, so he knew she had to be around somewhere. When he made it inside, he stopped at the stairs and stared up for a while. He was not looking forward to the climb nor what was going to greet him when he finally made it up there.

To ease his nerves, he went into the kitchen first to see if there was any cheese to snack on. He found a pack of yellow American and pulled a box of crackers out of the cupboard. As he sat at the kitchen island, preparing his quick snack, he looked at the pile of papers strewn across the table. Sorting through them, he saw one that looked important. It was a notice of a request for $1,250 to fix damage to Jason, the tutor's, car. Jack read the entire letter, which detailed Marsha's little visit to Jason's apartment building and the fact that there was an eyewitness to her punching a large dent into the hood of his Infiniti sedan.

Jack had always been a very mild-mannered, calm, and patient person who preferred to avoid conflict at any cost. He wanted to keep the peace by any means necessary. But to find out that his wife was not only potentially cheating with another man, but now that she was publicly stalking and harassing him was too much to bear.

He threw down the cheese, grabbed the notice, and made his way to the staircase as quickly as he could. He put one foot in front of the other and made it to the top in a matter of seconds. After catching his breath for a moment, he continued on to the bedroom and swung the door open. Marsha was completely hidden under the covers.

"Marsha," he called out as he went over to the bed. He pulled the comforter back to get her to wake up. She was curled up on her side wearing a pair of ugly, patterned pajamas.

"What's this Marsha?" Jack asked as he clutched the paper. "Did you read this whole thing about damage to Jason's car?

"Go away Jack," Marsha said as she tried to pull the covers back over her face.

"No. It's four o'clock in the afternoon and it's time for you to get up!" Jack commanded as he pulled the covers completely off the bed. "Get up!"

"Just who do you think you're talking to?" Marsha sat up and yelled back.

"I'm talking to you!" he said, matching her tone. "Did you damage Jason's car?! He used the word 'stalking' in this complaint!"

"I didn't stalk anyone," she protested as she turned away from him and laid back down. "Just ignore that, it's nothing."

"You can't ignore things like this, I have to pay for this! What is going on with you Marsha?" Jack asked, sitting down on the bed. "First, you're throwing tantrums in our bedroom, and now you're chasing after Tommy's tutor?"

Marsha was silent, hoping that he would just go away.

"And they tell me you haven't been to see Tommy in over a week. Don't you care about what's going on with him?"

"You sure have a lot of nerve!" she said as she jerked her head back around to look at him. "When's the last time *you* went to visit him? His dad?"

"I work Marsha! Someone has to!"

"All you care about is that job and eating everything in sight. Don't lecture me about our son Jack," Marsha said as she turned back around and put her head into a pillow.

"Well I went to visit our son yesterday, and he's not happy at that place," Jack said as he stood up. "They're planning on keeping him there longer, did you know that?"

Marsha was quiet again.

"And I'm tired of you making comments about my weight Marsha.

Yes, I eat a lot. But I also work *really* hard to keep this family afloat in spite of it. I'm under a lot of pressure and you aren't making things any easier."

When Marsha didn't respond again, Jack stood up slowly and went over to a drawer to grab some things.

"You need help Marsha—professional help," he told her as he retrieved a small luggage bag from the closet. "This is partially my fault because I should have said something much sooner."

Marsha just scoffed as she went to grab the sheets and comforter off of the floor. She pulled them onto the bed and covered herself back up.

"I'll be staying at a hotel for a while. When you're ready to talk to me like a grown up and leave your pity party long enough to go visit our son, you call me," Jack said as he zipped up his bag.

Before he left the room, he turned back around and paused for a moment.

"I love you, Marsha. I'll always love you. Please remember that, no matter what," Jack said. "But you have to do better. *We* have to do better. If not for anything else, for the sake of our son."

Brendan and Sophia had just finished practicing swings at the local batting cage. Now they were laying back on a grassy hill in the park, staring at the clouds swirling above.

They had been hanging out just about every day after school and on the weekends. After spending more time together, they learned that they had a whole lot in common. They both had large families and loved sports. Brendan kept her on her toes and had helped her improve her batting average. Sophia helped him with his math homework. She was on the track to become an honors student in advanced classes by the time she reached high school. Sophia was still too young to have a boyfriend, but she felt the type of bond with Brendan that could lead to a lifelong friendship. She was relaxed and comfortable with him and they talked about everything under the sun.

"Hey, Brendan. What do you think is the meaning of life?" Sophia asked as she twirled a colorful leaf between her thumb and pointer finger. The cool November air breezed through their hair and seemed to blow a circle around them.

"The meaning of life?"

"Yeah. Like what are we doing here?"

"Man, who knows? To find out how to be happy I guess," Brendan said with a shrug.

"Okay, so if that's true, then why does it seem like so many adults are unhappy?" she asked him.

"I guess...because they haven't figured it out yet?"

"Or maybe because they aren't sure they're living a life that has meaning?"

"Hmmm. Maybe. Or maybe they're just missing the whole point," Brendan replied. "Maybe they're just focused on all the wrong things?"

"Or maybe we should stop thinking so much and just…live the best way we can."

"You're so deep," Brendan said, and they both laughed.

"I think a lot about this stuff," Sophia said.

"You know Sophia, I'm really glad I got to know you," Brendan said. "You've taught me a lot. And not just school stuff, but like, life stuff too."

"Okay Brendan, don't get all sappy on me now," Sophia said.

"No, seriously. I used to like you because, you know, you're super pretty, smart, and all," Brendan admitted, sounding a little shy. "But now that we're friends and I know more about you as a real person, I'm just like...wow, you're just awesome. Seriously."

"Thanks Brendan. You're pretty awesome too."

Sophia took a deep breath in, feeling a bit overwhelmed by the unexpected compliment. It was nice to know that someone like Brendan could see her for who she was beyond her appearance, her grades, and her status as an up and coming star on the school softball team. Sometimes she felt that nothing she did was ever quite enough—that even being perfect wasn't enough. And being less than perfect at any moment, like losing that important game to the Lady Bengals in front of everyone, was just too much to bear. But hearing those words from Brendan made her smile on the inside. They made her feel like she could let her guard down a little—maybe she didn't always have to be "pitcher perfect."

CHAPTER 16
Thanksgiving Revelations

Mia was fully dressed in her pink ballerina costume as she twirled and pirouetted around the living room with a classical piano melody playing in the background. Her hair was tied tightly into a bun and her tiny ballet shoes were just as securely tied to her feet. Jill had cleared the front of the room to be her stage as the whole family watched her Thanksgiving Day performance.

When Mia finished her short routine and the music stopped, she was on the floor with her foot pointed one way and her hand elegantly pointed in the opposite direction. At just five years old, she really seemed to have a knack for remembering and executing the movements. The entire room erupted in applause and gave her a standing ovation.

Mia stood up, smiled and bowed low as if she had just performed at Carnegie Hall.

"Yay Mia!" Joey said as he jumped up and down joyfully, happy for his sister.

"Bravo!" Grandma Ella, Joseph's mom, raved over and over. Everyone said that Mia was her twin from another time, and now Mia was following in her footsteps by taking up ballet.

"You're a natural Mia!" Grandma Ella told her as she reached out her hand. Mia grabbed it and went to sit by her.

"Thanks, Gramma!" Mia said as she sat down next to her on the couch.

"When is your first recital?" Grandma asked.

"In December. Can you make it??" Mia asked.

"I most certainly can," Grandma assured.

"I'll call you and Dad with the exact date to see if you guys can make it," Joseph told her.

"Grandma, Grandpa! Are you coming to my play?" Joey said as he tugged on Grandpa Joe's sleeve. "I'm Clarence, the angel!"

"Well. It looks like our holiday calendar is booked solid," Grandpa Joe said as he winked at his wife. "You bet Joey T."

"Yes!!" Joey exclaimed as he pumped his fist in the air.

"Okay guys, I'm going to check on the roast," Jill said as she grabbed her apron again. Her parents had decided to take the trip to Florida that year to visit her older sister's family for Thanksgiving.

"It smells delicious," Grandpa Joe commented.

"Thanks, Dad," Jill said with a smile.

"I'll help," Joseph said as he started to follow her into the kitchen. He noticed that his wife had been a little quiet that day and wanted to talk to her.

"Where's Grace, honey?" Grandma Ella asked Joseph.

"Oh, she's in her room. She'll be down for dinner later to grace us with her presence for a while," he said with a smile and a playful eye roll.

When he went into the kitchen, he saw Jill quietly chopping vegetables at the counter. He tiptoed toward her and gave her a hug from behind.

"How are you?" he asked as he rested his chin on her shoulder.

"Alright. Dinner should be ready by 4:30," she said as she scraped the choppings into a bowl.

"There's no rush," Joseph said. "But I am starving. How can I help?"

"You could finish this salad," she said. "Chop up the Romaine lettuce, the rest of those tomatoes and these olives, then toss. I'll make the dressing."

Joseph grabbed the large bowl and got to work. "So you're upset that your Mom and Dad couldn't be here."

"No, no. They've spent Thanksgiving with us the past three years. It's only fair."

"But you still miss them," Joseph said. "It's okay to say so."

"You know me better than anyone," Jill admitted. "I just wanted them here so that we could tell them about our plans as a family."

"Yea, I know."

"And then Grace still isn't talking to me. I hoped that Mom could get through to her, you know? Break the ice at dinner," she continued.

"Yea, Teresa definitely has a way with words."

"She's closer to Grace than I am," Jill said and her voice cracked a little.

"That's just not true Jill," he told her as he rubbed her back affectionately. "Mothers and teenage daughters always bump heads at some point, then later on in life they become the best of friends. Look at you and *your* mom."

"It sure doesn't feel that way. I feel like I'm losing my grip on things. I don't like this feeling Joe," she said.

"I know, but it's a part of life. The kids are growing up. We have to let them," Joseph told her.

"Mommy, are you okay?" Joey T asked as he stood in the doorway of the kitchen. He was like a radar, immediately picking up the signal when someone in the house wasn't happy.

"Oh Joey T, of course I'm okay!" Jill said, quickly regaining her composure. She laughed when she saw that he had gone to change into his Thanksgiving Day dinner outfit—a pair of pin-striped pants, a matching vest, and a large red tie that was reminiscent of the fashion in 1930s Chicago.

"You look great buddy, give me five up high!" Joseph told him. Joey jumped up on cue and slapped his father's hand.

At dinner, Joseph and Jill finally revealed to the family that Joey was accepted into a special treatment program for children with Williams Syndrome. No one was happy to hear that Joey would have to be away from the house for two weeks and Joseph's parents, in particular, were skeptical about everything.

"How much do you really know about this Dr. Meron guy?" Grandpa Joe asked.

"I've done research into his history. He's a graduate of the medical school at Columbia University and has been doing this kind of work for over 10 years," Jill told them.

"But what do you really know about him other than his resume?" Grandma asked. "What do you know about his character? Is he trustworthy?"

"We've met with him on several occasions, Mom. He's assured us that Joey will be in good hands and he's shown us evidence that the treatment works," Joseph told them.

"Plenty of medications work son, but what about the side effects? That's what I'm concerned about," Grandma said.

Joseph glanced over at Joey who was trying to secretly transfer his green beans to his sister Mia's plate. "We'll talk more about this later, Mom and Dad."

Grace had been quiet throughout most of the dinner and had barely eaten anything on her plate. She now had an idea of what had caused the tension between her parents.

"Are you not hungry, honey?" Grandma asked her.

"Not really," Grace replied with an awkward smile.

"You look a little different. Have you done something new to your hair?" Grandma said, trying to get her to open up.

"Not really. Carlie just added a few extensions," Grace answered politely.

"It looks pretty, sweetie," Grandma said with a gentle, but concerned smile.

"Thank you, Grandma. Dad, Carlie invited me over and we're going out later, can I be excused?"

"Sure honey, just be careful out there tonight," Joseph told her after exchanging glances with Jill. Grace agreed and quietly made her way up the stairs to grab her things.

"Daddy and Mommy, can I be excused too?" Joey asked.

"For what?" Jill asked him.

"I have to do something," Joey replied. "It's important."

"Tell you what. You finish up what's on your plate first and then you can go do what you have to do," Jill said with a knowing smirk. Joey sighed but started to scoop the food up from his plate. When he got to the vegetables, he held his nose and shoveled a spoonful of the green stuff into his mouth, but then coughed it right back onto his plate.

"Joey T!" Jill scolded and everyone at the table laughed.

Grace came bounding back down the stairs with her bag strapped across her shoulders and waved to everyone in the dining room.

"Princess Grace, I have to give you something. Can you wait?" Joey asked her. He had been trying to give her his gift for the longest time, but she was always busy or out of the house.

"Just give it to me tomorrow, Joey T. Love you, buddy," she told him right before closing the front door behind her. "See you guys."

"Is she doing okay?" Grandma asked after she had left the house.

"She's going through a little bit of a phase," Joseph answered, and his parents just nodded.

Joseph's parents decided to get on the road soon after dinner so that they could rest up for their annual after-Thanksgiving holiday party at the local senior center. After they left, Joseph called Sophia, Mia, and Joey into the play room for a special surprise that he was calling their "very first Christmas gift." Jill put a blindfold over their eyes and led them inside. Joey and Mia were giddy with excitement.

"Okay, take your blindfolds off kids!"

Joey ripped his blindfold off first and it took a second for his eyes to adjust to the light. There stood his Dad, holding a furry, caramel-colored puppy.

"Surprise!" Jill and Joseph shouted at the same time.

"A dog!!" Joey screamed as his father put the puppy down on the floor. He ran over and started to play with their new pet.

"Yup, and you three are responsible for him," Joseph told them.

"Be gentle Joey, he's still a baby," Jill cautioned him.

"So cool!" Sophia said with a delighted laugh as she went over to greet the new family pet. Mia hung back and held onto her mother's pant leg.

"It's okay, Mia, he's a friendly puppy," Joseph told her as he tried to encourage her to come over. She was still hesitant, so Jill put her on her hip and carried her closer.

"Look, sweetie," she said as she leaned down slowly to pet the puppy. "You just pet him on the head like this."

After a few minutes of seeing that the dog wasn't going to bite her mother, Mia finally joined in and started to pet him too.

"What's his name?" Mia asked.

"That's up to you guys. What do you think?" Joseph asked them.

"Rocket! No. Barney. No. Clarence!" Joey volunteered some names. "No, Jeffrey!"

"How about Ramsey? I've always liked that name," Joseph suggested. Sophia nodded her approval.

"Cool!" Joey agreed. "Welcome to your new home Ramsey!"

Joey T and his dad had a Thanksgiving Day tradition of watching NFL football games until they fell asleep on the couch. They had a full spread of chips, dip, and Joey's favorite candy. Jill and the girls watched holiday movies upstairs in her King-sized bed while eating cake and drinking hot cocoa until they all fell asleep. It used to be Grace's favorite thing to do—that was until she joined the popular crew at school and started hanging out with her friends every Thanksgiving night.

"Touchdown!!" They jumped up and yelled at the top of their lungs whenever someone scored. Since their team wasn't playing, they celebrated every score just for the fun of it. They did a special dance that Joey had come up with that was a mixture of the Running Man and the Urkel Dance. By halftime, Joey was starting to wind down and rested his head under his father's arm. Ramsey had already fallen asleep on the floor next to the couch.

"Daddy, do I really have to go away next month?" Joey asked out of the blue. The question caught Joseph a little off guard, and he paused for a moment before answering.

"Only for a couple of weeks. You'll be back home before you know it," Joseph assured him.

"But why do I have to go?" Joey wanted to know.

"It's…something that will help you do better in school and with other things," Joseph tried to explain.

"What if I don't want to go?"

The question alarmed Joseph. For the first time, he realized that he and Jill hadn't considered how Joey might feel about the treatment and what it entailed. It was a question that he didn't have an answer to at the moment. He was saved from having to answer it when someone scored a touchdown.

By 11 p.m., they were both fast asleep on the couch together, but Joseph's sleep was disturbed by troubling dreams. In one dream, he was trying to get Dr. Meron's attention to ask a question, but the doctor just smiled devilishly and started laughing maniacally.

Joseph woke up suddenly and looked around frantically. It was 1:15 in the morning and the television had turned off automatically. He looked over and relaxed a bit when he saw Joey curled up by his side.

As he looked at his son, he thought about the expressions on his parents' faces when he and Jill were trying to explain the experimental treatment to them. To say they looked less than enthused was definitely an understatement. Everyone adored Joey and wanted the best for him but no one was excited by the news.

As time went on, Joseph was seriously starting to question whether participating in Dr. Meron's trials was the right thing for Joey and his family.

CHAPTER 17
Brave Face

Marsha sat in the parking lot at Dr. Meron's facility trying to get up the energy and courage to put on a brave face for Tommy. She felt a mixture of intense guilt and shame for not seeing her son for weeks as she recovered from a depressive episode. She hadn't even gone to see him for Thanksgiving. Tamara had gone out of her way to organize a big dinner for the families of children who were participating in Dr. Meron's trials. Jack was there, but Marsha didn't even answer the phone when he and Tamara tried to call.

Despite her resolve to finally go see Tommy that day, Marsha still was deep in the throes of self-pity. For weeks, she had been unraveling under the heavy pressure of a voice telling her that she didn't really matter and that her life was pointless. Young Jason had awakened an old fire within her, and when he put it out so abruptly, it left her feeling cold, empty, and useless.

Deep down, she loved her husband Jack. But she also couldn't help feeling that he was holding her back from something better. She worked tirelessly to build the "perfect life" with her husband and son, despite Tommy's Williams Syndrome diagnosis and Jack's eating disorder. But the more she tried to be perfect, the more imperfect everything became.

No matter how many tutors she hired for him, Tommy still wasn't doing well in school. He was mostly disruptive in the classroom and resistant to learning new things—a fact that she had withheld from Jill and the other Williams Syndrome mothers in their parent's group. As soon as Marsha left the room, Tommy started acting out. That was a significant reason why she was eager to get him in Dr. Meron's program.

Meanwhile, Jack had officially become a food addict and it was starting to get out of control. She secretly worried about his health, and instead of confronting the reality head-on, she joked about it in an attempt to discourage him from eating more and more. But her plan wasn't working. Instead of prioritizing his health, Jack was only becoming more and more detached from the family unit. Now, Marsha's "perfect family" was scattered and rife with confusion.

Ever since Jason rejected her, Marsha was sleeping 14-16 hours each day. She only got up from bed to answer the door when she ordered takeout food on her cellphone app. She ate in bed and then watched television until she fell backasleep.

But that particular morning, Marsha woke up from a disturbing dream about Tommy at 5 a.m. and it shook her back to reality. It made her realize that despite the oppressive thoughts and feelings she was having that her life was meaningless, she did have a purpose. And that purpose was to be there for her son.

Marsha put her head back on the headrest in her car and took a deep breath as she prepared to go in to see Tommy. She looked in the rearview mirror and practiced her winning smile. It was the smile that made everyone in the room feel comfortable and confident in her ability to get the job done. It was the smile that made Tommy happy. No matter how she felt, she knew that Tommy needed that smile right now. She put a few stray hairs back into place around her bun, put her large, dark sunglasses on and opened the car door. She could have been Audrey Hepburn's twin in *Breakfast at Tiffany's*.

When Tamara buzzed Marsha into the facility, she was so excited to see Tommy's mom again that she almost wanted to give her a hug. Tamara was becoming increasingly concerned about Tommy's behavior and lack of motivation. He spent most of his day staring at the wall or throwing a tantrum when the facility's educational consultant came into work with him on his school assignments. He was clearly unhappy and there could only be one explanation—his mother's disappearing act.

"Mrs. Rogers, it's so good to see you. How have you been?" Tamara asked as she pointed her in the right direction.

"I'm doing wonderful!" Marsha said with that winning smile plastered across her face. "How is my son doing?"

"Well, as I explained over the phone, we've been having some challenges, which is why we've wanted to keep him here a few more weeks for monitoring," Tamara admitted. "But I'm sure he'll be much better when he sees your face. Wow, I just love those shoes, Mrs. Rogers. And that bag."

"Thank you," Marsha said graciously. "I found them both at Nordstrom Rack for 50 percent off retail."

"Amazing! I see that I really have to get there one day," Tamara said, trying to keep the mood light and positive. Ever since Dr. Meron unceremoniously took her top position away, she had been reading more books on ways to improve her relationships at work. She understood that the last thing Marsha would want at that moment was any sort of judgment for not coming to see her son.

"Here's Tommy's room," Tamara said with a gentle smile as she led Marsha inside.

When Marsha walked into the room and didn't see Tommy, she panicked for a moment. Then she saw Tamara walk around to the other side of his bed where he was sitting on the floor. When her eyes finally fell on him, her smile dropped for a moment. He looked drained of color and energy. He was staring down at the ground.

"My Tommy!!!" Marsha exclaimed, quickly recovering her smile. She knelt down on the floor and opened her arms wide to embrace him.

"Mommy!" Tommy shrieked back. He hugged her back and there was an exchange of warmth between them.

Marsha sat on the floor right next to her son. "Oh. I've missed you so much."

"Where have you been Mommy?" Tommy asked.

"I've had to take care of some things, baby," she said hesitantly. "But Mommy's here now."

"Will you stay? Can I come home with you, now?" Tommy asked.

Marsha looked into Tommy's sad eyes, and those feelings of intense guilt and shame returned. She couldn't believe that she had been away from him for that long. She knew that it was time she got back on her feet and put things back together for her family's sake.

"You'll be coming home with me very soon, my love," she told him. "But in the meantime, I promise you that I'll be here every day to see you."

"You promise?" Tommy said with a little skepticism in his voice.

"I promise. Every day, no excuses," Marsha said as she caressed the side of his little face. "I promise."

"Okay, Mommy. I trust you," Tommy said before reaching over to hug her again.

Tamara had to step out of the room after seeing Marsha with her son. Tears of relief were streaming down her face and she had to compose herself. She quickly made her way to her office and locked the door behind her. Before she could sit in her chair, there was a knock and then the sound of someone trying to turn the knob.

"Who is it?" she called out while quickly wiping away her tears.

"Tamara, you're needed in Subject A's room," Dr. Richards yelled from the other side of the door. "Now."

To make the environment in the facility more formal, Dr. Richards had taken to referring to the children as "subjects," which drove Tamara crazy. Billy, Dr. Meron's son, was "Subject A."

"I'll be right there, Dr. Richards," Tamara replied. She stared out the window for a moment and sighed.

When she arrived at Billy's room, he was standing next to his bed ripping the pages out of a paperback book and tossing them all around the room. Dr. Richards was standing at a far corner of the room with his hand on his hip. The facility's teacher, Mrs. Jones, was trying to get the book out of Billy's hands.

"He refuses to do any sort of school work," Dr. Richards complained. "What is his problem, Tamara?"

"I want my video games back!" Billy stopped for a moment and declared. "I don't feel like studying. It's stupid!"

"It's alright Billy," Tamara said as she sat on the bed near him.

"It's not alright. They took all my video games!"

"I told him he could play them again as soon as he finished his assignment for the week," Mrs. Jones explained. "Just a few pages of reading and a vocabulary quiz. That's it."

"From what Mrs. Jones tells me, he's a month behind in his assignments. Why aren't you on top of this Tamara?" Dr. Richards wanted to know.

"Well he's capable of completing the work, he's just been very distracted by his games and television," Tamara said as she managed to get the book away from Billy. "I've talked to Dr. Meron about this for months."

"And?"

"And, he keeps telling me that it's just normal teenage behavior. That it will pass," she answered.

"The thing is, it hasn't passed. It's getting worse. He should ideally have a thirst for knowledge at this age, and at this stage of the treatment program," Mrs. Jones interjected. "All that he wants to do is play, not learn. It's just not normal."

"I will talk to Dr. Meron again," Tamara said defensively, feeling as if she was being double-teamed. "But I need him to hear this from you two as well."

Dr. Richards shook his head, disapprovingly. "This is precisely why Dr. Meron brought me in."

"Why is that?" Tamara asked.

"You're completely unqualified to manage this program, Tamara. I can't believe he hired you in the first place!" he said as he threw his hands up.

"What? I've been working with Dr. Meron for over five years. I know this research better than anyone besides him," Tamara said as she stood up to face him.

"You may know his research, but you're horrible at managing these trials," Dr. Richards accused. "Have you ever managed anything in your life?"

Tamara took in a deep breath and crossed her arms. "I've managed to put up with your complete lack of professionalism for the past month. I think that's a major accomplishment."

"Oh, that's very clever," Dr. Richards said with a chuckle as he walked towards her. "Very witty Tamara. But not very smart, because now I suddenly have a whole lot that I need to talk to Dr. Meron about when he returns."

"Oh, is that so?" Tamara said, knowing that she had probably crossed the line of no return with him. She realized that the likelihood that she would ever get along with Dr. Richards was slim to none. "And what exactly will you tell him that he doesn't already know, *Manuel*?"

"I'll tell him what I know, that you're probably not right for this team. That you need more training," he said as they continued their stare-down. "And please refer to me as Dr. Richards."

"Well, Dr. Richards. I'll save you one thing on your list of to-dos," Tamara said as she took off her white lab coat. "I quit the program, effective end of day today. I'll get my things together and I'll be sure I leave my notes."

Dr. Richards looked dumbfounded as he realized that he had lost his advantage. He bumbled over his words as he tried to think of a reply.

"You need to give us at least two weeks' notice before leaving Tamara," he finally managed to say. "There's still a lot that my staff needs to learn from you about the subjects."

"That's not an express part of my original arrangement with Dr. Meron. Come on Billy, Mrs. Jones will take you to the calming room. I think there's an iPad in there with a special game you can play," Tamara said. "Mrs. Jones, I also have something I want to give you before I leave today. I believe it will help you work more successfully with Billy and the other children. But you'll have to get Dr. Meron's final approval to use it."

"Certainly," Mrs. Jones replied as she led Billy out of the room. "I'm open to anything at this point."

"Oh, and Dr. Richards?" Tamara said as she turned back to face him. "What is it?" he said in an annoyed tone.

"They are not subjects. They are children. Please remember that they are special, wonderful, young human beings who we are trying to *help*," Tamara told him. "And also, my name is *Doctor* Goodwin. I received my M.D. at Columbia, just like Dr. Meron. That's how we met. Just so you know."

Dr. Richards sighed and crossed his arms disapprovingly as Tamara left the room. She followed Mrs. Jones to the calming room with Billy and had an extra pep in her step. For the first time in a long time, she felt good about what she was doing.

Joseph and Jill were enjoying a rare moment of quiet in the house on a Saturday afternoon. Mia was at ballet practice, Sophia was at softball practice, and Grace was shopping with her friends. Joey was at Suzy's house practicing their lines. He insisted on bringing their new puppy along to meet Suzy. It took a lot for Jill to agree to drop him off at the play date with his friend by himself, but she knew that this was an important first step toward giving Joey a little more independence. She was also becoming very close with Suzy's mom, Alison.

Jill was resting comfortably on a pillow on her husband's lap as he caressed her hair. She dozed in and out of sleep as they watched reruns of the 90s show *Home Improvement*. She was awakened once again by the sound of Joseph's cellphone ringing.

"Sorry about that, honey," Joseph said as he looked at the screen. "It's my mom, she's been trying to reach me all week. I'll talk to her in the other room. You keep resting."

Jill murmured something under the breath as she re-positioned herself on the couch, then fell almost immediately back to sleep.

"Mom, how are you?" Joseph said after he stepped inside of the kid's play room and closed the door behind him.

"Hi, son, I'm doing fine. What about you?" she responded with a bit of concern in her voice.

"Oh boy. What's wrong, Mom," Joseph said, knowing just about every inflection of his mother's voice.

"Nothing's wrong...really," she said slowly. "I've just been wanting to talk to you about a few things."

"Like?"

"Like, your Thanksgiving news. About Joey," she said.

"What did you want to talk about, Mom?" Joseph asked, eager to get right to the point.

"I want to talk about this treatment program you're thinking of putting Joey in. I didn't want to make a big deal of it at the table, but I'm concerned, son," she blurted out.

"What are you concerned about? I really thought you all would be happy to find out about it," Joseph said as he sat on the edge of a table. "It could help him."

"I don't know. Something just doesn't feel right. I've been trying to reach you all week. Have you gotten any of my calls?"

"I did but it's been really hectic this week. Bulk holiday orders are pouring in," he explained. "Why do you say that something doesn't feel right?"

"I know you want Joey to be the best that he can be—we all do. But there are so many risks with medical trials. It's just..."

There was a pause and then suddenly his mother broke down in a fit of tears. She could be very emotional at times.

"It sounds like this treatment could change who Joey is. And I don't like the sound of that," his mom finally managed to say.

"Mom," Joseph said, trying to fight back his own emotions. He hated hearing his mother cry. "He'll still be our same Joey. He's just going to have better health, have an easier time in school, have new interests. He might also look a little different..."

"But it just doesn't seem natural to me. An injection that changes how he looks and thinks? Joey is just how God made him. He's wonderful. Who are we to play God?"

Joseph paused at that last remark and closed his mouth tightly. It stung. He hadn't considered whether he and Jill were trying to play God. He thought back to the moment when he saw the before and after picture of Billy, Dr. Meron's initial patient. It looked like pictures of two different people.

"Mom...I'm a little too tired to get into this now. I have to go, but I will tell you that Jill and I have thought this thing through for months. It's a once-in-a-lifetime opportunity," he explained. "Know that anything we decide to do is for his benefit."

"I love you son. Please think this thing over more," his mother pleaded with him.

"I will, Mom, I promise. Please get some rest. I love you."

"I love you too, son. Please give Joey and the kids a special kiss from Grandma tonight."

CHAPTER 18
Forced Transitions

"Who told you about my research in the first place?" Dr. Meron yelled angrily into the phone. He had only been back in town for five hours after another week of schmoozing in New York City and had found a stack of messages on his office desk.

"Well Damarus knows nothing about the program and he had no right to disclose that information. I have every right to the privacy of my studies..."

"Who appointed you the moral chieftain of medical research? … And what cause do you have to talk to the FDA about my study? Based on what information?"

"I've been doing this work for eight years! How dare you question my ability to run my own program? I am not your student anymore, you can't *grade* me!"

Dr. Richards and his assistant stood outside of his door listening to the entire tirade. Ever since the day that Tamara quit, it seemed like everything was going wrong at the facility. The children constantly asked for her or for their parents, and their unmet requests almost always devolved into long tantrums. Two of the patients had health emergencies due to allergies to strawberries and peanuts that were accidentally included in their lunches. And now, Dr. Meron was suddenly getting a number of phone calls from his colleagues and medical organizations around the state. At the moment, he was being berated by one of his medical school professors who he'd always had a contentious relationship with.

"You've never had confidence in anything I do, so I'm really not surprised...You know exactly what I mean...Damarus was always your favorite student. I bet you talk to him every day...you would believe *anything* he said...I'm being disrespectful? What am I, 23 years old again?"

Dr. Richards looked at his assistant with raised eyebrows. There was a buzz on his cellphone notifying him that there was a problem with a patient. He rolled his eyes, told her to go handle it, and went back to listening through the door.

"Well, rest assured that if either you or Damarus try to visit my facility unannounced, you will absolutely be denied entry. You are not welcome here, so don't even bother making the trip," Dr. Meron said and then immediately slammed the phone down on the receiver.

"They're all just jealous," he mumbled under his breath as he put the stack of messages in his drawer and slammed it shut. "They just can't stand the idea of seeing *me* win at something."

Dr. Richards lingered outside for a few more minutes before knocking on Dr. Meron's office door. If he knew anything about communicating effectively with people, Dr. Richards would have known that it was not the right time to bring more problems to Dr. Meron's plate.

"What? Who is it?" Dr. Meron's voice boomed through the door.

Dr. Richards let himself in.

"It's me, Doctor. We really have to talk about a few things."

"Did I invite you to enter? Now really isn't the time," Dr. Meron snapped at him as he paced back and forth behind his desk.

"Please tell me when will be a good time, because I haven't been able to get in touch with you for nearly a week," Dr. Richards replied curtly. "There are things you need to know."

"Oh are there?" Dr. Meron asked with a snarky tone. "Go ahead, tell me what I just *need* to know."

"Well for one, I've learned that several of your patients are way behind in the educational part of their therapy, namely Subject A."

"You mean my son, Billy."

"He refuses to complete his assignments and frequently throws out-of-control tantrums to get his way. I've just learned that we have no valuable data regarding his progress in speech, spelling, math, or reading from the past three weeks."

"You should be talking to Dr. Goodwin about this," Dr. Meron said, waving him off as he sat back down at his desk. "I hired you all, the best and brightest, because you're supposed to figure these things out without my help!"

"Um. That's another thing you need to know Dr. Meron," Dr. Richards said as he crossed his hands on his lap. "Tama—I mean Dr. Goodwin has decided to quit the program."

"What?!" Dr. Meron exclaimed, finally giving Dr. Richards his full attention. "What do you mean she *quit*?"

"She decided a few days ago that she no longer wants to participate in your program."

"Well, she can't just quit. She's been at my right hand with this research for years!" Dr. Meron yelled as he slapped his hand on his desk angrily. "Why would she leave without telling me anything?"

"Just a difference of opinion, I suppose. And she left me and my team with quite a load to carry."

"Please leave my office, Dr. Richards," Dr. Meron said bluntly. "If there's anything else you need to tell me, draft an email."

Dr. Meron's day had gone from challenging to unbearable. He had become so accustomed to having Tamara around that he couldn't imagine her not being available to him. He picked up the phone and called her office line. It rang and rang until going to voicemail. He then called the work cellphone he issued her. That went directly to voicemail. He then realized for the first time that he didn't have any other way to contact Tamara. He didn't even have her address offhand—she spent most of her days and sometimes long nights at the facility.

Dr. Meron sat at his desk for a long time holding the phone in his hand, staring into thin air. For the first time in a while, Dr. Meron was feeling an all-too-familiar feeling that he despised: helplessness.

John couldn't believe that Debra actually had Thanksgiving dinner without inviting him over. It was the first time in close to 20 years. Instead of having dinner at the family house, she took the kids and went to visit her sister's family in another state. She wasn't even that close with her sister Beatrice, but Beatrice was Debra's chosen companion for Thanksgiving Day.

In fact, instead of getting a dinner invitation from Debra, he received a letter in the mail from her lawyer the week after Thanksgiving initiating the first step in an official separation. When he received the letter, he had a mild panic attack and found himself in the local bar drinking his thoughts and troubles away.

His mother was driving him nutty to the point where he had booked a room at a local motel for a week. It wasn't really in his budget, being that he was still paying the mortgage on two homes and his workload had unexpectedly lightened. But he needed the time away from the constant motherly nagging, demanding, and nitpicking. He wanted desperately to go home and talk things over with his wife, but now he felt as if he had trapped himself between a rock and a hard place.

What if Debra didn't want him to come back home anymore?

What if Debra was dating someone new that she met at the school she wanted to attend?

If he begged to come home, would that eventually cause Debra to become just as controlling and demanding as his mother?

What if it was too late?

All of these questions haunted him and kept him up at night. His one hope was to see Debra at the upcoming Williams Syndrome meeting to try to patch things up. He knew that she didn't like to miss the meetings, and it was the perfect excuse to get together in one place for an extended period of time. It would also show her that he was just as committed as she was to exploring new solutions for Patty.

❧

"*Let it snow, let it snow, let it snow...*" the pretty red-haired performer sang as she danced around the stage wearing a shimmery ballroom gown. The smell of egg nog, apple pie, and peppermint filled the air. The sound of over 200 people fluttering about filled the expansive room.

It was the evening of the elaborate, much-anticipated company holiday party that was hosted annually by Jill's company. They threw the affair at a classy chandelier-lit St. Louis hotel ballroom and spared no expense.

Mia loved going to the annual party more than anyone because she got to dress up. She was looking very polished in a sparkling champagne-colored sleeveless gown and a pair of matching Mary Jane shoes—a young fashionista in the making. She and her dad were in the middle of the room dancing to the live holiday music along with Grace and Joey. Whenever Joey wanted to spin Grace around, she leaned down a little and made it happen flawlessly. Joey was over the moon at the chance to show everyone his moves.

Everyone in the family was surprised and happy when they found out that Grace was coming to the party—she and her mom had been talking more, though Jill still wasn't very happy about her relationship with Scott. Sophia had invited Brendan to the party, and they quickly found a group of their peers to hang out with.

Jill had a craving for a few of the catering company's famous cocktail meatballs and headed over to the far end of the room. On her way, she was surprised to see Marilyn, the facilitator of her local Williams Syndrome parent meetings, heading in her direction.

"Marilyn, how are you?" she asked as they embraced. "I didn't know you worked here?"

"Oh, I don't. My granddaughter, Dorrine, does," she said and then turned to find her. When she did, Dorrine flashed a wide, beautiful smile and immediately started heading over to meet with them.

Dorrine was 32 years old and had been diagnosed with Williams Syndrome when she was a baby. She was born to a young mother who couldn't handle the pressures and financial strain of having a special needs child, so she transferred parental rights to Dorrine's paternal grandmother, Marilyn. Marilyn, also on her own, sacrificed a lot to take care of her granddaughter and to raise her to be a well-adjusted, mostly independent adult.

"Hello," Dorrine said politely when she arrived.

"Dorrine, this is my friend Mrs. Todaro. Jill, this is Dorrine," Marilyn introduced.

"So nice to meet you!" Dorrine exclaimed as they shook hands. Jill admired her bright smile and starry green eyes.

"Nice to meet you too, Dorrine," Jill said with a smile.

"Dorrine is an associate at the location on Hodgkins Lane. And she has her own studio apartment right down the street," Marilyn explained.

"Really? That's amazing Dorrine, congratulations on your success!" Jill said, impressed.

"Yes. She's a part of an independent living program for adults with Williams Syndrome. She has access to job and life skills training, cooking classes, shopping trips, and plenty of group activities," Marilyn explained.

"I've heard of those programs," Jill said, nodding her head. "It sounds like they're doing great work."

"Yes, Dorrine is very happy and she's always into something," Marilyn said. "But of course I still worry—it's what we mothers do. She's put me on a strict limit of four visits per week now."

"Remember, three visits per week starting next year Mom," Dorrine reminded her. Marilyn rolled her eyes knowingly and Jill laughed.

"I know, I know. I'm just so proud of you," Marilyn said with a smile as her eyes started to fill with water.

"I'm going to get more punch, Mom," Dorinne said, excusing herself when she spotted a friend from work at the food table.

"I know it must be hard to let her have so much independence," Jill commented as they watched her give her co-worker a hug.

"Of course. She'll always be my little Dori. But I have to let her spread her wings," Marilyn responded as she wiped away a few tears.

"Here you go," Jill said as she pulled a pack of tissues from her purse. "I've needed these a lot lately myself."

"Thank you. So will you be at the upcoming meeting?" Marilyn asked, trying to change the subject. "It's the first one in a while. Everyone has been so busy lately—especially with that new treatment program that all the parents are joining."

"Yea, we'll definitely be there," Jill answered. "Joseph's actually looking forward to it for once. You say that all the parents are joining?"

"Well, most of them. There are a few who have refused. I believe four from our group have already begun the process," Marilyn confirmed.

"We've decided to take Joey in after Christmas. Already submitted the paperwork."

"Oh is that so? Well, you'll have to tell me how everything goes. I've barely heard from anyone since our last meeting."

"I definitely will. And we will definitely see you at the next meeting," Jill said as she reached over to give Marilyn another hug. She then watched as Marilyn turned to look for Dorrine. When Marilyn saw that her granddaughter was still chatting it up with her friend from work, she hesitated, thought for a moment, and then decided to go back to their table to sit by herself.

"Mom," a familiar voice said. Jill whipped around and saw her daughter, Grace.

"Yes, honey, how are you enjoying yourself?" Jill asked, relieved that they were back on speaking terms.

"It's really great, Mom, but I've gotta go," Grace said. "Carlie invited me to this party and…"

"It's fine, honey, I understand," Jill immediately said. "I'm just so glad you could make it tonight. I love it when we're all together as a family. All of us."

"I know Mom. I do too," Grace said and then leaned over to give her a quick peck on the cheek. Before she had a chance to turn around, Jill grabbed her arm.

"Grace," Jill said, not really knowing what she wanted to say next.

Grace looked at her and for the first time in a long time, there was a connection between them.

"Grace, I see so much of myself in you. I think that's why we bump heads so much— we're a lot alike," Jill told her with a smile as tears started to fill her eyes. "And I see so much in you. I just want everything for you."

"I know Mom, I know," Grace said, looking down at the ground to stop herself from getting emotional. "I just need you to trust me more."

"I do, and I will," Jill replied as she enveloped her daughter in a hug. "But I'm still your mother, so please bear with me. And please be safe out there. I love you so much."

"I love you too."

"What took you so long, girl?" Carlie said when she saw Grace walking up the walk in her black cocktail dress, three-inch heels, and hooded bubble coat. Loud 90s music was blaring from the windows throughout the house along with the sound of a hundred teenagers talking at the same time. "You look hot."

"Thanks. I just left my mom's holiday party," Grace said as she gave her friend a half hug. "Who's here?"

"You mean, is *Scott* here?" Carlie teased. "No he's not, but his tool of a friend is. That slimy jock, Mark. Ugh. His breath smells horrible and he's a close-talker."

"Great news," Grace said sarcastically as she followed Carlie inside.

The inside of the house was almost completely dark except for the strings of colorful holiday lights around the staircase, fireplace, and archways. Some of the kids were dancing while others were engaged in loud conversations. Still, others were having intimate moments with their significant others in quiet corners of the house. Grace noticed a large fire pit in the back where a group of teens was gathered around toasting marshmallows.

Carlie went straight to the drink counter where their other friend Vanessa was pouring potato chips into a large bowl. It was her parent's house. Grace trailed behind.

"Grace!" Vanessa said when she saw her. "So glad you could make it! You look so nice."

"Thanks. I'm loving the playlist," Grace said with a smile as she took her coat off. "Where's your coat room?"

"Right down the hall there," Vanessa said as she pointed.

Grace made her way down the hall, as she searched for her keys in the pockets of her coat. She'd learned long ago that things had a way of coming up missing when inside of a pile of coats at a party. When she finally found them, she looked up and saw Mark standing in front of her.

"Hey...Grace," he said with a sly grin on his face. His eyes were halfway closed, he was swaying a little, and he was holding a red cup full of beer in his hand. He was eyeing Grace like a cat with a perched bird in its sights.

"Hey," she said while pushing her way past him into the coat room. To her dismay, he followed and closed the door behind them.

"You look so great," he said as he came closer.

"What do you want?" she asked, pushing him away.

"Nothing, just wanted to talk to you for a minute," Mark said as he reached over to play with her hair. Carlie was right—his breath smelled like 10 piles of rotting garbage.

"Ew. We don't have anything to talk about, get out of my way," Grace said, again trying to push past him, but he stepped in her path.

"You know, you can do so much better than Scott, Grace," he told her, slurring every other word.

"What, like you?" she said with a scoff. "Get real, Mark."

"So pretty with an attitude. I like a girl with spunk," Mark commented as he tried to move in closer again. He stumbled a little but recovered his footing. "You wouldn't be so mean to me if you knew what your little boyfriend does behind your back."

Grace looked at him for a moment and frowned. "What are you talking about?"

"Don't get me wrong—you're his main girl. But to be honest, he pretty much has a different girl at every school where we play away games. I gotta give it to him, he's quite the player—and I don't just mean on the lacrosse team!" Mark said with a laugh.

"Whatever, you're just jealous of him," Grace said, waving him off.

"Believe what you want," Mark said. "But I just want you to know I like you, Grace. And I can do a lot more for you than Scott. Just know that I'm here when you're ready."

"What is this, some kind of competition for you?" Grace asked. "You want everything that Scott has, don't you?"

"Nope. Just one thing right now," Mark said as he grabbed her chin and kissed her before she had a chance to escape him. She quickly pulled away and wiped her lips.

"Ugh, you're disgusting," she said as she went for the door. "Now I might have to get a tetanus shot."

As soon as she left the room, she ran right into Scott coming down the hall with Carlie. Mark left the room right behind her, wiping Grace's bright red lipstick from his face. Scott looked at them both curiously as he put two and two together in his head.

"What were you doing in there with him?" he finally asked Grace.

"Dude, she totally hit on me," Mark said, trying to look innocent as he threw his hands up in surrender.

"What? You're out of your mind!" Grace protested and they started arguing back and forth.

"You know what? It doesn't even matter anymore," Scott said shaking his head, feeling embarrassed by the small crowd of kids that were watching them. "We're done Grace."

"What are you talking about Scott? He followed me into the room and—" Grace tried to explain.

"I've been looking for the right time to tell you. Then I come here and you're hanging out with my best friend? I should have never left Amanda's house just now," Scott said, his voice trailing off at the end. It was obvious that he had been drinking.

"You just left whose house?" Grace asked.

"You might as well know now. Yup, I have a new girlfriend," Scott confirmed. He watched as tears slowly started to well up in Grace's eyes.

"You promised me that there wasn't anyone else, Scott. I asked you time and time again," Grace said, trying to hold it together. "You told me I was the only one you were with."

"Well, stuff happens," Scott said coldly. "I changed my mind."

Grace stood there quietly, feeling that same feeling she felt in elementary school when her classmates laughed at and shunned her. Watching Scott take her feelings lightly in front of everyone caused something to spark inside of her. She decided that this time she wasn't going to be the victim.

"Well, you know, if that's how it has to be," Grace said with a shrug, suddenly regaining her composure and wiping away the tears that were building up at the corner of her eyes. Her reaction caught Scott by surprise.

"So, no hard feelings?" Scott asked, having prepared himself for Grace to have a meltdown.

"No hard feelings. We had a nice time while it lasted. And like you said, stuff happens," Grace said as she started to walk past him. "And by the way Scott, there's something on your shoe."

"What, where?" he said, upset that someone might have scuffed or stained the new pair of tennis shoes Grace had bought him. It was his first time wearing them. Grace leaned down to point at his shoe and he picked up his foot to get a closer look. She quickly and easily pulled the sneaker off. In the same motion, she turned around and headed out to the patio where people were still gathered around the fire pit.

"Hey, what are you doing?" Scott protested. He stumbled as he followed her outside. He watched in horror as Grace tossed his brand new white sneaker directly into the pit.

"What is your problem!! Why did you do that?!" he screamed as he tried to save his shoe, but it was too late. The group of spectators laughed at him as he stood around the fire with one shoe on trying to fish the other one out of the flames.

"Well, you know, stuff happens Scott," she said with a shrug as she turned to leave.

"Those tennis shoes are so hot, Scott!" Carlie said with a laugh as she followed Grace outside. They locked arms in solidarity and left the party together.

As much of a strong face Grace had put on inside of the house, she couldn't keep it all together in time to make it to her car. She was about to fall down on the sidewalk in tears, but Carlie caught her in time and managed to lead her the rest of the way to the driver's seat.

"I can't believe I didn't see this coming," Grace said after a few quiet minutes of sobbing into her steering wheel. "What was I thinking!?"

"You were in love," Carlie said. "It happens to all of us, Grace. Trust me, it's going to be okay."

"No. But that's the thing, Carlie," Grace said as she wiped her face, thoroughly streaking her makeup. "I didn't love him. I never loved him. I just loved the *idea* of him."

Carlie nodded, listening quietly.

"Everyone told me he was a jerk, and I knew he was. Of course, I did. But I just couldn't let go of what he represents, you know? Like, everything that we think we want, you know?"

"I know exactly what you mean, Grace."

"Who doesn't want to be with one of the hottest, most popular guys in school? And he wanted *me*," Grace explained. "How could I say no to that?"

"Not many girls would."

"I guess I've always thought I could be different from those other girls. Stronger. Smarter. But I fell right into his trap," Grace admitted. "Do you know how much stuff I bought him, Carlie?"

"Grace, it's okay. I totally get it, and it doesn't make you a bad or stupid person. Like you said, anyone can fall victim to that."

"No, no, I'm not comfortable with being a victim. God, I can't stand that word," Grace said as she shook her head and roughly ran her hands through her hair. "I am not a victim. I just went into this with my eyes wide shut."

Carlie reached over to give her friend a hug and Grace collapsed into her embrace, breaking down into a fit of tears. She wasn't crying so much for the loss of Scott, but more-so because she was finally openly admitting to herself that she had lost touch with who she really was for a moment. She felt sadness, but also a sense of relief. She knew that it would take some work and plenty of time to recover from this blow.

CHAPTER 19
The Beauty of Acceptance

"Our Jamie has been with us since she was five. We knew what we were getting into when we adopted her, but we didn't care. We knew it would be a challenge due to how old we are, but we figured it was better that we're there for her as long as possible instead of leaving her to the foster system in her formidable years..."

Everyone in attendance at the Williams Syndrome meeting was fully tuned in as the soft-spoken, older, white-haired man named George Collins spoke. He sounded and looked a little like Father Time telling a story to a room full of eager listeners. George was telling the tale of how he and his wife came to adopt their now nine-year-old daughter with Williams Syndrome. The entire time, he sat relaxed in his seat tenderly holding his wife, Carla's, hand. They were new to the group and brought a comforting aura to the room.

"...Having her with us has been a challenge to us mentally, physically, and emotionally, but it's also been a blessing in so many ways. She keeps us on our toes and gives us a reason to keep going strong," George explained.

Across the room, Jack and Marsha sat looking like the exact opposite of George and Carla. Marsha was dressed in an expensive blue dress, high heeled shoes, and her hair freshly styled. She appeared to have had some type of cosmetic procedure because her face looked frozen in a questionable expression. Her leg was crossed away from Jack, who was sitting with his chair almost a foot away from her. He had his arms crossed tightly over his belly and looked like he would prefer to be anywhere except sitting beside his wife.

A few seats away, John was sitting next to his wife Debra. It was the first time that they had been together in one room for more than a few minutes in months. Despite being happy to see her, John still pretended to be detached. He leaned back in his chair and tapped his foot impatiently while rapping his fingers on his thigh. Debra looked like a brand new person, and everyone noticed. She usually boked tired, stressed, and at the end of her rope. But today, she looked mellow, well-rested, and nicely-groomed. She had highlighted her usually dark blonde locks and was even wearing makeup.

"That was quite the introduction. Welcome to our group George and Carla," Marilyn said as she began clapping and everyone joined in. After the applause ended, Marilyn clasped her hands together and looked around the room to see who else might want to share the news.

"Jill, I was so happy to see you at my daughter Dorrine's company Christmas party. Did you have anything you wanted to share?" Marilyn asked.

"Yes. I just wanted to say that seeing your daughter that night really inspired me. She looked so happy and full of life. It made me think a lot about Joey's future, and it helped me see that maybe I need to let

Joey have more freedom and independence. He's a teenager now and it's hard to believe, but it won't be long before he turns 18."

"That's wonderful news. I know how hard it can be to let go of the reigns. As you can see, I'm still struggling with it to this day," Marilyn said with a chuckle. "But Dorrine is happy and that makes me happy."

Marilyn looked around the room again, searching for another couple who wanted to share. She was trying her best to hold back her own emotions.

"So, John and Debra, we haven't heard from you two in a while. How's little Patty?" she asked.

"Patty's doing great. We've been thinking about enrolling her in that special treatment program soon," John spoke up. Debra looked at him curiously because this was news to her.

"Interesting. Maybe you could talk to Jack and Marsha about it," Marilyn said as she glanced over at the pair. She could sense that there was some tension between them. "Tommy's in the program now, right, Marsha?"

"Yes, he is," Marsha said with a slight nod. Her facial expression revealed nothing and she didn't look like she was very eager to share. She met eyes with Jill. Jill smiled at her, hoping that they could talk about it after the meeting. Marsha looked away as if they were strangers.

"George and Carla, have you guys thought about going to see that doctor? I think they'd say your daughter is the perfect age for it," John asked. "It might give you some peace of mind since you're getting older."

"John," Debra said in a scolding tone.

"No, no, it's fine," George said as he squeezed his wife's hand. "I've heard about it. I've heard about the amazing results. But Carla and I decided together that we're definitely going to pass."

"Why's that?" Debra asked. "Have you at least spoken to Dr. Meron about it?"

"There's no need. We believe that God has a hand in everything that has happened to us up until this point. From adopting Jamie to finding this group," George said confidently. "We believe that God made Jamie unique for a reason. And we also believe that God will provide for her in every way. What we don't believe is that a solution can be found in any artificial drug."

"And just why not?" Marsha asked. "There are countless drugs on the market that are helping people every day."

"Yes, but this one seems different. Especially since it involves children," Carla spoke up. "In any case, we're not going to continue to preach about it to you all. We just all have to go with our own instincts about what's best for our children."

"That's right," Marilyn said with a nod as she thought of how to redirect the conversation. "So. What are everyone's plans for the holidays and the New Year? Any events we should know about?"

"For anyone who's in the area, our son Joey will be in a Christmas play at his school. It's his big role before we take him in for the treatment," Joseph said. "They gave us a few extra tickets."

"So, you've decided to put him in the program?" Marsha suddenly asked.

"Yes," Joseph answered. "Can we talk with you guys about how Tommy's doing later?"

"Tommy's doing just fine," Marsha said curtly. "Not much to tell."

"Right, just fine," Jack said under his breath and then rolled his eyes. He had perspiration on his brow and under his arms that was seeping through his dress shirt. He looked like he hadn't had a very good day.

"Yes. *Fine*," Marsha said as she shot an icy look in Jack's direction. It was the first time they had been together in one place since Jack moved out of the house. Marsha had kept her word about going to see Tommy every day, but she was still doing battle with her emotions and feelings of insecurity. It had prompted her to go on a shopping spree, get Botox injections, and have a filler injected into her lips. Jack was livid when he logged on and saw the credit card bill.

"Since when have we been thinking about putting Patty in the program?" Debra whispered to John while the others were talking.

"You said you wanted us to talk about it," John replied back in a low tone.

"But we never did. This is *you* making decisions for *us* again," Debra scolded.

John was at a loss for words when he saw the look of dismay in Debra's eyes. He had hoped that making this declaration to the group would make her happy.

"Okay, everyone. I'm so glad that we could meet here one more time before the holidays. And if anyone wants to attend Joey Todaro's

Christmas play, please get the information from Joseph and Jill," Marilyn said. "Remember, we're stronger together. I'll see you all in the new year!"

"Has anyone seen or spoken to Mary Ellen or Ray?" Jill asked as everyone was standing up. Everyone shook their heads to say no and continued on their way.

"I haven't heard from them either, but I have their phone number if you need it," Marilyn said. "I was actually going to call them too—it's so out of the ordinary for them to miss a meeting."

"Yes, I'll take it," Jill said, getting out her cellphone as she and Marilyn approached each other.

Joseph and Jill had gone to the meeting together after work. Joseph made it a point to take off from work early despite his workload to ensure they got there on time. On the way home, they had plenty to talk about.

"That was the strangest group meeting I've ever been to," Joseph observed. "Everyone seemed so weird."

"Yea, except for the new couple. They looked so happy and relaxed. Did you see the body language between Jack and Marsha?"

"Yea. Jack didn't look too happy. And Marsha looks...different," Joseph said.

"To say the least," Jill said with a knowing look. "What about John and Debra? They usually hold hands throughout the entire meeting."

"It's like there's something in the air," Joseph said.

"Everyone seems so different. Are we different too?" Jill wondered aloud. Joseph looked over at her and grabbed her hand tightly.

"Of course not," he said. "We're fine honey. Like Marilyn says, we're stronger together. We're in this together and we're going to stay strong through it all."

❧

Tamara knew that it was risky to pop up on the Smiths unexpectedly, but she didn't know any other way of reaching out to them. She had memorized their address as she did many of the other children's parents. She sat in her car for a long time, debating on whether this was a good idea or not. The last thing she wanted was to ruffle the Smiths' feathers anymore or to cause them to call in a complaint to Dr. Meron's office. She hoped that they would hear her out.

Finally getting up the nerve, she got out of the car and nervously made her way up to the front door. She was a little surprised when she saw Mary Ellen Smith raking a few stray leaves near the garage. Mary Ellen seemed distracted, yet very focused on her task.

"Mrs. Smith?" Tamara said timidly. There was no reply. She cleared her throat.

"Mrs. Smith," she said again, louder. Mary Ellen still didn't look up. Finally, Tamara decided to go over and tap her on the shoulder. Mary Ellen jumped and clutched her rake defensively.

"Oh, my God!" she exclaimed as she put her hand on her chest and got her bearings. She immediately recognized Tamara from the clinic.

"Dr. Goodwin, you scared me!"

"I'm so sorry Mrs. Smith. I was calling you but...are you very busy?" Tamara asked.

"Yes, a little. What is this about?"

"I just wanted to talk to you and your husband about a few things. I hate to impose, but do you think we could sit down for a few moments?"

"If this is about Sammy going back to that place, then no. Absolutely not," Mary Ellen said, shaking her head as she resumed scraping the leaves into a tidy pile.

"No, it's not about that. Actually, I'm not working for Dr. Meron anymore. I'm doing my own research."

"Well, good for you," Mary Ellen said.

"I wanted to show you something I've been working on that I really think will help Sammy, and it doesn't have anything to do with medicine or serums or injections. It's a more...holistic approach," Tamara told her.

"My husband is resting, Dr. Goodwin. I don't think he'll be in the mood for a conversation right now," Mary Ellen said.

"Mrs. Smith," Tamara said. She walked up close to Mary Ellen and put her hand on her shoulder. Mary Ellen turned to look at her and they locked eyes.

"I am so sorry for what you and your husband had to go through. I should have done more to prevent it from happening that way, and I'm so ashamed of myself for that," Tamara said as her eyes began to well up with tears. "Please, let me try to make things right."

Mary Ellen looked at her for a while more, then let out a deep sigh. She leaned the rake up against the garage door and motioned for Tamara to follow her inside.

"Just have a seat here. I'll go talk to my husband," Mary Ellen told her and disappeared into a back room.

Tamara looked around the living room as she waited. There were crayon drawings on the floor in one corner of the room along with a toy fire engine truck and Lego blocks. She saw a partial Lego creation that Sammy was working on and it piqued her interest. As she leaned down to examine it more closely, Mary Ellen and Ray walked into the room.

"What can we help you with, Dr. Goodwin?" Ray demanded. He looked a bit annoyed by her presence.

"Oh, sorry, I was just admiring Sammy's creation. He was always interested in building things while he was at the facility," Tamara said as she got up to greet them.

Ray looked less than amused. He was trying his best to be patient with this person who he had partially blamed for the quiet distress he and his wife had been going through since Sammy was kicked out of Dr. Meron's program.

"Okay. Well, I can tell you want me to get right to the point, so I will," Tamara said as she sat down on the love seat across from the sofa. They followed her lead and sat down to hear her out. She opened her briefcase and pulled out an iPad, a chart and two manuals, which she handed to Ray and Mary Ellen.

"I've been working with a programmer I went to school with who's helping me to develop a program designed to sharpen the skills of children with Williams Syndrome and similar conditions," Tamara explained as she lit up the iPad and opened an app. "I was actually showing Sammy the early version of the program before he left the facility, and he seemed to be making some impressive progress with it."

Ray scanned through the manual carefully as he listened to her talk. "What kind of skills does it help sharpen?"

"Well, that's an important part of the app. It first identifies the areas of need through testing, then creates a custom learning solution that the student only needs to navigate for about five hours per week. I'm confident that after just a few months of use, Sammy's mental and cognitive skills can improve by 20 percent."

"Interesting," Mary Ellen said, starting to perk up at the news of something that could help her son.

"What's great is that it will do more than just help students with reading, writing, and spelling. It will also help them fine tune some of the skills they already have. For instance, in Sammy's case, it can provide him with guidance on creating building projects, construction, architecture, and engineering."

Ray's interest increased when he heard it could help Sammy develop his interest in architecture. "How can it do that?"

"Through well-thought-out educational games. This app will include a comprehensive array of games that will help develop Sammy's knowledge of certain topics at his pace. Studies have found that educational games help give children a deeper knowledge of targeted subjects. They develop both cognitive and non-cognitive skills," Tamara continued to explain. "I just want to perfect it, and I'll need Sammy's help to do that."

By the time Tamara finished her presentation to the Smiths, almost two hours had passed. A lively discussion filled the room and it was as if the light had returned to Ray and Mary Ellen's eyes. They felt a glimmer of hope being renewed within them that something could help their son's progress, and they were eager to find out what Tamara's program could offer.

Sophia and her team had pulled it out and won the big championship game. As fate would have it, their final game was against the Lady Bengals, and it was a nail-biter. They won by just one run after a member of the opposing team made a major error, letting a ball slip under her glove into the outer field. Unfortunately for the Bengals, a girl who was a member of the track team at Sophia's school was on second base. She managed to slide right into home base for the game-winning run. It was the first softball championship the school had won in over 20 years.

Sophia pitched an amazing game and had been recruited by the varsity coach to attend their spring training sessions with high school softball players. They were planning to groom her to be one of their go-to pitchers as soon as she entered the eighth grade.

The team's big win prompted Joseph and Jill to throw a huge celebration the next day. They invited all of Sophia's teammates, the kids' friends, and their neighbors to their favorite pizza restaurant for a night of pizza, cake, ice cream, and music. The owners let them have the entire back room.

Sophia and her team were posing at the table with their brand new trophy, which was almost as tall as they all were. Sophia caught a glimpse of Brendan coming into the room to join the festivities and called out to him.

"Brendan! Come check it out," she said, waving him over. He gave her a hug and then inspected the trophy from top to bottom.

"Man look at the size of this thing! We need to win one of these next year," Brendan said with a smile. "You deserve it Soph, congratulations!"

"Thanks so much, Brendan," Sophia said. She was glowing.

"Hey, where's Joey? I've got something to show him," Brendan said as he looked around.

"Joey T!" Sophia called out over the noise in the room. He jumped to attention and ran over to where they were standing.

"What's up, Joey!" Brendan said as they slapped hands. "I brought you those cards I told you about."

Joseph watched from across the room as Brendan and Joey sat down together at a table and started sorting through a stack of baseball cards. He watched as Joey examined each one closely while Brendan told him more about each famous player. He had promised to help Joey start his own baseball card collection. The look on Joey's face was golden.

"Hey, neighbor!"

Joseph had been so distracted watching his son that he didn't notice his next door neighbor Paul approach him.

"Paul, you made it," Joseph said with a smile as he shook his hand.

"Yup, the wife wanted to stay in, but no way I would turn down this invitation. Championship team huh?" Paul said with genuine excitement in his voice. "You know, I heard there are some really great opportunities in women's softball after college."

"Yea, who knows. Maybe even the major league someday," Joseph agreed as he slapped Paul's arm and got ready to rejoin his wife at their table. But Paul kept the conversation going.

"It's rare for a player Sophia's age to pitch that fast," he said. "You know, I used to be quite the pitcher in my day. I started for my high school's varsity baseball team in five games back in '83."

"Really? That's pretty great, Paul," Joseph said, trying to be polite, but not really wanting to hear the whole story.

"We came this close to winning a championship ourselves," Paul said with a chuckle. "Those were the days. You know, high school. Did you play any sports?"

"Uh, yup I sure did! Well, Paul, I'm so glad you could make it. Please help yourself to some pizza and a slice of cake," Joseph said, cutting him off abruptly as he patted him on the back.

"Oh, okay. Well, thanks, Joseph. Thanks again for inviting me," Paul said, looking like someone had let the air out of him.

Joseph nodded, then something made him glance back over to where Joey and Brendan were sitting together. Brendan had just offered Joey a few of his cards to start his collection and they slapped hands together to seal the deal. At that moment, Joseph felt a twinge of guilt. He realized how special it was when people accepted and embraced Joey for exactly who he was. The look of joy on his son's face was everything. Paul just wanted the same acceptance.

"Hey, Paul?" Joseph said suddenly, calling out to his neighbor before he disappeared into the crowd.

"Yes?" Paul said, turning back around. Joseph made his way over to where he was standing.

"I played basketball and track in high school. Basketball was my favorite, though," Joseph said. Paul perked back up.

"I always wanted to play basketball, but I never had the height," Paul said with a smile.

"That's a myth that you have to be tall to play b-ball," Joseph said as he led Paul over to the pizza table. "Look at Muggsy Bogues and Spudd Webb! You just gotta have technique. I can show you a few moves on the court one day if you want. A few of us guys get together on Sunday afternoons from time to time."

Even in the dim room, he could see Paul's eyes light up. "I'd love that. Thanks!"

CHAPTER 20
Getting Confirmation

It was out of the ordinary for Grace to spend one Friday night in the house, let alone the entire week. She was usually out with her friends, hanging out with Scott at a party or spending the night over at Carlie's house.

But ever since she was publicly dumped by Scott, Grace had barely wanted to leave her room let alone be in social environments. What was worse was that people were still talking about their breakup on Facebook. Every time she saw a snarky comment from one of their mutual friends online, it felt like she was reliving the moment over and over again. The only ray of light was seeing the post someone put up of Scott's sneaker being roasted on the holiday fire.

She also couldn't stop herself from stalking Scott's page on a daily basis. He had been shamelessly posting photos of him with his new girlfriend Amanda. He was even bold enough to refer to her as his "main girl" on the public forum, indicating that there were other girls. Amanda apparently thought it was cute, because she liked every post and gushed about him in the comment area. It made Grace feel nauseous.

Grace's cellphone rang and she silenced it immediately. All of her friends had been trying to get her out of the house, but all she wanted to do was sit in her room, watch, TV, eat pizza, and drown out her sorrows with sad music. She felt comforted by the fact that her friends cared enough to try to reach her, but she still wasn't ready to meet up with them. She needed time to sort things out by herself.

As she flipped through the channels that Saturday, securely tucked beneath her heavy comforter, she came across a motivational speaker on television. The lady was very pleasant-looking and had a comforting voice with a delightful southern accent. She was talking about knowing yourself. The message written across the bottom of the screen read: "Who Are You?"

"It can be difficult to navigate this world when you feel like you're all alone in it," the lady said.

Grace nodded a little as she clutched the remote control tightly.

"But sometimes when we think we're all alone, it's just an illusion. It's a story we've been telling ourselves so long that we've accepted it as the truth," the woman continued. "There are people all around us who would walk with us, who would listen to us, who would intervene for us, if only we allowed them to."

Grace was skeptical about that last tidbit, but she put the remote control down and continued to listen.

"You want people to know you and to understand you. But if *you* don't even know who you are, how can anyone else know who you are?"

Her audience applauded. Her simple words got Grace to thinking about her own life. Two years prior, she was spiking volleyballs, getting

As in all of her classes, and headed down the path to college. Most of all, she was happy and content with her life then. Now, she was just confused.

Who am I? What do I want?

Grace thought about how for the past year or so, she was someone unrecognizable. She had gone out of her way to be someone different for other people. She wanted so badly to continue to be a part of the popular crowd at school that she had totally lost touch with herself.

Down the hall, Joey sat in his room with his back up against the door. He had a large box of Honey Nut Cheerios in his lap and the baseball cards that Brendan gave him spread out in front of him on the floor. Every now and again he'd toss Ramsey a bit of cereal.

Joey could tell that something was up with his sister Grace because she had barely come out of her room in almost a week. Instead of knocking on her door, he decided to wait patiently until she came out of her room to go to the bathroom or to the kitchen for food to talk to her. He had been waiting in that spot for over two hours.

Joey stood up and peeked outside the door just in case he hadn't heard her leave her room while chomping on his Cheerios. Her door was still closed. He wondered if he should just sit outside on the stairs, but then his mom might come home and take the cereal box from him. She didn't know he knew her hiding spot for his favorite cereals in the kitchen.

Just as he was closing his door back, he heard Grace's bedroom door swing open, then the sound of her descending the stairs. Joey immediately sprang into action.

"Hey, Grace," Joseph said when he saw his daughter pass by on her way to the kitchen.

"Hey, Dad," she said with a sheepish smile as she shuffled her way to the kitchen. Joseph was about to follow her in to see how she was doing, but before he even had a chance to stand up, Joey came speeding down the stairs like lightning.

Grace stood in front of the refrigerator door for a while staring at the food choices before her. Her mind was occupied with other things. Finally, she grabbed a green apple. When she closed the refrigerator door, there stood Joey holding a colorful volleyball.

"This is for you, Princess Grace!" he said innocently as he presented her with his gift.

Grace looked at her little brother and then at the ball. She hadn't held a volleyball in her hands for over two years.

"Thank you, Joey, what's this for?" Grace asked as she took the ball and started examining it.

"You used to like volleyball. I thought you might like it," he answered.

Grace's eyes fell on the drawing and message on the back of the volleyball. Soon, tears were streaming uncontrollably down her face.

"Why are you crying, Princess Grace?" Joey asked. "Did I do something wrong?"

Grace chuckled. "No Joey T. You did everything right. Thank you so much."

Grace leaned down to give her little brother a hug. At the door of the kitchen, Joseph watched his first born children and felt himself getting emotional. This was the type of thing that made him so proud and happy to be a dad. It made him realize that while he and Jill weren't perfect, they were doing a pretty good job raising their kids with love.

"Come on little bro, you wanna go do a few drills? Remember what I taught you?"

"Pass, set, hit! Pass, set, hit!" Joey repeated as he jumped up and down in excitement.

"Right. Okay, it's kinda nice outside, but still go put on a hoodie so Mom won't complain," Grace told him as they slapped hands in agreement.

"Hey, can I join you guys?" Joseph said. Grace looked up and smiled at her dad. He hadn't seen that smile for months.

"Yeah!" Joey exclaimed as he made a mad dash for his bedroom. Grace fell into her father's arms and he held her head under his chin.

"You guys are so awesome," he said, then kissed her on the top of the head. "Are you okay Princess?"

"Not really. But I will be Dad," Grace said as she continued to cling to her father for support. "I promise."

Sounds of glee could be heard outside in the backyard as Grace and Joey hit the volleyball back and forth. Their father volunteered to be the ball retriever to keep the action flowing. Soon, the noise drew Mia out of her playroom and Sophia out of her bedroom. Joseph went to retrieve a net from the garage and soon the drills turned into a two-on-two volleyball game in chilly 40-degree weather. About a half hour later, Jill returned from the grocery store and found her whole family playing in the yard like it was a sunny summer day. She watched them for a while, then her motherly instincts kicked in. She went to the coat closet to retrieve a few things.

"Here, guys," she said when she returned with a pile of hats, scarves, and gloves in her arms. She watched closely until everyone had one of each. Finally, she put a set on herself and then furtively stole the volleyball from Grace's hands.

"Mom!" Grace protested with a laugh. "You don't play volleyball!"

"What?? Where do you think you got your skills from? I'll serve," Jill said as she squared up behind her daughter. Joseph took the position on the other side of the net.

All the kids were surprised when they saw their mom toss the ball up, jump and do an almost perfect overhand serve. Sophia and Mia were so surprised that they couldn't return the serve.

"Wow, way to go, Mom!" Grace said as she gave her mom a high five.

"We're gonna win this!" Joey proclaimed as he also smacked hands with his mom.

"You guys had better stay on your toes over there," Jill taunted.

"Don't worry about us. That was a lucky shot," Joseph trash-talked back.

The family laughed and played together for the rest of the afternoon until the sun went down. It had been a while since they all had a chance to bond as a family in that way. Having Grace there, smiling and enjoying herself once again, was like finding the missing piece of a puzzle.

Joseph had a pile of work to do and people to call that morning, but he was a little distracted. He kept scrolling through his phone looking at the photos he took of his family that weekend playing volleyball. Everyone was smiling ear-to-ear, wearing their skully hats, scarves, and gloves. Joey stood in the middle holding the volleyball he had given Grace. He was trying to figure out which photo to pull and have printed up to feature on his desk.

In one photo, Joey was giving his cheesiest smile with his eyes closed tight. It made Joseph smile every time he scrolled to it.

"This is definitely the one," he said with a chuckle as he sent the photo off to be printed and framed at his favorite copy shop. Even though he had made his choice, he still went back and kept looking at the photos as his office phone rang off the hook.

There was something really special about Joey and everyone knew it. It went beyond just his Williams Syndrome diagnosis. He was always polite, thoughtful, and cared for others. Joey would literally give the shirt off of his back to a stranger. It was rare for a 13-year-old boy to have his level of intuition and compassion.

Joseph was increasingly becoming worried about how Dr. Meron's treatments might change his son's personality. The unexpected call from his mother definitely triggered the concerns. She wondered if they were playing God by trying to change Joey. The more he thought about it, the more he wondered the same thing.

"Mr. Todaro," Joseph's assistant Amy said, knocking before she peeked her head inside of his office. "There's a gentleman who says he's from a doctor's office on the phone. He says he wants to confirm your appointment?"

"Tell him I'll call him back, please," Joseph said as he finally put down his cellphone. "Be sure to get his name and number."

"Sure thing," Amy said, and then promptly left. A minute later, she came back to the door. "Um, Mr. Todaro, I apologize but the gentleman insists on speaking with you. His name is Dr. Manual Richards. He's on line three and said he'd hold."

Now a bit annoyed, Joseph picked up the receiver and nodded for Amy to go back to work. She instinctively closed the door behind her.

"Yes," Joseph said.

"Is this Mr. Joseph Todaro?" the voice said. "Yes, what can I do for you?"

"Hello, Mr. Todaro, this is Dr. Manuel Richards. I just wanted to confirm that you're still planning to enroll your son Joey into the facility on December the 29th at 9:00 am."

"That's the plan," Joseph answered. He didn't appreciate being bullied into taking Dr. Richards call for such a minor issue. "Is there a reason why this call couldn't wait? You're calling me at work."

"Well, I'm at work also, Mr. Todaro," Dr. Richards responded. "I tried you on your cellphone earlier but there was no response. We need to get this list confirmed as soon as possible."

"And I could have called you back in an hour on my lunch break," Joseph replied.

"You could have, but you might not have, and we have a schedule to keep here," Dr. Richards said, matter-of-factly.

Joseph was a little taken aback by the doctor's rudeness. "Who exactly is this anyway? Where is Dr. Goodwin? She's the one who helped us when we came in."

"Dr. Goodwin is no longer with our program," Dr. Richards said flatly. "I'll be working with you from now on."

"What about Dr. Meron?"

"Hold on a moment please. *What do you need, Denise*?" Dr. Richards whispered to someone in the room with him.

Joseph could clearly hear the person in the background telling Dr. Richards that he was needed in one of the patient's rooms. Faintly, Joseph could hear what sounded like a child screaming and having a tantrum. Dr. Richards was talking to Denise in a hushed tone, but Joseph could hear every word.

"*Why do you come to me every time this happens...do your job and put him in the calming room or give him what he wants...yes, you have permission to call in help. I'll check in on him later*," he said, then finally turned his attention back to Joseph. "Okay, what were we discussing Mr. Todaro?"

"I asked about Dr. Meron. Is he still going to be a hands-on part of Joey's treatment process?" Joseph asked impatiently.

"Well, *obviously* Dr. Meron is still a part of the program. He's the creator of the treatment. But I'm the lead researcher now and I'll be dealing with you more directly. Is that okay?" Dr. Richards said in a patronizing tone.

"You know what? Hold off on confirming that appointment until I speak *directly* with Dr. Meron. *That* would be okay with me," Joseph said, trying to control the anger that was building in his stomach.

"There's really no need for that, Mr. Todaro. Dr. Meron is a busy man," Dr. Richards said.

"Well, so am I, Doctor. But I'll make time in my schedule to speak with him. Pass my message along to him, will you? Thanks a lot," Joseph said then slammed the phone down before Dr. Richards could get another word in.

"The nerve of that guy!" Joseph said to himself. He had gone from a blissful moment reliving the fun time he had with his wife and children that weekend to feeling as if he wanted to throw his phone across the room.

Joseph frantically started going through the paperwork on his desk, trying to calm down and occupy his mind with work. After 15 minutes of fruitless activity, he finally put the papers down and looked into space. He sighed, leaned back in his chair, and grabbed his cellphone again. The photo of his happy family with Joey's cheesy smile came right back up on the screen. He looked at it carefully for a while. He wanted to make sure that Joey always had that same smile, positivity, and free spirit. Did he really want to put his son under the care of someone like Dr. Richards?

❧

Jill finally found a moment to sit down and call Mary Ellen Smith. Though they weren't close friends, she and Mary Ellen had spoken a few times in the past. Jill wanted to talk to her about the recent meeting she missed, and also find out how Sammy's treatments were going.

"Hello?" Mary Ellen said, picking up on the first ring. She sounded cheery.

"Hi Mary Ellen, how are you? It's Jill Todaro, from the Williams Syndrome meetings?"

"Oh, Jill! I'm doing okay, how are you?"

"Pretty great. I just wanted to call you up, see how you and Ray are doing. We missed you at the last Williams Syndrome meeting."

"Yea I know. We needed some time to ourselves after...well I don't know if I want to get into it. But suffice it to say that we've had a challenging couple of months," Mary Ellen said, choosing her words carefully.

"Do you mean with Sammy? How is he doing with Dr. Meron's treatments?" Jill asked, not being able to hold her curiosity in any longer.

"Sammy's no longer getting those treatments," Mary Ellen said abruptly. “It wasn’t for him.”

“Oh. Sorry to hear that,” Jill said, suddenly realizing why they didn’t go to the meeting.

“Oh, please, don’t be. We’ve actually found another solution that may help Sammy in the long-term. But I don’t want to turn you against Dr. Meron’s program since I know you guys are participating,” Mary Ellen said. There was silence on the line for a few moments.

“How did you know we were participating?” Jill asked. She was torn between wanting to know more about the solution Mary Ellen was referring to and trying to figure out when she told the Smiths their plans.

“Well, I saw your husband at the facility that day. He said you couldn’t make it,” Mary Ellen said.

“When was this?” Jill asked.

“Uh. Back in September maybe? It was shortly after Dr. Meron first came to our group meeting.”

Jill was quiet for a while as she thought about it. “Okay. Well, I sure would love to hear about that other solution you guys found. Can I call you at a later date?”

“Definitely. I hope everything works out for you guys.”

“Yea, me too,” Jill said as she ended the call. She sat in silence for a while as she slowly came to the realization that Joseph had consulted with Dr. Meron without her.

CHAPTER 21
The Lovely Intangibles

"How could you do that!? Without me? Were you going to just sign him up without my consent?"

Joseph's worst nightmare had come true. It was a concern that he had put on the backburner after Jill agreed to sign Joey up for Dr. Meron's treatments. After a while, it seemed to be water under the bridge. But somehow, some way, Karma had found a way to let Jill find out about his solo visit to Dr. Meron. He felt immense guilt as he sat on the edge of their bed, listening quietly and watching Jill pace back and forth in front of him.

"Do you know how silly I felt when Mary Ellen told me that?" Jill said as she finally sat down on the other side of the bed. "I was clueless. Why didn't you tell me you already went there without me?"

"I was wrong, Jill. And I knew it right after I did it. I tried to tell you, but I..." Joseph tried to explain, but he knew there was nothing he could really say at the moment.

"We're supposed to be a united front. We do *everything* together as a unit. That's what makes this family work," Jill said as her voice began to crack.

"Jill, I..." Joseph tried to say again, but the words wouldn't come to him.

"I just don't know what to even say to you right now. I thought we had everything figured out, but now...I don't even know what to think!"

"I know what you mean," Joseph admitted.

"Ever since we heard about this treatment program for Joey I feel like we're just not on the same page. And it scares me. We tell each other everything and yet you kept this from me for months," Jill said as she threw her hands up in the air.

"I wish I would have just told you. But I guess I was afraid you might change your mind again," Joseph said.

"You know what, I'm too exhausted to even argue. There's all this stuff going on at work, and now this. I need to be alone. I need some time to think about things," Jill said. She and Joseph stood up at the same time.

"You stay here and get some rest. I'll go downstairs," he told her as he tried to comfort her. She dodged his intended embrace and went into the master bathroom without saying another word. Joseph took that as his cue to leave the room.

Joey peeked out of his door just in time to see his father come out of his parent's bedroom. Though Joey couldn't make out what they were saying inside, he could hear them talking and he could sense that something was off. Joey watched as his father closed his bedroom door gently and quietly behind him.

"Daddy?" he called out down the hall. "Are you okay?"

Joseph looked up and walked over to his son's bedroom, trying to put on a cheerful face. "What are you doing up, buddy? It's way past your bedtime."

"Where are you going? Downstairs for cocoa?" Joey asked. Ramsey jumped up from his place on Joey's bed and ran to the door when he heard Joseph's voice. "Can I come?"

"No, actually I'm going down to the den for the night," Joseph answered as he reached down to pet the dog.

"Can Ramsey and I go with you?" Joey asked.

"No, your mom doesn't like it when you sleep downstairs," Joseph said, trying to sound upbeat.

"Then can you sleep in here with us? We can camp in!" Joey suggested. The look on his face was so full of excitement at the idea that Joseph couldn't help but smile and nod his head.

"Okay buddy, let's do that."

"Yesss!" Joey said. He made a mad dash for the linen closet in the hallway and took a large stack of sheets from the shelf. He ran back to the room and started setting everything up with his dad.

About 15 minutes later, Joey's room had been transformed into a grouping of tents that draped from the bed to the dresser to the nightstand. Joseph turned on the starry light machine so that the ceiling looked like the sky at night. They laid back on the floor, head-to-head, looking up at the "stars" shining through the sheets. Ramsey finally settled down between them and went to sleep.

"Daddy?"

"Yea, buddy?"

"Daddy, do you and Mommy love each other?"

"Of course we do, buddy, what makes you ask that?"

"I don't know," Joey answered. There was quiet for a while as they continued to look at the stars.

"Daddy, what is love?" Joey asked, breaking the silence. Joseph considered his question for a moment before answering.

"Love is... caring about someone no matter what. Being there for them no matter what. Happiness. Spending time together."

"Why do you and Mommy love each other?"

"I don't know if I can explain why. It's just a feeling you have when you're with someone. I've loved your mother since the moment I met her. She makes me happy. And our love is what brought *you* here."

There was another long silence between them as they continued to watch the stars move around the room. After a while, Joseph started to doze off.

"Do you love me, Daddy?" Joey suddenly asked, waking his father back up.

"Yes, I love you. Your Mom loves you. We love you with all of our hearts buddy. You and your sisters are everything to us."

"And you love me... *no matter what*?"

Joseph looked over at his son and saw that Joey was looking right back at him with his eyebrows furled. His starry eyes sparkled in anticipation, waiting for an answer. He wondered

what would prompt his son to ask those questions.
"Son, I love you no matter what, from now until infinity. Always remember that."

"Debra! Welcome to my humble abode," Carla said cheerfully as she held the door open for her new friend to enter. Debra had Patty on her hip. She was excited to have someone to visit and talk to who wasn't a minor.

"Thank you so much, Carla," Debra said as she looked around the house.

"And this is Patty, I presume," Carla said with a smile as she reached out her hand. Patty shook it, then shyly tucked her head into her mother's neck.

"Come on into the sitting room. I made some tea and I have these delicious little Dutch butter cakes," Carla told her. "And if you're hungry, I tossed a fresh Caesar salad with chicken."

"Oh wow, that really sounds delicious," Debra said as she settled into her chair.

"Patty, do you want to meet Jamie? She has new toys," Carla asked as she held out her arms. "She's in the next room."

"Go ahead Pattycakes," Debra told her as she pointed her toward Carla.

Right after the last Williams Syndrome meeting, Debra made it a point to introduce herself to the new couple, George and Carla Collins. She was intrigued by their story of adopting their daughter Jamie when she was five and impressed by how calm and content they seemed. She wanted to connect with them to learn more about their experiences and possibly get a nugget of wisdom from them.

Carla sat the tray of tea down in the middle of the table and then took her seat next to Debra. The tray was polished silver, and the matching tea set looked like it was made of the finest porcelain with a floral pattern and silver detail.

"How beautiful," Debra commented as she admired the tray. "And so formal."

"I know you probably can't hear much of my accent anymore, but I'm British. We take tea time very seriously," Carla said with a smile as she poured Debra a cup.

"Really? I've always wanted to visit," Debra said. "When did you move here?"

"I met my husband there 39 years ago. He was visiting on business. A year later, we were

married in the states," she said. "He was quite handsome in those days. How long have you been married to your husband?"

"17 years. But it seems like longer," Debra said with a smile.

"I know what you mean," Carla said and they laughed together.

For the next hour, the two sat together and talked about everything from marriage to their children to their professions. Carla was still a teacher at a local elementary school and was thinking about retirement.

Debra told her about her plans to go back to college for an associate's degree.

"How do you juggle your job with taking care of Jamie?" Debra asked.

"Good question. Thankfully, Jamie attends the elementary school where I teach, so I can check in on her whenever necessary. Before that, we had to rely on special needs child care providers. We went through four before finding someone we could really trust," Carla explained. "We still call on her from time to time."

"I'll likely have to do that also, but I know it can be expensive."

"It is, but you and your husband should be able to afford the expense. It's worth it," Carla said as she took another sip from her cup.

"I'm sure it is. But I'll probably be dealing with that expense on my own," Debra said.

"What do you mean?" Carla asked.

"Well," Debra said, thinking about whether she should go into detail. She felt comfortable with Carla—it was like talking to a motherly figure. "My husband and I are separated at the moment."

"Oh no," Carla said, genuinely looking concerned. "For how long?"

"A little over three months."

"I'm sorry to hear that." They were quiet for a while and just sat together.

"Can I say something to you?" Carla said, breaking the silence.

"Yes, of course," Debra said.

"There are three things that have helped me get through every major challenge in my life. My belief in God, great music, and my husband," Carla said.

Debra nodded and continued to listen as she poked at the butter cake on her plate.

"If I had to, I would find a way to care for Jamie on my own. But having my husband by my side allows us to truly thrive as a family," Carla said. She reached over to tenderly put her hand on top of Debra's hand. "So if there *is* a way that you and your husband can work things out, I implore you both to put in the work."

Debra was a little taken aback by Carla's forwardness, but she was touched by her sincerity. Deep down, she knew that she was right. She just didn't know if she could go back to living the way she did before. She needed more support and understanding from her husband.

Jack had been staying at a hotel located in between his office and his home. The bed was uncomfortable and it made his back hurt, and he hadn't had a home-cooked meal in weeks, but he at least had some peace.

Marsha hadn't called to talk to him since he left, though on a few occasions he got a hang-up call from a restricted line. She sent him one text to remind him of the Williams Syndrome meeting so that she could keep up appearances with him by her side. Tommy had recently been released from the facility with instructions on how to administer the weekly injections at home.

The elevator was on the fritz at his hotel that evening, so Jack had to walk up the three flights to his floor. He held a bag from a local deli that contained an extra-large pastrami hero, a large bag of chips and a 1-liter soda. It was his fifth meal of the day—he liked to eat right before going to sleep.

When he finally arrived at his hotel door he was panting and had to pause to catch his breath before entering. He shuffled his way over to the King-sized bed, threw his bag of food down and then flopped down on the bed. He leaned forward and grabbed his knees, still trying to relax. Finally, he unbuttoned his dress shirt and swung his legs over onto the bed to rest.

He flipped through the channels and ended up watching a holiday movie, *Miracle on 34th Street*, as he ate his pastrami hero. He became nostalgic for his childhood when everything seemed so magical and possible. He also longed for that feeling of having a normal, loving family to go home to during the holidays. He wasn't even sure if he would be spending Christmas with his own family that year.

He finished off the first half of his hero and then took a long swig of soda. He promptly started in on the second half. A few minutes later, he let out a long, loud belch that his next door neighbor may have heard through the walls. One minute later he was feeling a pain in his chest that he assumed was more gas. Another minute went by and the pain was getting worse. He clutched at his shirt and started to lean over to the side. By then he was panicking because the pain was intense. He dropped the sandwich in his lap.

Instinctively, Jack reached for the hotel phone and managed to get it off the hook. He panted and struggled to catch his breath as he tried to press the "0" button for the front desk. Finally, he touched the right key and rested his head on the headboard, waiting to hear a voice on the other line.

"Front desk?" a pleasant voice finally said.

"Help. Help." he tried to say over the sound of the television playing in the background. As he lay there, unable to move, all he could do was listen to the scene from *Miracle on 34th Street* where Fred and Doris were having an argument about faith, common sense, and the "lovely intangible" things about life.

"...don't overlook those lovely intangibles," he heard Fred say. "You'll discover they're the only things that *are* worthwhile."

CHAPTER 22
Regrets and Repentance

Jill was one of a few moms who volunteered to help Mia and her ballet classmates get ready for their first recital. The dressing room was all abuzz with the sounds of 10 little girls in orange tutus jumping, pirouetting, and chattering away.

"Mommy, is Daddy here yet?" Mia asked as Jill put the finishing touches on her makeup. She gently swept a large brush across her face to give her face a glittery shine.

"I'm not sure, honey, he might be a little late from work. But your Grandma Ella's here. Grace picked her up."

"Mommy, are you and Daddy mad at each other?" Mia asked out of the blue. Jill was caught off-guard by the question. She cleared her throat as she thought of an answer.

"What would make you ask that?" Jill asked instead.

"Daddy's been sleeping downstairs," Mia said. "Why isn't he sleeping in your room?"

"Well…"

"Girls, it's time to get to your places!" Mia's ballet teacher called out as she clapped her hands in a rhythmic beat that they all seemed to recognize. Jill was "saved by the bell."

"You do your best Mia, we'll be out there cheering for ya, hon," Jill told her as she leaned down to give her a hug.

"Okay, Mommy!" Mia said as she jumped down from her chair and followed her classmates. Jill watched with motherly pride as her daughter joined the group of girls.

When she came back to where the audience was sitting, she was a little surprised to see Joseph sitting there with Sophia, Grace, Joey, and Grandma Ella.

"Hi," he said as she stood up to greet her. They had an awkward embrace. Grandma Ella examined them.

"I thought you would have to work late tonight," Jill said as she reached down to hug Ella.

"I took off early. I wouldn't miss this for the world," he said with a smile.

"Is Mia ready for her big debut?" Grandma Ella asked as she started to stand up to let Jill sit in the seat next to her son.

"Yes, she looks perfect," Jill answered. "It's okay, Mom, you can stay there. I'll sit right here."

Grace could sense that something was going on between her parents. She glanced over at the both of them curiously as she thought about what could be the matter. She deduced that it was somehow related to Joey going into the treatment program they had planned for him. She assumed that they were probably still arguing over the details.

"Daddy, I wanna be a dancer too," Joey suddenly declared.

"Oh, yea? Tap dance?" Joseph asked. "Or maybe breakdancing?"

Everyone laughed as he did a snake move with his arms, then The Robot. Joey tried to mimic the same movements.

"Not bad guys," Grace said approvingly with a nod. The lights in the room went down and the stage lit up. Within moments, Mia's ballet teacher came out with the girls—they were all holding hands in a straight line.

"Yea, Mia!" Joey screamed out at as the audience welcomed them on stage with a round of applause. Some of the girls froze in terror, while a few standouts, including Mia, bowed and prepared themselves for their performance.

The 20-minute recital was an amusing scene, to say the least. A few of the girls completely forgot the routine and stood completely still with deer in headlights looks on their faces. The others mostly struggled to follow the movements of their teacher, who was coaching them from the sidelines. The standouts in the bunch added extra flair and pizazz to their performance, encouraged by the laughter and clapping from the audience.

When the routine was over, the girls got a standing ovation, and most of them gladly took a bow. The teacher led them off the stage and the lights in the auditorium came back on.

Grace's eyes quickly adjusted to the light as she grabbed her coat. She had just received a text message from Carlie to meet their group of friends for pizza. She hadn't seen her girlfriends in a while after the breakup with Scott, and was eager to get back together with them.

"Mom, Dad?" she said to them as they were gathering their things.

"Will you be able to drive Grandma? I'm going to meet Carlie to get something to eat."

"Sure, honey. Just be safe," Joseph said as he reached over to give her a kiss on the forehead.

"Remember you have that quiz tomorrow," her mom reminded her. They had been studying together again on weekends to help Grace get back on track with her grades.

"I'm going to ace it, no worries. Kiss Mia for me," Grace said with a smile as she made her way out of the aisle. She looked down at her phone to type a quick reply to Carlie as she headed for the exit. She opened the double doors and went outside, heading for the parking lot.

"Hey, Grace."

She heard a familiar voice say her name as a hand grabbed her arm from behind. She looked around and was surprised to see Scott standing there. One of his friends was standing nearby with his hands shoved in his pockets.

"Hey, how are you doing?" Scott asked. "Can we talk?"

Grace immediately thought that this was some kind of stunt to try to corner and embarrass her for social media, so she looked around frantically to see if someone was recording her. The coast looked clear and the look on Scott's face seemed genuine.

"I really have to go. What are you doing here anyway?" Grace asked.

"I had to see you…I saw your post on Facebook about the recital," Scott answered.

Grace was surprised to hear that he had been watching her on social media. Every time she saw a post from him it was either a photo of his new girlfriend or a lacrosse meme.

"What do you want to talk about?" she asked.

"You and me. I miss you, Grace," he said plainly. "I want to try to work things out."

"What? I…I can't, Scott," Grace said, looking surprised. She felt a familiar feeling of helplessness and vulnerability. Scott had a way of making her let down her defenses. His piercing blue eyes seemed to be looking right into her soul. He could tell when he had her in his trap.

"Come on. Let's just talk about it. You at least owe me that much," Scott said as he grabbed her hand.

"Wait, what?" Grace said as she looked back up at him. "You think that I owe you something?"

"Well, you did roast my sneaker in a bonfire," Scott said with a laugh. "Those were limited editions and I had to go home in my socks that night! But I have to admit, it *was* pretty funny."

Grace just looked at him for a long time. For the first time, she was truly starting to see Scott for who he really was. And she wasn't amused.

"Look, don't think about it so much. Let's just go somewhere and talk," Scott said as he pointed to his car.

"No thanks, Scott," Grace finally said. "You should go talk to your *girlfriend*. This isn't fair to her."

Scott stood open-mouthed as Grace turned and headed to her car. He was completely confident that he could convince her to come back. His relationship with Amanda was only superficial—a "Facebook romance" meant to make Grace jealous and insecure. He never had any intention to stay with her. The truth was, he had developed genuine feelings for Grace over the time they were together. She was strong-willed, smart, and thoughtful. He had never dated a girl who was anything like her.

"Grace, wait. Please," Scott said, becoming more desperate. He ran to intercept her path.

"I have somewhere to be," she told him.

"I know you're upset with me, Grace," Scott said as he took her hand. "I messed up okay? I know that now. I was just so jealous when I saw you that night with Mark. He's always joking around, telling me how he's going to steal you from me."

"I would never waste my time with a guy like that," Grace said, unable to hide a look of disgust. "You should have known that."

"I know, and that's why I like you so much. You're not like other girls," Scott said. "I don't want to let you go. I really want you back. Come on."

"You see that's just the thing though, Scott. You say I'm not like other girls, but you're just like other guys. I wanted so badly to believe you were different, but you're not. And I deserve better."

Scott started to say something in defense of his character, but then just looked down at his tennis shoes—yet another pair that Grace had purchased for him. He knew that she was right.

"I gotta go. Take care of yourself, Scott, I wish you the best. Enjoy college next year," Grace said as she leaned forward and kissed him on the cheek. Then she turned around and went on her way.

"Yea. I'll see you around, Grace," Scott said.

Marsha roughly pushed her way through the double doors into the emergency room even though they were automatic. The sound of her high heels click-clacking through the hallway was all that could be heard as she looked for a nurse to help her.

"Excuse me!" she finally yelled out when she saw a nurse cross her path. "I'm looking for my husband, Jack Rogers??"

The nurse casually pointed to the main station where a group of nurses was behind a desk checking their computers and talking on the phone.

"Nurse, I got a call that my husband is here. Jack Rogers?" Marsha asked frantically. The nurse was on the phone so she put up her finger to tell Marsha to wait. "No, I won't wait. I want to see my husband!"

An orderly came through the restricted doors that led into the emergency room and Marsha went right in before they had a chance to close again.

"Miss! Miss! You can't go back there right now. The shifts are changing!" the desk nurse yelled out to her.

Marsha went to the triage area and started pulling back curtains checking each bed for her husband. At one point, she stopped and reached down to take off her heels so that she could move more quickly. After checking several beds, a security officer caught up with her and led her back to the main desk.

"I want to see my husband!" she yelled at the top of her lungs.

"Ma'am I understand but you have to wait until the shift change is over," the officer told her.

"Where is he? I need to know where he is!"

"The nurse can tell you, ma'am. Please calm down."

By the time she was back at the nurse's station, the nurse was off the phone and ready to assist her.

"What was his name again?" she asked.

"Jack Rogers. He's my husband. I got a call that he was brought here an hour ago," Marsha told her. The nurse did a search on her computer.

"He's in surgery at the moment. After that, he'll be transferred to the ICU," the nurse told her. "It'll be a while before you can see him, ma'am."

"What happened to him?"

"His doctor will come talk to you soon. Please have a seat, Mrs. Rogers," the nurse told her as she led her to a seat. "Would you also like to talk to a counselor?"

"No, I'd like to talk to my husband!" Marsha yelled at her.

After five minutes of waiting, Marsha became so restless that she had to get back up from her seat. She paced back and forth in the waiting room.

"Where is that doctor!" she screamed. The nurse came back over to her. "I need to see my husband!"

"Mrs. Rogers, is there someone that I can call for you? A family member? A friend?" the nurse asked in the sweetest, calmest voice she could muster. Marsha looked at her for a while, feeling as if she would burst out in a fit of tears at any moment. She became aware of herself and the fact that she was making a huge scene. Finally, she reached into her purse and pulled out her cellphone. Her hand shook as she handed the phone to the nurse.

"Jill. Please call Jill Todaro."

The nurse took Marsha's phone and looked up the name in her contacts. She then gave the phone back and went to the nurse's station to make the call.

Jill hustled her way to the nurse's station as Joseph parked the car. She was dressed in a jogging suit with sneakers and had her hair pulled up in a ponytail. As soon as she received the 11 o'clock call from the hospital's ER saying that her friend was in distress, she jumped out of bed and hit the road. Joseph was still up in the den watching television and insisted on going with her at that time of night for that long of a drive.

"She's right over there," the nurse told her. "I've asked her several times if she wanted to see a counselor but she refuses."

Jill went into the waiting room and saw Marsha staring out of the window looking terrified.

"Marsha?" Jill said gently. "It's me, Jill."

Marsha turned around. As soon as she recognized a familiar face standing there, the tears came.

"Oh, Jill!" she shouted as she fell into Jill's arms.

"It's okay. It's going to be okay, Marsha," Jill said.

"They said I can't see him yet. They had to perform emergency surgery and he's in recovery now," Marsha explained as the tears fell freely down her face. "Jill, I can't lose him. I can't, I can't."

"You won't, come on, let's sit," Jill told her.

She led Marsha to a more secluded section of the waiting area to sit down and held her hand tightly as she listened to her talk. The words were flowing out of Marsha's mouth as if a dam had been broken—she was no longer holding anything back. She told Jill how much she had missed her husband but was too prideful to contact him. When Joseph came into the waiting room, Jill waved him off, knowing that this was a moment that was meant to be shared between two girlfriends. He waved back, then went to sit in the main waiting area.

"He hasn't been staying at the house for a while now, actually," Marsha confessed as she rested her forehead in her hand. "He left me after he found out that I went to visit Tommy's tutor."

As curious as she was about that tidbit, Jill stayed quiet and just let Marsha talk. She had suspected that Marsha's interest in Jason went beyond his professional expertise, but she didn't know that she would actually take action on it.

"And I just let him go. I didn't even try to make him stay," Marsha said. "I haven't spoken to him in weeks! What if I don't ever get a chance to speak to him again!"

"Don't think like that. You will Marsha, you will," Jill said reassuringly.

"What was I thinking chasing after Jason? He's just a kid, Jill. What's wrong with me?" Marsha continued. "I've probably known Jack longer than Jason's been able to walk and talk."

Jill just looked at her friend and continued rubbing her back tenderly.

"He was in that hotel room all by himself. He should have been home with me. I'm his wife, I'm supposed to be there for him," Marsha said. "I knew he was eating way too much and getting huge, but I didn't really try to help him. I just watched him in disgust and ridiculed him. I'm supposed to take care of both of my boys."

"How is Tommy doing?" Jill asked.

"I dropped him off at the sitter's house on my way here. I think he's spent enough time around doctors in white coats for a while," Marsha said as she wiped away tears.

"Do you want me to go get him? He can stay with us for a while—Joey will love it."

Marsha looked up at Jill as if she was seeing a new person. Her eyes were red and raw from crying non-stop for hours. "God, you're a saint, Jill. You guys drove all the way here at almost midnight to be here for me. I can't believe how I've behaved over the past couple of months. I'm so embarrassed."

"It's okay."

"No, it's not okay," Marsha said with a sigh. "Jill, Jack was right. I need professional help. I know it—I've known it for a long time now but I was in denial. And Jack has just put up with me for all these years. He's such a good man."

"That he is," Jill said, nodding in agreement.

There was a long silence between the two as Marsha tried to pull herself together. She was tightly grasping tear-soaked tissues in both of her hands.

"Jill," Marsha finally said weakly. "Will you be my friend again? I'm so sorry for everything. I just need a friend right now."

Jill reached over and hugged Marsha tightly as she started to sob again. "Of course."

CHAPTER 23
Holiday Magic

The volleyball season had ended, but Grace's old coach, Mrs. Ephraim, still had intramural games after school for girls who wanted to play for recreation and practice. She also was responsible for getting teams together for volleyball games in the summer. Grace could have waited until the following spring to try to rejoin the team, but something was compelling her to take action before the new year. She wanted to enjoy the holiday season knowing that she was back on the squad.

When Grace came to the gym after school and asked if there was room for her to join a game, Mrs. Ephraim was eager to put her on the court. After a few minutes of warming up on the sidelines, she rotated Grace in as an outside hitter—her usual position.

"Okay Todaro, let's see if you still got it," Coach Ephraim called out from the sidelines and clapped loudly.

The opposite team served the ball and it was easily passed to the setter. When Grace saw her bend down low to set the ball, she knew it was probably coming her way. She wound up, got into position and soared in the air right as the ball came toward her. She slammed the ball down with such force and trajectory that no one from the opposing team even went for it. Her team celebrated and slapped hands. The coach smiled and signaled for Grace to come back to the sidelines.

"Wow, that felt great!" Grace said as she rolled her arms back and forth to loosen them up more.

"You've been practicing haven't you, Todaro?" Coach Ephraim asked with a laugh. "Come into my office for a moment, I want to talk to you. Keep playing, ladies."

Grace forgot how much she missed being around Coach Ephraim. She was a short and feisty lady who always made time to talk to her girls one-on-one when there was a concern. She would let team members stay in her quiet office for a nap or to study when they needed to get away from the everyday pressures of high school life. Going to the coach's office to tell her she was quitting volleyball was one of the hardest things Grace ever had to do.

"So, Grace," Coach Ephraim said as she reached into her mini fridge to grab a cold water for her. "What have you been up to lately?"

"Well, just trying to get my grades back up."

"Trying, or doing?"

"Doing," Grace corrected herself. "I'm working on it. I think my teachers are annoyed by how much I ask for extra credit."

"Keep annoying them. What are your plans?"

"Well, I've actually been looking at this art school. They have a program for students who want to get into photography."

"Photography. That's an interesting choice. When are the applications due?"

"Soon. I have an appointment with my guidance counselor tomorrow morning."

"That's great, it sounds like you're on top of things. I'm really happy to hear that, Grace," Coach Ephraim told her. "To be honest, you had me worried there for a minute."

"Yea I know. But I'm getting back on track. There's so much I want to do! Starting with getting back on the team next season, if you'll have me?"

"You know you're always welcome on my court, kiddo," the coach told her as they slapped hands. "And let me know if you need a reference letter or anything. We're going to get you into that school."

"Thanks, Coach. I'll keep you updated," Grace said with a smile. Coach Ephraim could see a familiar excitement in her eyes.

"Okay, get back out there and rotate in. Next time you come late, I'll have you running laps until you drop!"

"Yes, Coach Ephraim," Grace said with a smirk as she got right up and headed back out to the court.

"I love it!" Tamara said as she reviewed her new website with her computer programmer. "It integrates so well with the app design."

Tamara had been working tirelessly with a small team of people to develop her new company which was focused around helping children with Williams Syndrome and similar conditions. The goal was to give parents holistic ways to help their children including diet recommendations, training programs, learning software, educational games, and chat rooms where registered users could interact and support each other.

Ray and Mary Ellen Smith had been crucial in helping her develop the entire program. She still had a long way to go, but progress was being made.

Tamara had never been so happy in her life. This was despite the fact that she had to give up her cushy apartment in downtown St. Louis for a one-room studio in a more affordable part of town. She had to cut back her shopping budget drastically and use her savings to pay her team. But she was happy because she was doing something that mattered and that she enjoyed.

"I'll call you tomorrow after I get a chance to review the entire thing," Tamara told her designer over the phone. "I'm going to see the Smiths right now. They invited me over for dinner."

Tamara hung up the phone promptly and grabbed her keys. She and the Smiths had gotten much closer over the past weeks. She finally had the opportunity to sit with Sammy in a more comfortable environment where he was happy and opened up to her more. Since Sammy was one of her first patients, she wanted to spend as much time with him as possible to better understand his condition, his thought processes, and how he learned new things.

When she pulled up to the Smith's house, she could smell a casserole baking from the outside. The thought of having a home cooked meal around a table made her want to sprint to the front door. When she worked for Dr. Meron, she would splurge on take-out and restaurants—now she mostly sustained herself on soup and salad. But she was confident that her personal sacrifices would be worthwhile in the future.

"Dr. Goodwin! Come on in, Sammy's been talking about you all day," Mary Ellen said cheerily when she opened the door. "Dinner will be on the table in 10 minutes."

"Thanks, Mrs. Smith. I have some things I want to show you guys."

"Tamara!" Sammy exclaimed when he saw her. He immediately ran up to her and grabbed her hand. "Come see!"

Sammy led her to his play area in the corner of the living room and pointed. There sat a Lego structure that was shaped like the beginning of a house.

"Wow, you did that, Sammy?" Tamara gushed.

"My Daddy helped me, but I did most of the work," Sammy explained as he sat down in front of the structure. He grabbed a couple of pieces and examined it for a few minutes. He then carefully placed the pieces where he thought they should go.

"You see that?" Ray said as he walked into the room to join them. "He's been doing that all week."

"Step by step and the job gets done!" Sammy said, quoting something that his father told him.

"That's right, son," Ray said with a glowing smile. "I think that building game you created is really helping him get the hang of this. He's also been using the other app you suggested to fine tune his guitar skills. He's learning a new chord."

"That's amazing news!" Tamara said as she knelt down next to Sammy and watched him work. She instinctively pulled out her writing pad and asked him a few questions about what he was doing.

"Dinner is served!" Mary Ellen called out to everyone from the next room.

"Come on, Tamara, you sit next to me," Sammy said as he grabbed Tamara's hand and then led her into the dining room along with his father. As soon as she sat down, Mrs. Smith put a hot bowl of Italian wedding soup in front of her. It smelled delicious.

"Thank you, Mrs. Smith. I haven't had a home-cooked meal in ages," Tamara said.

"Oh Tamara, we're always happy to have you over here. You've given us hope and we'll never forget that," Mary Ellen said as she reached across the table and grasped her hand. Tamara smiled and nodded her head. Then they all held hands and said a prayer over the meal.

"You know, my husband and I were talking the other day," Mary Ellen told her before taking a sip of her soup. "We were thinking about how Dr. Meron's treatment might have really changed our Sammy. We were so eager to get him help that we didn't think about what those injections might do to him over time."

"We didn't even fully investigate the possible side effects," Ray said.

"Right. And I would have never been able to forgive myself if those injections did something to my baby," Mary Ellen said, shaking her head. "We basically signed away all of our rights in the matter."

"But let's stay focused on the positive," Ray said as he leaned over to rub his wife's arm. "What we thought was a setback was a setup for something better. We met you. God sometimes works in mysterious ways."

Mary Ellen nodded in agreement as tears welled up in her eyes and she glanced over at Sammy. "Things are going to be great. I can feel it."

"And Sammy is still our Sammy," Ray assured her.

Tamara looked at the family and was overwhelmed with a feeling of joy. They were good people and they deserved the best that life had to offer. She made a promise to herself that she would work tirelessly so that families like theirs could have hope and see their children succeed, no matter the odds.

Marsha sat in the chair next to Jack's bed staring at him, monitoring his every breath in and out. Though the doctors told her that the surgery was successful and he was expected to make a complete recovery, she was still terrified by the sight of him laying up in a hospital bed. Jack had always been her rock, and now she had to watch him in a completely vulnerable state. She knew that she would have to gather the strength to be the rock for both him and Tommy now.

"Jack, are you awake?" Marsha said quietly and sat up when she saw him stirring. "Jack, honey?"

Jack moved around some more in the bed and then slowly blinked until his eyes opened fully. Marsha hopped up from her seat and came to his bedside.

"Hi, sweetie," she said as she caressed his face.

"Marsha," Jack said weakly.

"Oh, honey," Marsha said, feeling as if she might break down in tears for the hundredth time.

"Please, don't cry," Jack told her. "It's okay."

"You had me worried."

"I'm sorry."

Marsha readjusted herself on the bed and laid down next to him like a little girl. She rested her head on his chest.

"I'm the one who's sorry Jack. I've been so horrible to you," Marsha said. "You've always been good to me."

"I told you, I'll always love you, no matter what, Marsha. Both you and Tommy," Jack said.

"I know. And I promise you, things are going to be better from now on. I'm getting help," Marsha told him. "I went to talk to a therapist this morning."

"You saw a therapist?"

"Yes I did, bright and early this morning. And I really like her. I'm going back to see her next week," Marsha said.

"That's great to hear, honey," Jack said, then let out a huge sigh.

"But, Jack. You have to promise me that you're going to be better too. We have to get you healthy too."

"I will do whatever you say," Jack said. "You're the boss."

"No. We're partners," Marsha said as she leaned her head up to look her husband in his eyes. "We're going to do it together, as a team."

John strolled up to the door of the place he used to call home and rang the doorbell without hesitation. He never thought he would find himself feeling like a stranger there.

Something came over him that morning when he woke up and went upstairs to find his mother's kitchen a complete mess. Ever since he came back to live with her, she had been slacking off of her household duties. She now expected him to take care of everything as he did when he was a kid. When he looked at the pile of dishes in the sink, plates on the table and empty wine bottles on the floor, he realized that nothing could be worse than finding himself stuck in this situation for the rest of his life. He had to go get his family back by any means necessary and it was absolutely crucial that he did it before Christmas—he couldn't spend another holiday without them.

"Hey John," Debra said, unable to hide a look of confusion when she opened the door. "The boys aren't here. They're out with friends."

"I know. Can we talk?" John asked as he gazed at his beautiful wife. She looked just as young, confident, and full of life as she did when they first met all those years ago at his trucking company.

"I'm kind of in the middle of something," she resisted.

"It will only take a few moments," John insisted.

"John, if you're just going to start an argument..." Debra started to say. Before she could finish her sentence, John took a step forward into the doorway and put his hands gently on either side of her face. He looked at her for a few moments and then leaned in to give her a kiss.

"I don't want to argue with you ever again," John told her. "I just want my wife back. I need you, Deb. You and the kids."

Debra looked at him with new eyes, feeling as if she might melt in his embrace.

"Do you mean that?" she asked.

"Of course I do. I'll do whatever's necessary to make this work," John told her sincerely. "I'll stop trying to control everything. You do whatever you need to do to be happy, go to school, put Patty in that treatment program, whatever you want. I trust your judgment."

"Oh, John. You don't know how happy I am to hear you say those words," Debra said, becoming emotional. "But I decided I don't want Patty to get those treatments. I think you were right all along about that."

"What changed your mind?" John asked.

"I've been talking to Carla and George—you know that new couple we met at the last Williams Syndrome meeting? They gave me a new perspective. God made Patty a special little girl and I don't want to risk changing that with some experimental drug."

"I totally agree. She's our baby. She's happy and full of life, and we'll do whatever we have to do to keep her that way," John said.

"I've been doing some research. There are a few alternative options

I want to explore for Patty. But I want you to come with me so that we can look into them together."

"I'll be there. What else do you need from me?" John asked. It was like music to Debra's ears.

"I just need some more support from you, John. I can't do it all alone. And I have to have a say in all decisions that affect our family," Debra told him.

"Of course. But you have to help me help you. Tell me what you need me to do. I'm not always aware of myself and how I might be neglecting you. Call me out when I'm wrong," John said.

"And you do the same for me. What's the point of being together if we're not going to be honest with each other? But we have to show respect for each other at the same time. That's what a marriage is all about."

"I agree. We're going to do this. We're going to make this work, honey," John told her. "I promise."

"Yes. I believe you," Debra said with a smile. She reached up to hug her husband and they both felt an indescribable sense of relief. Debra stepped back and grabbed John's hand tightly as she welcomed him back into their home.

CHAPTER 24
Decision Time

"Dr. Richards!"

Dr. Meron stood in his son Billy's room watching him as he sat glued to the television. Billy barely noticed that his father was in the room at all. He looked back down at the most recent report he had received from Billy's tutor and couldn't believe what he was reading.

"Yes, Dr. Meron," Dr. Richards said when he finally entered. His office was across the hall from Billy's room. It used to be Tamara's office.

"Why are my son's reports showing that he's two months behind on his assignments?" Dr. Meron wanted to know. "What has he been doing for the past two months?"

"Well, the last I heard his teacher said he simply refuses to do the work," Dr. Richards said with a slight shrug. "She's been trying to get in touch with you about it for some time now."

"Why didn't you *make* him do the work?"

"He throws a fit if anyone even touches his television. We can't make him want to learn—he's completely disinterested in anything involving school work," Dr. Richards answered.

"My boy has always had a thirst for knowledge. And he barely even acknowledges my presence! What has changed?"

"There are theories…" Dr. Richards started to say.

"Doctor, my patience is being tested. If you have a theory on this matter spit it out!" Dr. Meron demanded.

"The length of the treatment period. Dr. Goodwin theorized that maybe he's been given the injections too long. That maybe the formula is dulling his senses somehow," Dr. Richards answered with another shrug. His nonchalance enraged Dr. Meron.

"And how long have you known this?" Dr. Meron yelled.

"Not as long as you have. I reviewed the reports Dr. Goodwin sent you months before she left and she mentioned her theory several times in them."

"I'm constantly on the road, how could I have time to fully read those reports?" Dr. Meron said, knowing that he was wrong to ignore her messages but still trying to save face. "You felt no need to back her theory to me in person? We could have stopped treating him months ago."

"I'm constantly here, taking care of the very constant problems that turn up in your facility, Dr. Meron. I don't have the time to read your reports and dictate them to you as well," Dr. Richards said with a snarky attitude.

"You are out of line, Doctor!"

"I'm just being honest, Doctor!"

"Your honesty could come with a modicum of respect! Dr. Goodwin may have challenged me from time to time, but she was always very respectful."

"Well as you can see, Dr. Goodwin isn't here. I'm here and I'm doing her job the best way I know how," Dr. Richards replied.

"Yes I see," Dr. Meron said as he clenched his fists angrily at his sides. "I see that I made a mistake in hiring you. Your services will no longer be needed here, Dr. Richards."

"What?"

"You heard me. I'm just being *honest* with you Doctor," Dr. Meron said, mocking him as he turned to leave. "Please clean out your desk and leave by end of day."

"You can't be serious. I'm the one who's been holding this chaotic excuse for a medical facility together!"

"And the insults continue. Goodbye, Dr. Richards."

"You'll regret this, Dr. Meron," Dr. Richards called out behind him. "I know people who know people at the FDA."

"Oh really? Well, you signed an airtight confidentiality agreement doctor. If you reveal any private details about these trials, I will do everything in my power to make your life even more miserable than it already is," Dr. Meron threatened.

Joseph waited in a booth at his favorite diner for his fraternity brother to arrive. He picked at the cherry pie on the plate in front of him, leaving it mostly untouched. There were a lot of thoughts and burdens weighing on his mind.

Phil was in town for business and it couldn't have been more timely. Phil had a way of putting put things in the right perspective. He also had a way of taking even the worst situation and making it seem like it wasn't that bad.

As Joseph took another sip from his coffee mug, he looked up and saw Phil approaching his table.

"Hey, brother," Phil said in his usual jovial tone as they slapped hands.

"Good to see you, bro," Joseph said as he stood up to give him a man-hug. "How'd that meeting go?"

"It went. Should hear something from them next week, but it's looking good," Phil answered. "Let's not talk about business. I wanna know what's up with you."

"How do you always know?" Joseph said shaking his head and chuckling.

"I just do. Your voice gives it away every time," Phil said with a shrug. "So what's up?"

"Jill's upset with me," Joseph told him. "She found out that I went to see that doctor without her."

"Crap! That wasn't supposed to happen."

"Tell me about it. I meant to tell her myself but…" Joseph started to say. "Well let me just say I should have told her myself."

"Yea. My wife hates it when she feels like I kept something from her. Which is pretty much all the time," Phil said with a little chuckle as he got the waitress' attention. "Coffee please."

"Not only do I feel horrible that she's upset with me, now I'm not sure we're on the same page as far as these treatments anymore," Joseph explained. "We're supposed to take Joey to the facility a few days after Christmas."

"So you're definitely doing that?" Phil asked, unable to hide a look of surprise.

"Yea, why do you say that?"

"I don't know," Phil said with a shrug. "I just didn't know you were seriously thinking about it."

"You know," Joseph said scratching his head. "You're like the third person in a week to say something like that to me."

"I'll be honest—the whole thing just seems strange. And you and Jill never fight, but this is the second time I'm hearing about you guys being on the outs since you told me about this doctor guy," Phil said.

"So, you think we're making a mistake going to him?"

"I can't tell you either way because I don't know anything about the guy or his research. All I know is that I don't like hearing about you and Jill arguing. I look at your relationship as a model, and all is not right with the world if you guys aren't getting along."

"Wow. Didn't know you felt that way."

"Of course," Phil said. "You know, Josie and I barely even talk these days if it isn't about the kids. I don't know when that all started. You guys gotta keep talking man. Don't let the world distract you from what's really important…"

As he listened to his best friend continue to talk, Joseph suddenly had a very strong desire to get home. He needed to have a serious conversation with his wife.

~

"Hey, Mom," Grace said. She startled Jill, who was standing at the kitchen counter in her robe stirring a cup of cocoa much longer than necessary. She had drifted off into her thoughts for a moment.

"Hey there, didn't know you were home," Jill said as she leaned over to give her daughter a kiss on the cheek.

"Yea, I've been filling out applications all afternoon," Grace told her.

"Really?"

"Yea, I finished five already. I'm really hoping I get into this art school in St. Louis. They have a great photography program."

"Oh, honey!" Jill exclaimed, feeling as if she wanted to jump for joy. She hugged her daughter tightly. "You don't know how happy I am to hear that. I always thought you'd be great in visual arts."

"Thanks, Mom. Coach Ephraim is helping me too. She said I could rejoin the volleyball squad next year," Grace said with a smile.

Jill stepped back a little and looked at her eldest daughter. She now understood what her own mother had told her—that daughters are usually a reflection of their mothers. She looked at Grace and saw herself when she was 17 and just getting ready to experience life. Jill remembered how important it was for her to feel love and acceptance at that age.

"Mom, can I talk to you about something totally unrelated?" Grace suddenly asked.

"Of course. Go ahead."

Grace went over to the kitchen island and sat down, inviting her mom to do the same. When they were both settled, Grace looked down at the table for a while as if she were trying to choose her words carefully.

"Mom. I don't know what exactly is going on between you and Dad right now. And I don't really have to know the details. But whatever it is…please, just work it out."

Jill gave her daughter a knowing look and then nodded in agreement.

"We're a family. Nothing else matters more than that. We should be able to get through anything together," Grace said with sincerity as she grasped her mother's hand and then stood up from her chair. Jill was still speechless as her daughter kissed her on the cheek and then left the room as quietly as she came in.

Nothing else matters…

Grace's words rung in Jill's ears like a bell going off as she sat in the kitchen letting her hot cocoa get cold. She and Joseph had been through countless trials that led them to where they were at that moment. She knew that she couldn't let anything compromise all of the hard work they had put into building their family and keeping it strong. Tears started to come to her eyes as she thought of the struggles they had been through with doctors, teachers, therapists, nannies, and tutors to help Joey grow into the thoughtful, smart, well-adjusted boy he was.

Just then, as if on cue, Joey skipped into the kitchen with Ramsey, the family dog, close behind him.

"Hi, Mommy," he said as came close to her. "Can I have some cocoa too?"

"Sure, buddy," Jill said as she quickly tried to wipe the tears away.

"Are you okay, Mommy? Why are you crying?" Joey asked as he looked up at her, his bright green eyes full of concern.

"Mommy was just thinking about some things. But I promise you, everything is fine. Everything is better than fine," Jill declared with a smile as a feeling of relief washed over her. She knew what she had to do—nothing was going to stand in the way of her keeping her family together.

Jill stood up from her seat and reached down to pick Joey up. She swung him around like she used to do when he was just a toddler. He shrieked with joy. She finally set him down and took his hand to lead him to the counter so that they could make another hot cocoa.

"You know how to do it," she said as she reached up to grab the box.

"Yup!" Joey said eagerly. "I want to make it with milk this time."

They heard the front door open and then the sound of Joseph's voice.

"Jill!" he yelled. "Jill!"

"Joey and I are in the kitchen," she called back.

Joseph went to find them. As soon as he saw his wife he walked straight up to her and gave her a hug.

"Well, hello to you too," Jill said, sounding surprised.

"Jill, listen. I was wrong not to tell you about my meeting with Dr. Meron. I will do whatever I have to do to make it up to you. But please, let's get past this one thing? Let's move forward."

"I'm already past it," Jill said with a gentle smile.

"You are?" Joseph said. Now he was the one who looked surprised.

"Yes. We can't let petty things get in the way of what really matters."

They separated for a moment and Joseph took both her hands. He looked over at Joey, who was standing there with the milk container in his hand and a Kool-Aid smile spread across his face, then back at his wife. "I've also been thinking. I don't think we should take Joey in next week. Let's just cancel everything."

"I've been thinking the same thing," Jill said, immediately feeling as if a weight was lifted from her shoulders. Somehow, they had gotten back on the same page without ever having to have a full conversation about it. That was the magic that kept their relationship strong.

"So, I don't have to go anymore?" Joey asked.

"No, Joey, you're not going anywhere. You're staying right here with us. With your family," Jill said definitively.

"That's right, buddy," Joseph confirmed. "Come here."

Joseph reached his hand out for Joey to join them in a circle. He pulled his wife and son close to him and they embraced for a long time. At that moment, he knew without a doubt that they had made the right decision.

CHAPTER 25
In the Zone

"Are you ready?" Jill said as she joined Joseph in the foyer. He was standing in front of the bay window, looking at the street but not looking at anything in particular.

Marilyn was having a small holiday get together at her house for the parents in her Williams Syndrome group. She wanted them to have a way to mix and mingle one more time before the new year. Joseph and Jill were bringing Joey with them. Grace decided to take her sisters Mia and Sophia out for pizza that night. She was making more of an effort to spend time with them.

"I sure am. You look so beautiful," he commented as he turned and looked his wife over. She blushed a little and winked at him.

"Joey!" Jill called out. "Come on, buddy, it's time to go."

Joey came out of the playroom where he had been watching television with Ramsey. Ramsey followed him everywhere he went in the house.

"Can we take Ramsey with us?" Joey asked.

"No, not tonight, buddy," Joseph told him.

Just then, the house phone rang. Joseph was just about to pick it up when he heard the caller ID state that it was Dr. Meron's office. He turned and looked at his wife, knowing that it was probably Dr. Meron himself finally calling to confirm Joey's participation in the program. They had previously submitted the paperwork, but Jill made sure that there was a clear clause at the end that allowed them to cancel the arrangement at any time.

"Don't answer it," Jill told him. "Let's just enjoy this evening. We'll call Dr. Meron in the morning and tell him what we decided."

"Okay, let's go," Joseph agreed.

Jill opened the front door and nearly tripped over a large, heavy box that was sitting on the porch.

"What is this?" Jill asked rhetorically.

"Not sure, I ordered some things for Christmas, but I already received them all," Joseph shrugged.

"Me too," Jill replied, then looked curiously at Joey as she leaned down to open the box with her keys. Inside there were five 10-pound boxes of Milk Bones.

"Joey!" she said as she pulled one of the boxes out to examine it.

"I saw them on TV," he said proudly. "They're my Christmas present for Ramsey."

"I don't even think he can eat these yet though, sweetie. He's just a little puppy!" Jill said, shaking her head. "And why so many? There are like 100 in a box."

"Okay, I think it's time to turn off the one-click setting," Joseph said with a wink. He picked Joey up, playfully tossed him over his shoulder and headed to the car.

When they arrived at Marilyn's house, they were welcomed by her daughter Dorrine at the door.

"Hi, I'm Dorrine. Please come in!" she said with a pleasant smile. The room was filled with the parents from their group, their children, and some of Marilyn's family members.

"I'll take your coats," Dorrine offered.

"Thank you, Dorrine," Joseph and Jill said at the same time.

"Thank you!" Joey repeated as she took their coats and went to the closet.

"That's Marilyn's daughter," Jill leaned over and told Joseph.

"Jill, Joseph!" Marilyn said as she approached them. "So glad you could make it!"

"We wouldn't miss this. As always, you've done so much for us this year. Thank you for keeping the meetings active. They help keep us balanced," Jill told her. Joseph nodded in agreement as he held Joey close to his side.

"It's my pleasure," Marilyn said. "Please come over and get something to eat."

"Quite a spread," Joseph commented as he followed her to the long table covered with food. "I'm starving."

"Dorrine helped me do the preparations. She's quite the chef!" Marilyn explained.

"Hey, Joey!" Sammy called out from across the room. Joey let go of his father's hand and ran like lightening to join his friend.

"I guess Marsha and Jack couldn't make it," Jill said when she didn't see Tommy or his family in the room.

"No, but Marsha sent over a huge platter of food. She called me today and said that Jack is doing much, much better," Marilyn assured her.

Marsha had decided to keep Tommy with her instead of taking Jill up on her offer. She was concerned because Tommy had been behaving differently ever since they checked him out of Dr. Meron's facility and she wanted to keep an eye on him. Dr. Richards sent Marsha home with a series of injections and instructions for continuing Tommy's treatments.

"Did she say anything about how Tommy's doing?" Joseph asked. Marilyn just shook her head and then changed the subject. She preferred to stay neutral and save group updates for meetings.

"So, I was actually about to say a little something to the families. Holiday wishes and such. I'll open the floor to anyone who wants to do the same," Marilyn said. "Enjoy yourselves."

Marilyn went up to the front of the room near her fireplace and began clinking her glass with her cocktail fork to get everyone's attention. She motioned to her daughter Dorrine to come next to her. Jill and Joseph went over to greet Mary Ellen and Ray. They were a little surprised to see Dr. Goodwin there with them and Mary Ellen immediately read the confused expression on Jill's face.

"I'll tell you all about it later," Mary Ellen whispered to Jill. "So much to talk about."

"I just wanted to take a moment to thank you all for coming out tonight," Marilyn said loud enough for everyone to hear. "I know this gathering was a bit last minute, but I felt compelled to bring you all together one last time before the new year. A lot has transpired this year that I'm sure has put a strain on your families, but you got through it. I am so happy to see you all here tonight."

The room filled with the sound of applause.

"I pray that we all have a joyous holiday season and a new year that's full of enlightenment, happiness, and love. We're stronger together."

"Amen," everyone said in agreement.

"Would anyone else like to say something?"

Everyone looked around at each other shaking their heads. Marilyn waited a few moments, but there didn't seem to be any takers.

"Okay, well everyone, enjoy yourselves. Please eat all of the food and take some home with you!" she finally said.

"Wait, Marilyn," Joseph said from the back of the room. "I have something I want to say."

"Sure, the floor's all yours Joseph."

Joseph grabbed his wife's hand. They slowly and carefully made their way to the front where Marilyn was standing, meandering through the small crowd of people. Joseph was nervous because he wasn't 100 percent sure what he was going to say. When he arrived there, he took a moment to look around at the other parents, their children, and a few other faces he hadn't seen before.

"Joey can you come up here, son?" he asked. Joey ran to his father's side immediately and hugged his hip. His presence gave Joseph an extra jolt of confidence.

"Hello, everyone," he began. "Some of you know me, my wife, our son, and our family—our story."

Many of the attendees nodded silently in agreement. You could hear a pin drop in the room.

"When my son was first diagnosed with Williams Syndrome, the doctor told us that he had a 'failure to thrive.' And at that time, I didn't want to believe it, but I eventually accepted that as the truth. But today, with what I know about my son…what I've learned about him, what I've learned *from* him, I want to say that that doctor's diagnosis was a load of nonsense."

Jill squeezed her husband's hand tightly and looked up at him.

"…I say that because my son has thrived in ways that even us so-called 'normal' people haven't yet. He's lightyears ahead in so many ways. He loves unconditionally, he lives boldly, and he's not afraid to be exactly who he is. He also knows that he's loved and that has made all the difference."

"I wanted desperately to help my son become more 'normal'—to make him more like other kids his age. But I realize now, I don't want that. I want my Joey T. Children with Williams Syndrome aren't normal—they're *exceptional.* And I think we use that word 'normal' way too loosely. What makes *us* normal? In fact, I think we're pretty average compared to these amazing kids."

Every parent in the room was wiping tears from their eyes at that point. They grabbed their children and pulled them closer. Even John was teary-eyed—he picked up his daughter Patty and gave her a kiss on the cheek. Debra looked at them lovingly and tugged at Patty's shoe playfully. George and his wife Carla were settled in on the couch with their adopted daughter, Jamie, sitting between them.

"I want to take this moment to thank God for my son Joey, for my wife, and for my family. Every day is a blessing when you have a loving family. We're also blessed to have such a powerful network of people that we can reach out to. Thank you so much. We're looking forward to a happy new year and many more to come. Cheers everyone!"

"Cheers!" everyone exclaimed as they lifted their glasses in unison. Jill, overcome with emotion at that moment, reached over and gave her husband a long hug. She sobbed into his dress shirt.

"Everything is going to be alright," he told her. "We made the right decision."

"You've been given a great gift, George. A chance to see what the world would be like without you in it," Joey said calmly, reciting his line almost perfectly.

"This is just a dream. I'm going home," the boy playing George Bailey said angrily and then left the stage. When everything went dark to signify that the scene was over, everyone in Joey's section jumped up from their seats, clapped and whistled. They knew that it was the last line he had to say in the play.

Joseph had to reserve two rows for the family and everyone they knew who wanted to come to Joey's Christmas play. Both sets of grandparents came along with Joseph's brother James. Mary Ellen and Ray came along with Sammy. At the Smith's recommendation, Jill and Joseph were now working with Dr. Tamara Goodwin to help Joey develop his proficiency in the area of communication using her new educational program. Joey seemed to have an interest in talking to people, so, for now, they were working on developing his public speaking abilities. Joey also made it a point to personally invite his teacher's assistant, Jemma, to the play—she sat with the family, along with her husband. And of course, his teacher, Mrs. Moldestad was there to support all of her "cherubs."

"He was so great!" Grandma Ella gushed about her grandson's performance and grabbed Grandpa Joe's hand tightly. He nodded his approval.

"Yup. That's our Joey!" Grace yelled out and then whistled loudly.

The audience loved every moment of the play—it was pure entertainment. There were moments when the kids would forget their lines and have to improvise, prompting laughter. Joey remembered every one of his lines and even had a few moments where he interacted with the audience. When the play was over, Joey and his classmates came out for one final bow and the audience gave them a standing ovation. It was the perfect evening to get everyone in the spirit of Christmas, which was coming in two days.

The entire family filed out of the auditorium and gathered outside the door where the student actors would exit after changing. Joseph was holding a small wrapped box.

"What did you get him?" Joseph's brother James asked.

"You'll see," he replied with a wink. "You're a part of it."

Joey and Suzy came out of the door and everyone shouted with excitement. Joey jumped back, then smiled and blushed when he saw that it was his family. They started to chant his name.

"You did great up there, buddy," Jill told him as she leaned down to give him a hug. "You too, Suzy!"

"Thank you, Mrs. Todaro!" Suzy said before going over to her parents.

"I got the whole thing recorded," Grandpa Marv said as he fiddled with his clunky old camcorder.

"I hope you remembered to put in the tape this time!" Grandma Teresa teased.

"Here you go. This is from your sisters, mom and me. Another early Christmas present," Joseph told Joey as he handed him the small box. Joey grabbed it eagerly and started tearing it open.

"Tickets to Sky Zone!!!" Joey shouted when he saw what was inside.

"Yup, and the whole family's going. Including your Uncle James," Joseph said as he looked over at his brother.

"Hey, I'm down!" James agreed.

"Thank you! Thank you! Thank you!" Joey yelled as he jumped for joy.

"You deserve it, buddy," Joseph told him. "We're all so proud of you."

"Can we play dodgeball?"

"Sure," Joseph answered as he put his arm around his son's shoulder and walked with him to the exit doors.

"And a game of SkySlam?"

"Yup."

"Can we stay all day long? From morning to night-time?"

"We'll see."

"Can we go right now?"

"Uh, no not tonight buddy. I think they're closing soon."

"Can we go tomorrow?"

"Tomorrow's Christmas Eve. I think they're closed then and on Christmas Day too, Joey T."

"Are you sure 100 percent sure about that Daddy? How about the day after Christmas?"

EPILOGUE

The Williams Syndrome Walk was an annual event held at locations all around the country to raise funds and awareness. It was a big day for the families and their children—they came out, walked together for miles and enjoyed fun and food all afternoon long.

Joey stood between his parents and held their hands the whole time they walked. Mia was holding her mom's hand. Grace brought Carlie along, and Sophia walked with Brendan. At the end of the route, they all gathered together around picnic tables that were covered with fresh fruits, foods, and beverages provided by event sponsors. It was a perfect 80-degree summer day.

"Hey, Mommy, there's Tommy!" Joey said suddenly and pointed. He was right—there on the other side of the crowd stood Marsha, Jack, and Tommy. Jack looked like he had lost a lot of weight, but Tommy was the one who looked the most different. He was a bit taller and the shape of his face had changed slightly. Marsha was fussing at him because he was playing a portable video game and barely paying any attention to what was going on around him. He looked like he wanted to be anywhere but there.

"Wow, you're right, that is Tommy," Jill said. "Let's go say hi."

They walked over with Joey. He immediately ran to Tommy's side and tried to get his attention. Jill tapped Marsha on the shoulder.

"Oh wow! Hey, Jill," Marsha said as she leaned over to give her a hug. Jack and Joseph shook hands. Joey looked a little confused because usually by then he and Tommy would have run off somewhere together. He was also confused by how different Tommy looked.

"It's great to see you. How is everything?" Jill asked as she glanced over at Tommy, who seemed to be ignoring Joey.

"We're doing okay," Marsha said as she closed her eyes and nodded. "We're okay. Jack just got a good report at the doctor's office. And he lost 50 pounds."

"That's amazing! Congratulations, Jack," Jill said.

"Thanks, Jill. I feel 10 years younger."

"Hey there Tommy, what's up with you?" Joseph asked. Tommy still didn't look up. Instead, he brushed the hair away from his face and continued playing.

"Nothing," he replied.

"He's being a little difficult today. He didn't want to come out to the event," Marsha explained, looking embarrassed.

"Really? He's always loved going to these walks," Jill commented. There was an awkward silence between them.

"We had to stop the treatments," Jack explained, knowing that they were wondering about it. "Apparently, Dr. Meron was forced to shut down his clinical research trials and the facility. There are concerns that he didn't fully investigate potential side effects. Tommy's doing okay, doing better in school, but there are some challenges from time to time."

"I guess he's your average teenager now," Marsha said with a nervous chuckle. "He mostly wants to play video games all day and browse the social media sites. This is the first time he's been outside in a while."

Jill and Joseph nodded quietly, then looked at each other.

"What are you playing Tommy?" Joey asked curiously as he tried to lean in to see the game. Tommy finally looked up and tried to hide the screen. Joey noticed something different about his eyes—they didn't look the same. They looked cold and they had somehow lost their starry pattern.

"Tommy?" Joey said his name again.

"My name is *Tom*," he replied in an annoyed tone, then he turned and left the group. He walked over to a tree and sat down by himself, resuming his video game. It was completely out of character for Tommy to act so rudely toward anyone.

"Come on buddy," Joseph said as he patted Joey on the back. "Let's go get something to eat."

"Well…it was nice seeing you both again," Jill said to Marsha and Jack.

"Same here," Jack replied as he wrapped his arm around his wife. Marsha looked a little embarrassed as she smiled and waved.

Joey's thoughts shifted from Tommy's strange behavior to the large, heated platter full of chicken nuggets he had seen sitting on the picnic table. He skipped ahead of his parents toward his sisters and their friends, who were already sitting down with their plates.

Joseph pulled Jill close to him as they slowly strolled back to the picnic area together. Instead of thinking or talking about what just happened, he decided it was best to just enjoy the beautiful day. It was a day of family, reflection and looking ahead to the future. He looked ahead at Joey who was doing a happy dance in front of the picnic table with his plate. Grace playfully started tickling him to keep him away from the food.

"He is going to *demolish* those nuggets," Joseph finally said.

"Yep. He loves them almost as much as his father does. You'd better get some before he eats them all," Jill said playfully.

"Ah, he can have them. I've got everything I want right now."

Psalms 139: 13-16

New Living Translation (NLT)

13. You made all the delicate, inner parts of my body
and knit me together in my mother's womb.

14. Thank you for making me so wonderfully complex!
Your workmanship is marvelous—how well I know it.

15. You watched me as I was being formed in utter seclusion,
as I was woven together in the dark of the womb.

16. You saw me before I was born.
Every day of my life was recorded in your book.
Every moment was laid out
before a single day had passed.

Made in the USA
Columbia, SC
01 July 2019